FOOD FOR THE GALLOWS

By

Suzanne Downes

Also by Suzanne Downes

The Underwood Mysteries
A Noble Pair of Brothers
Food for the Gallows
Behind the Horseman
An Aria Writ in blood
Yield Not to Misfortune
A Place for Repentance
In Prospect of Death

DI Matt Piper Series
The Devil Drives a Jaguar
Blood and Stone
An Empty Handed Traveller
A Devoted Sister

The Inspector Lazarus Mysteries
A Troublesome Woman
A Spice of Madness
A Woman Scorned

The Thora Scattergood Mysteries
Small Matters
Small Crimes
Small Minds

Children's Books
Cassie's Quest
Cassie's Quandary
Cassie's Queen

Bold Brian

DEDICATION

For my good friend Jan Riley

CHAPTER ONE

'Quieta Non Movere' – Do not move settled things

"Cadmus ..."

Mr Underwood folded down the edge of his newspaper and raised an enquiring eyebrow at his wife.

"Yes?" he responded promptly.

Having so easily claimed his attention, Verity now seemed at a loss how to continue. Her gaze transferred itself from his face to her nervously twisting fingers. He noted her diffidence, but kindly made no comment upon it, merely laying his paper down on the breakfast table and waiting patiently for her to proceed.

"I had a letter from Gil yesterday," she said at last, the words tumbling out in her hurry to get them over with, her voice slightly breathy and high pitched.

"Did you indeed? How is he?" If he was in any way surprised that his brother, the clergyman, should have written personally to his wife of only a few months, and not to himself or their mother, he declined to remark upon it.

"He is well – and happily settled in his new parish. He says it is a charming place. He wrote to me about it because he recalled that Hanbury lies only a few miles from the Pennine village where my dear Papa had his living and I grew up."

"Really?" It did not occur to Underwood to find it odd that his brother should be in possession of this knowledge, whilst he was largely unaware of her childhood. He had no doubt he and his wife had often discussed these things, though he could not, at that precise moment, remember any of it. Verity was too relieved by his appearance of genuine interest to feel offended by his evident ignorance of her past life.

"Gil described it so well, I was quite overcome with homesickness," she continued eagerly, then lapsed into blushing silence as she became cognisant of the fact that her words could be construed as criticism of their present circumstances, living, as they were, with his mother and step-father. Even now she had waited until the Milners had left the table before she could have a private word with her husband. However Underwood merely smiled and patted her hand in his affectionately absent-minded way.

1

"I don't wonder at it. The area has a way of gripping the imagination. I find myself thinking of it quite frequently."

It was, perhaps, fortunate he was not paying particular attention to her expression, for he would have been astounded by the look of sick distress which passed over her face, as though he had reminded her of something exquisitely painful. He had put from his mind, as she had not, the memory of their last sojourn in the Pennines and it would appear she was inclined to read rather more into his words than he ever intended to convey.

He remained oblivious, however, and went on, "Did Gil have anything else to say?" Whatever else escaped him, it had not gone unnoticed that she did not offer him the letter that he might read it for himself, but far from being annoyed, he was inclined to find this air of secrecy rather amusing. Knowing his brother as he did, he imagined Gil had set Verity a task of persuading him to do something which he feared would provoke a refusal from himself. Mr Underwood was prepared to feign ignorance of their plotting – but only for the moment.

"Oh, just the usual messages of goodwill and affection to your mother, and his regards to your step-father," she made an attempt at airy unconcern, which was almost his undoing.

"Naturally," he said, nodding his head seriously, as though to emphasize his acceptance of these filial and fraternal greetings, but he eyed his wife with good-natured wariness from beneath his heavy lids, alert for any signs which would prove his suspicions correct. "I should have expected nothing less from so dutiful a brother and son, but I must own, I am surprised he found so little to say, postal charges being what they are."

Verity looked suitably guilt-ridden, "Well, that was not quite all," she ventured hesitantly.

He was, by now, having the greatest difficulty in hiding his amusement. Verity was the most transparent of women and he doubted her ability ever to lie to him successfully. She was evidently struggling to hide her purpose from him and he wondered vaguely if it would not be kinder to admit that he knew Gil had set her an unsavoury task and simply request that she tell him outright what it might be. On reflection, however, he decided he was enjoying the situation far too much to end it prematurely.

"Perhaps you might like to let me read the letter for myself?" he suggested tentatively.

"Oh no," she answered swiftly before realizing how this emphatic denial might look to her husband. She amended hastily, "I do believe I have misplaced it."

"Oh? How very unlike you to be so careless, my dear. You make me more and more eager to know what was contained in this mysterious missive."

"No, no! Oh, pray don't tease me any more. I wish Gil had never written to me. I am hopeless at subterfuge."

Underwood laughed outright, "No, you are not. Heaven help you if you ever have anything of real importance to keep from me. Now, tell me what Gil has asked of me."

Verity sighed heavily, half in relief and half in exasperation at her own pathetic performance, "He wanted to know if you have yet made any decisions about the future."

"What sort of decisions?"

She knew he was being deliberately obtuse, hiding, as usual, behind his famed absent-mindedness, but after his tormenting of the past few minutes, she was determined not to rise to the bait, "Where we are to live, to begin with, and what form of employment you intend to take, now that you have left the University."

The events of the previous year in Bracken Tor had not only caused Underwood some unhappiness, they had also deprived him of his employment. Tutors at Cambridge University were normally expected to be a member of the clergy and whilst Underwood had managed to avoid that fate, he could not ignore the stricture that they must certainly remain unmarried.

Unfortunately for those around him, he was a man who could quite easily bury himself in books and rarely raise his head to notice what was going on around him, unless it be something which would challenge his intellect. Being cosseted by his mother and an adoring and accommodating wife, he had found life very pleasant and had failed to notice the quietly simmering frustration in his dear Verity.

Gil, however, had picked up every nuance from her frequent letters and now hoped they would be responding to his invitation to pay a prolonged visit to his new parish. No mention was made of the fact that Underwood's interest in the murder in Bracken Tor had not only lost Underwood his position but had also cost the Reverend Gil Underwood his living too. One could hardly remain as vicar when one's brother had proved the Lord of the Manor was a murderer; a cheat who had substituted an illegitimate child for an unwanted

3

daughter and had finally committed suicide when his secret had been uncovered.

"From all that, I deduce my brother has something in mind for me?"

"Yes, he does," she replied frankly.

"Then why did he not write to me?"

"Because he says you always do the exact opposite of anything he suggests," she retorted, then, too late, reflected upon his possible reaction to this candid criticism. She glanced covertly at her husband, but he did not seem to be unduly annoyed by his sibling's assessment of his character.

"Nonsense," he said decidedly, then noticed a distinctly quizzical expression on his wife's face. "You would appear to agree with him," he added, severely.

"I'm afraid I do. I have never known you to take his advice in anything."

"I married you, didn't I?" Underwood smiled as he made this remark, intending that she should see it for the jest it was meant to be, but the stricken look in her eyes ought to have warned him that she had not heard anything to amuse her.

"You married me because Gil told you to?" she asked, her voice so low he could scarcely hear her.

Underwood was a kindly man, but there were times when he lacked a certain sensitivity to the feelings of others. This was one such occasion. Without thought he merely laughed and answered, "But of course."

"Oh," he should have heard the anguish in the softly spoken monosyllable, but he was wavering between mild irritation that his brother should be meddling in his affairs, and curiosity to know precisely what Gil had suggested for him.

"You may as well tell me the whole," he prompted her, aware only that she had fallen silent, but heedless of his own role in her distress. "What exactly has he in mind?"

She shook her head slightly, as though to dislodge unwelcome thoughts,

"There is a house – a large house, in need of some repair. He thought it would be the ideal place to start our school."

"School?" He looked startled, "Good gad, who ever mentioned a school?"

4

"Gil says you did. When you spoke of leaving Cambridge, you said teaching was all you could do."

Underwood had to admit the truth of this, "I very probably did, but that was before I was married. Where does he intend you should come in all this?"

Verity was not a fool. She knew without doubt that if her husband wanted to do something, he would give very little consideration to her opinions. He was not an unpleasantly selfish man, and certainly not a tyrannical husband, but he had lived so long alone, pleasing only himself, that he had not quite grown accustomed to consulting another person. As for herself, she knew she was far too acquiescent for his good, but she adored him so much it was hard to gainsay him. That he should mention her now merely pointed to the fact that he did not want to travel north to start a school. Verity, however, did. For the first time since their marriage she was not prepared to follow his lead without protest. She was very fond of her mother-in-law, but she did not want to spend the rest of her life under the same roof, forever in her debt. She wanted a home of her own, and a chance to grow to know the complex man she had married. She was also fully aware that Underwood was a man who needed to be kept occupied, as did she. The holiday had been a long and pleasant one, but it was time to go back to work. They did not belong to a class which could fill its days with leisure and pleasure, and before long the inactivity would drive an insurmountable wedge between them. Their marriage had had an inauspicious beginning, being, for her a love match, but for him, more a convenience and certainly his second choice. She had no intention of allowing 'familiarity to breed contempt'. Underwood could not be permitted to spend his days in idleness with her forever at his side, growing bored simply because there was no novelty in her presence.

"Naturally I shall be helping you. Little boys need a woman sometimes, to nurse them when they are ill, and to teach them polite behaviour. Boys left to themselves are mere savages."

Underwood was not unfamiliar with the savagery of the male sex and he laughed. "Very well, we shall travel north to investigate Gil's school, but be warned. If this parish is as isolated as his last, I shall feel no compunction in refusing to live there. Call me a coward if you will, but the thought of a winter entirely cut off from civilized society fills my soul with dread."

"Oh, no," she countered, her tone filled with enthusiasm, "Hanbury is not a tiny village like Bracken Tor. It is quite a large

5

town. It was once very small and quiet, a market town, then came the fashion for spring waters and Hanbury came into its own. It boasts a very elegant Pump Room, a Circulating Library, theatres and Assembly Rooms. I do not think you will find it at all isolated."

"Very well, it is decided. Can I leave the travelling arrangements to you?"

"Yes, I will take care of that, if only you will tell your Mama we are leaving. She will be so distressed, thinking I am taking you away from her."

With all the sensibility of a man who took his loved ones entirely for granted, Underwood airily replied, "Oh, mother won't be concerned in the least. But I shall tell her if it makes you feel better."

*

"Remind me once again, my dear, why I have subjected myself to the rigours of the road? One town, I find, is very much like another." Underwood was gazing out of the carriage window as they entered the spa town of Hanbury, and contrary to his comments, he was observing the view with avid interest.

"I do hope you are not going to provoke Gil with this mood, Underwood," answered Verity tiredly. It had been a long and arduous journey and much as she adored her husband, she was not much in the frame of mind to deal with his vagaries.

"I? I could not provoke anyone." Underwood assured her, "I am the most easy-going of men, but it is hardly my fault if Gil insists on taking parishes which are situated in the wilds of Derbyshire. I warn you, if this living is as remote as the past one, I shall be on the first stage home."

And that, thought Verity, is the crux of the matter. Underwood obviously felt quite at home living with his mother, but Verity, much as she liked and admired the older woman, most definitely did not want to continue living under her roof.

"I don't know why you imagine all civilised life ceases outside Oxford and Cambridge. We Northerners are not complete barbarians!" she snapped, suddenly irritable.

"My dear, no Cambridge man would ever admit that Oxford might be civilised," he answered mildly, "You seem a little under the weather," he added, "perhaps you should take the waters whilst we are here?"

"Why should I do so? There is nothing wrong with me." She was now thoroughly exhausted by both the journey and his teasing.

"Nothing but a fractured sense of humour," muttered Underwood, unwilling to provoke a quarrel, but unable to let the comment pass by.

Fortunately she was saved from having to make a response by the coach coming to a halt in the yard of the Royal Hotel, which was a large inn, but hardly deserved either the name Royal or Hotel. The Underwoods were only too glad to get out of the cramped interior and stretch their aching legs.

Whilst Underwood gave the coachman directions of where to send their luggage, Verity walked under the archway which led out of the yard and walked out into bright sunlight and a busy market place.

They skirted around the back of the market stalls, not being interested in purchasing anything, and thus managed to avoid the worst of the crush. They then had to pass the pens full of sheep and cattle and the noise of the frightened animals was deafening. The fulsome odours of cooking food gave way to the smells which tend to issue from nervous livestock, and they were both glad to hurry their steps until the din was left behind.

Through a narrow passage between two large and imposing buildings they found a slightly smaller square, tree-lined and pleasant. The edifices here were as obviously smart dwelling houses as the previous ones in the Market Square had been municipal. There had been the Town Hall, Library and Assembly Rooms and others. Here were the houses of the rich. They took a right turn out of this square and could see the steeple of the church in front of them.

The neighbouring parsonage was surrounded by a high stone wall and it took a few moments before they found the arched gateway which gave them access to the garden. The church was encircled by a lower wall and they were both impressed by the size and magnificence of Gil's latest acquisition.

They entered the gate and paused briefly to admire the house, which was probably only twenty or thirty years old, and considerably larger than a man alone could possibly need. It was built of the same grey stone as most of the other buildings in the town and the large, square-paned windows sparkled merrily in the unclouded sunshine. A colonnaded porch protected the front door and it was approached by a path made of stone flags. Verity and Underwood made their way to the front door and Underwood lifted the huge brass knocker and let it fall thrice against the oak panels.

Gil, who had evidently been expecting them, opened the door himself and before long they had exchanged greetings and were being ushered into a large, airy room, warm from the sun which poured through the tall windows.

Once settled into comfortable chairs in the parlour, Gil, as was his wont, had tea ready laid for them and required only the hot water to be brought by his housekeeper, Mrs Trent. Whilst he brewed tea for them all, Underwood and he exchanged news, mainly about the health of their mother and various uncles and aunts.

The meal over, polite enquiries ensued as to the health of all parties, then Gil turned to his sister-in-law and asked bluntly, "How is C H behaving, Verity?"

Verity blushed rosily and laughed self-consciously, "What on earth do you mean by that, Gil?"

Underwood glared at his brother, "Yes, what the devil do you mean, Gil?"

"You know exactly what I mean, Chuffy. You are a selfish creature, and I'm quite sure you have been treating your poor wife abominably."

Mr Underwood was a man who was always very much in control of his emotions, but if there was one man in the world who could reduce his stoicism to behaviour that would be more fitted to the nursery, it was his younger brother, and it was therefore a belligerent answer which flew back, "I would very much like to know what you think it has to do with you? If you must go about saving souls and giving sermons, keep them for those who appreciate your meddling."

Verity was appalled to be at the centre of this sudden squall, never having seen the brothers argue before, and wondered frantically how she could calm the situation. She would have been even more horrified had she known jealously lay at the base of their animosity. With his brother out of sight and therefore out of mind, Underwood had been able to forget that Verity and Gil were exceptionally fond of each other, but these unexpected comments from his brother roused a possessiveness which he would have been deeply ashamed to have to acknowledge.

For his own part, Gil had been as near to being in love with Verity as he had any woman, but had nobly stepped aside for his brother, knowing she was in love with him. That suppressed emotion now translated itself into a determination to force his brother, if necessary, to cherish the woman he had won.

Of course Verity knew Gil was fond of her, but she imagined the affection was brotherly, as her own was sisterly. It never occurred to her that he had ever really been in love with her. Vaguely it was borne upon her that this visit might not have been the best of ideas.

"Please, gentlemen. Let us have no more of this. It is very sweet of you to be concerned, Gil, but I assure you, Cadmus has given me no cause for complaint."

Gil glanced at her, taking note of her thin face and heavy eyes, then returned his gaze to his brother, "Do you hear that, Chuffy? No cause for complaint, but no mention of happiness, of fulfilment."

Underwood had regained his composure and was able to give a short laugh,

"Good heavens, Gil. Do you expect us to parade our private lives before the entire world?"

"I expect nothing but assurance of Verity's happiness," reasserted the vicar, with more determination than tact.

"Gil, I am happy. Of course I am happy," interjected Verity hastily.

"Satisfied, brother?" demanded a triumphant Underwood.

Gil grinned amiably, "That was all I wanted to know."

Underwood, realizing he had been successfully baited, allowed his expression to relax into a rueful smile, "Dammit, Gil! You almost had your claret drawn."

"You would not strike a man of the cloth," said Gil, feigning shock and horror.

"I'd gladly strike this one," grunted the seriously discomposed Underwood; "He shows an over-enthusiastic interest in my wife."

Gil said nothing, suddenly aware that he had gone too far, but was unable to entirely regret his behaviour. He felt that Underwood had married Verity for a dozen reasons, none of which included love. That would have been of no consequence had Verity felt the same way, but it could only cause her intense misery knowing her affection was not returned. From his uncharacteristically aggressive reaction, Gil felt sure that his brother was at least growing fonder of his wife, and with hard work and luck, a long and happy marriage might ensue. Gil had great regard for his brother, unresolved and unacknowledged feelings for Verity and he wished neither of them to suffer the anguish of an unhappy partnership.

The storm blown over, the brothers settled happily into an easy discourse in which Verity took no part. Neither seemed to notice that she had fallen unusually quiet and her demeanour was no longer placid. She wished Gil had not questioned her upon her marriage for, in doing so, he had forced her to ask herself the same questions, and she was not completely sure she could give herself the same answer she had given him.

She had been so happy in those first few weeks after their wedding, requiring nothing more from life than to be with Underwood, to be sincerely grateful that the miracle had happened, that he had married her and not the girl with whom he had fallen in love only months before.

Now, however, she found herself increasingly dissatisfied with their relationship. She thought more and more about Charlotte Wynter, wondering if Underwood too was thinking of her. She could not forget that she had been second choice, and that had things fallen out differently, he would never have seen her as anything other than a friend. In short he had never told her that he had fallen out of love with Charlotte and in love with her. She loved him still, perhaps more than ever before, for she had given herself completely to him, had lain in his arms at night and discovered the passion of which he was capable, but that had merely intensified the underlying misery which soured her feelings for him. How could she be sure that he was thinking of her, and not imagining another life?

She could not control her bitterness and found herself being critical of his actions, always looking for an ulterior motive when he said or did something kind or complimentary. She despised herself for it – and him more for causing her to do it.

Had she really been lying when she told Gil she was happy? She did not know, and it was not knowing which gnawed at her, cankerous and malignant.

CHAPTER TWO

'Verbum Sat Sapienti' – A word is enough to the wise

A chink in the curtains allowed a single strand of sunlight into the room, which shone directly into Verity's eyes, waking her with a start. After a considerable delay for blinking, stretching and yawning, she lay watching the dust motes dancing on the air. It was not until she realized how high the sun must be to shine in at this angle that she began to wonder just how late she must have slept. The little gold watch that had been a wedding gift from her husband and now spent its days pinned to the front of her dress, lay on the table beside her bed and she reached lazily for it. She gasped and quickly sat up when she had focused clearly enough to read the time – past eleven o'clock. No wonder the bed beside her had been long vacated by Underwood!

Once the curtains had been drawn fully back, the room was flooded with daylight and with a contented sigh Verity raised the sash, rested her elbows on the sill and looked out onto the garden.

It lay tranquil beneath her, full of the drowsy heat of the approaching noon. Well-kept lawns were edged with flower-filled borders, chaotic with colour and scent, here and there a heavy-laden bee blundered clumsily from blossom to blossom, and she was enchanted to see butterflies winging their erratic way across the path. A box hedge which divided the garden from the orchard beyond, rustled and filled the air with the high pitched squabbling of sparrows.

Their sudden panicked flight heralded the arrival of human disturbance, and Verity heard a door close beneath her. Presently Gil and Underwood appeared below her window and both hesitated, apparently to admire the garden, "Who does all this, Gil, for I'm sure it is not your handiwork?" asked Underwood.

"An elderly relation of Mrs Trent comes in twice a week, but you would not think it so idyllic on the days he brings his goat. It is supposed to keep the grass short, but the one idea in its head is to eat the flowers. The language is not fit for a clergyman's ears, believe me!"

Underwood laughed and Verity was about to call a cheery good morning to them when she heard her name mentioned and succumbed all too readily to a little harmless eavesdropping.

"Chuffy, are you sure Verity is quite well?" Gil continued, his voice full of concern. Verity shrank back slightly, almost holding her breath for fear they should become aware of her presence. She found that the answer her husband gave suddenly meant a great deal to her.

"What makes you ask?" Underwood sounded vague, as though his mind were on other things.

"I notice she does not look her usual self. She has grown a little thinner, has she not?"

"I have no idea – but after being jostled over bad roads for hours on end, and an appalling night's sleep in a less than salubrious posting house, it is scarcely surprising she looks a little jaded." He sounded more irritated than caring and Verity sank her teeth into her lower lip.

"Are you sure that is all?" pursued Gil anxiously.

"Humph!" snorted Underwood, "You show an avid interest in Verity's welfare – perhaps you should have married her when you had the chance."

Gil answered quietly, but with deep feeling, "There are times, my dear brother, when you are unspeakably insensitive!"

"So I have frequently been told. I apologize." They strolled away and any further conversation was lost to her. With a sharp intake of breath, she pulled herself away from the window, afraid that the brothers might give a backward glance and see her at the window.

She sat at the dressing table and gazed pensively at her reflection, thinking with hurt confusion of what she had overheard. Eavesdroppers never hear good of themselves, said the old adage – how true! Underwood had sounded so indifferent to her, so callous when he suggested that Gil should have married her. Did he perhaps now wish that things had been different? And to use the word 'jaded' in reference to her; it was a word one used for old, raddled women.

The face which stared palely back at her served only to cruelly reinforce his assessment. She was worse than jaded, she was positively haggard! The hair combed back off her face in her night time plait was altogether too severe a style, accentuating the strong shape of her physiognomy, the too determined jaw, the slightly heavy brow.

With a determination born of hurt and anger at her husband's dismissive attitude towards her, Verity loosened the plait, found a pair of scissors in her dressing case and began to hack at the front of her hair.

It took her only a few minutes to remember how to use the curling tongs, but a little practise to use them on herself – she had only ever used them before in her capacity as a lady's companion, and she found it was entirely different wielding them on her own hair. Had she but known it, she was extremely lucky to have such thick and resilient hair, for the inexpert coiffure could have been disastrous. As it happened, any errors she made in the cutting were hidden in the glossy ringlets she finally achieved. The back of her hair she left long, partly because she couldn't reach or see it, but also because she could not bear the idea of parting with all her tresses. This was coiled into its usual chignon, but her face was softened by the fashionable ringlets which now framed it, lending an unaccustomed and unexpected femininity and prettiness. A gentle pinching restored a little colour to her cheeks, and she decided that the time had come to doff the dark colours she had worn since her father's death and her occupation as a governess – after all, she was a governess no longer.

She was grateful now that her mother-in-law had persuaded her on several shopping trips just prior to her wedding, and had enticed her into purchasing numerous articles of clothing and adornment which she had been convinced she would never wear. Her present mood, however, was one of reckless abandon, and she delved deep into the trunk which she had, as yet, not managed to unpack.

*

When his wife walked into the dining room, having missed breakfast, but in good time for luncheon, looking stylish and much younger than she had the day before, Underwood's mouth dropped open in an exceedingly unbecoming gape. It was left to Gil to leap to his feet and hold her chair for her to be seated, saying, as he did so, "What a remarkably pretty dress, Verity. I don't believe I have ever seen you wear red before. I must say it suits you."

Verity managed to smile at him, but her eyes were fixed on Underwood, wondering what his reaction was going to be. She thought he was finding the dress too garish, though it was in fact a rather muted shade, more dark cherry than scarlet, and picked out with tiny gold spots.

Underwood, with all the tact of his sex, managed to say entirely the wrong thing, "What have you done with your hair?" he asked bluntly.

13

"Don't you like it?" she asked, a little breathlessly. He observed her dispassionately for several seconds, his head slightly on one side, "I liked it long."

Gil waited for the explosion of wrath from his sister-in-law which he felt Underwood richly deserved, but Verity said mildly, "It is still long, I have only trimmed the front a little." Then she added, rather stiffly, "You have never mentioned liking my hair before!"

He looked blankly at her for a moment, as though he did not quite understand the significance of this comment, then countered, in a tone which brooked no argument, "Of course I have." Upon which he began to serve himself from the assembled dishes.

Verity, however, was not about to relinquish the discussion. Too often in the past she had done just that, and had endured frustration and unhappiness, feeling that nothing was ever resolved between her husband and herself.

"In fact," she pursued in a quiet, though clear and slightly aggressive tone, "you never mention my appearance at all. I don't suppose you could even tell me the colour of my eyes."

It was a challenge and he immediately recognized the fact. Vaguely it was borne upon him that he was about to undertake some sort of a test, and his future comfort might very well depend upon his answer. He was not pleased for he was a man who cherished his peace, besides which he was hungry and wanted his lunch. After the slightest delay he lifted his eyes to her face, whereupon she closed the disputed orbs. His anger vanished in an instant and amusement replaced it. He smiled as he said softly, "You are placing ridiculous importance upon a trifle."

With her eyes screwed firmly shut, Verity replied, "You only say that because you cannot answer. If I am wrong and you do know, I shall retract and apologise, but I do not think I shall be called upon to do so."

Underwood threw his glance heavenward in exasperation, then looked in irritation at his smugly grinning brother.

"Very well, if you must play silly games. Your eyes are hazel, with intriguing specks of pure gold. The dress you wore yesterday was dark grey with a white lace collar. Your birthday is September the tenth and you will be twenty-seven years old. Our wedding day was the nineteenth of November and your height is five feet four inches. Does that satisfy you?"

14

Her eyes sprang open at the first of these revelations and now she looked at him, her eyes soft, her teeth sunk guiltily into her lip, "Oh, Cadmus!"

"*Oh, Cadmus*, is all very well, but I have been vastly maligned," he told her with mock severity.

She took his words far more seriously than he ever intended and tears glistened in her eyes, "Yes, you have," she admitted, "But you have no one but yourself to blame. I have not the gift of second sight. How can I know you see these things if you make no mention of the fact? It would be nice if you occasionally told me that I was dressed becomingly."

"But you are always neat and tidy, and I was not aware that such comments were required of me. I have never asked your approval or opinion, because the looking glass tells me everything I need to know."

"It is not the same for a man," she said helplessly, aware that he would never understand this vague protest, "My looking glass does not tell me if I seem attractive in your eyes."

As she watched his reaction from beneath lowered lids, her heart sank. His expression was one of complete astonishment – evidently he had never thought of the word 'attractive' in connection with his wife. She almost wished she had not initiated the conversation – and yet, was it not better to know than to be forever wondering? Of course he did not find her attractive, he had never done so, had never pretended otherwise. She only wished her humiliation were not about to be paraded before Gil.

In her misery she desired nothing more than to slink away, to hide and lick her wounds like an injured animal.

"Attractive to me? My dear girl, I had no idea you had any such ambition. I wish I had been aware of it, for I might have saved you a good deal of inconvenience," he said smoothly. Distress tightened in her throat in a painful lump which threatened any moment to burst forth in a torrent of weeping. Why had she started this? But he was still speaking and she forced herself to listen, though she thought she had never felt such pain as this before in her life.

"It is not your apparel which I find attractive, it is merely a decent covering. It is your heart and your mind which hold my interest. Your face and those lovely expressive eyes, the colour of which, despite your cynicism, I shall recall all my life, hold my attention more surely than any dress. I do not notice nor care what you wear, and I always thought it was the same for you."

It was Verity now who gaped in amazement. Never in her wildest fantasies had she imagined Underwood saying anything so charming or romantic.

Gil was rather taken aback. Had he realized Underwood intended to speak so frankly he would have vacated the room several minutes ago. He rose as quietly as he was able and swiftly left, but he need not have worried. Neither husband nor wife noticed his departure. They had eyes only for each other.

Verity swallowed deeply, unable now to prevent the tears spilling onto her cheeks, "Cadmus…" her voice broke on a sob and he rose so quickly that his chair fell over backwards and clattered unheeded to the floor. When he reached her, he took her in his arms and kissed her. It was as though their lips had met for the first time, so powerful were the emotions Verity was experiencing.

They could have remained thus for some considerable time had not Gil knocked at the door and called plaintively, "I trust all is settled between you, because I am passing out with hunger."

Underwood released her and laughing, tossed her his handkerchief, "I have never known a woman to have a handkerchief when she needs one! Wipe your tears. Gil wishes to show us Hanbury when we have eaten."

When the meal was over, Verity went to prepare for their walk and Gil faced his brother across the table, "You handled that situation very well, Chuffy. You have great charm when you choose to exert it, but tell me now, truthfully, did you mean a single word you said to Verity?"

Underwood gazed impassively at his sibling for several seconds before he replied bluntly, "You overstep the mark, Gilbert. Verity is my wife, kindly remember that!"

*

Hanbury did not disappoint them. It had expanded and prospered since Verity visited it last, several years before. The fashion for spas had been growing steadily for three or four decades and Hanbury had joined a little late, but with whole-hearted enthusiasm. The townsmen had built all that a spa required, Baths and Pump-rooms, theatres and Assembly rooms. There was even a small crescent of stone-fronted

16

terraced houses. The pretty tree-lined squares led to wide avenues of imposing hotels, inns, boarding houses and shops. The whole place was a bustle of activity, and because it was still the largest town in the district, it was the market for the whole area, as well as being the goal and focus for those who needed, or felt they needed, a restorative.

In her present buoyant mood, Verity thoroughly enjoyed her walk, but for Underwood, that inveterate observer of mankind, the highlight of the tour was the visit to the Pump-rooms.

Resplendent in marble and mahogany, the Pump-room itself was a triumph of the town-planners. Several dolphin-fashioned fountains spewed forth the clear, cold hill water into marble basins and those who wished, and were able to afford the charges, could help themselves to the magical cure-all. There were brass cups on chains provided for the purpose, but many of the richer visitors brought their own silver or crystal cups. Mahogany benches lined the walls, or made little round islands in the centre of the marble-tiled floors. Palm trees strained towards the glass roof, as though to feel the real sun on their feathery heads, and lent an atmosphere of sticky heat which could almost be mistaken, by those who knew no better, for the tropical.

It was not just this opulence which fascinated Underwood, but also the gentry who were enjoying it. There were a few poor souls scattered about who could be seen to be genuinely ill or infirm, but most of the wheeled chairs were occupied by women whose faces displayed the sourness of boredom, the disappointment of lives which were empty and without purpose, and who had consequently taken refuge in the small excitement of pretended illness, or by men who had spent their youths indulging in every kind of excess and were now paying the price of ill-health.

There was a sprinkling of younger people; unmarried and obedient daughters, who trotted dutifully to the gushing fountains to fill the cups; the idle young bucks, short of money and hoping to charm a little from the pockets of gout-ridden fathers by a show of filial affection. Then there were lady companions, bitter at their poverty and spinsterhood, who could be guaranteed to quell any show of humour or romance from the young.

Underwood found a seat for his wife and went to fetch her a glass of water – a glass provided by the ever-thoughtful Gil, who overlooked nothing. Verity was not particularly eager to try the waters, but Underwood had insisted, remarking that she had not been 'quite up to snuff' since they had left his mother. Verity had to agree with that assessment of the situation. There had been one or two occasions lately when she had felt quite ghastly, though nothing would have induced her to admit that to her husband.

She dutifully sipped the proffered drink and was pleasantly surprised to find it quite palatable. She relaxed into her seat and looked about her, listening to the two men discussing various other occupants of the room.

Gil had wasted no time in making himself at home in Hanbury and already had a following of long-term visitors and inhabitants. He tended to be particularly popular with the elderly ladies in his congregation, but Underwood and Verity kindly kept this observation to themselves.

Both Underwood and Gil would have strenuously denied ever indulging in gossip, but their conversation sounded remarkably gossipy to the amused Verity.

"The elderly lady in purple silk and the huge turban is Lady Hartley-Wells and the woman beside her is Miss Cromer, her companion. She lives in a gigantic mausoleum of a house just outside Hanbury. She lost her husband and only son twenty years ago in a carriage accident and has refused to move away from the town or out of mourning ever since. Rumour has it she intends to leave everything to the church, so I am under strict instructions from the Bishop to treat her nicely – and to be honest, it is not hard to do. She appears forbidding, but she's extremely kind-hearted."

"Perhaps I ought to be charming to her and steal her riches from under the Bishop's nose," said Underwood with a grin.

"I wish you would," returned Gil seriously, "I admit I resent the assumption that only the rich are worthy of notice. I didn't join the ministry to toad-eat the titled and wealthy."

"You didn't – but most of the others did."

Gil described a few others to his brother, then there was a sudden buzz of activity by the door and most heads turned to witness the advent of another elderly woman. She caused a stir not least because of the way she was dressed, which was a fashion which would have looked out of place on all but the youngest and most virginal of girls. She leaned heavily on a silver-handled, ebony cane on one side and a dandified youth on the other. She was laughing loud and hearty at some sally from her companion and sound was echoing in the vast room, drowning out even the sound of the constantly falling water.

"Mother and son?" enquired Underwood quietly. Gil shook his head and murmured back, "Believe it or not, husband and wife. She is nearing seventy, he is not yet twenty-six. Oliver Dunstable and his bride Josephine."

Underwood raised a quizzical brow, but he made no comment, merely watching Josephine and her husband as they made an almost royal progress across the floor to their accustomed seat. She called loudly to acquaintances and none tried to cut her, though several looked distinctly uncomfortable at having such attention drawn to them.

The Dunstables seemed entirely unmoved by such rudeness, raucously and obviously enjoying each other's company, and very possibly also enjoying the discomfiture they were inflicting upon their fellow man.

"Love match?" asked Underwood succinctly.

"I honestly could not say for sure," replied Gil. "They seem to have a tremendously good time together, but she has a great deal of money and it would appear he has none. She also has a daughter with a husband whom she heartily despises, and it has been suggested the marriage was contracted to spite the pair of them. All I really know is that the young husband is outrageously indulged and glories in it."

Verity chose this moment to speak, but only because it was a subject about which she felt strongly, "I think everyone has the right to happiness, even if it defies convention."

Underwood smiled at her; "I could not agree more, my dear. And for myself, I am always delighted to hear of a marriage which dwarfs the fifteen-year age gap which exists between us. I feel almost boyish."

The look in Verity's eyes told him that their difference in age had been her very last consideration.

Gil caught a glimpse of the look which passed between them and raised his eyes heavenward. He was beginning to wonder if he would not have been happier had he chosen not to interfere in his brother's concerns. He hated the suspicion he had that Underwood was not being entirely honest regarding his feelings for his young wife.

Being an outside observer of these complicated, and hitherto unknown, love games was going to be intensely wearing!

CHAPTER THREE

'Arbiter Elegantiarum' – *The judge in matters of taste*

The village in which Verity had spent her formative years was some five miles from Hanbury by road, but only about two and a half on foot across the moors. Accordingly, she rose early the next morning, leaving Underwood asleep, and told Gil over tea, that she intended to spend the day visiting old friends. She had not asked Underwood to accompany her, knowing he would find the whole expedition tedious in the extreme. He was not a man much prompted by sentiment, and he would never understand her wish to see again the places connected with a happy childhood.

The present incumbent of Draythorp was a youngish man, in his first position, and was only too delighted to meet the daughter of one of his predecessors. Reverend Chapell was still remembered with great affection and so was his only child. Reverend Mitchell insisted on showing Verity around the village, calling at several homes where he knew she would be welcomed. Verity had a delightful morning, renewing old acquaintances, especially one lady who had been particularly close to the motherless girl. Mrs Leigh had tears in her eyes when she saw Verity, for she had begged the young woman to stay with her when her father died, and had been most distressed by Verity's insistence that she must go out into the world and earn her own living. She was overjoyed to hear that Verity was now a married woman and extended invitations to both the Underwoods, should they grow tired of Hanbury.

Verity was both touched and heartened by her reception and promised to pay more visits whilst she was in the district. She returned to Hanbury in time for tea and found her husband waiting impatiently for her. He testily complained that his brother had bored him to death, talking of nothing but his plans for the future and Underwood's duty to his wife. She laughed gaily and assured him he would have found her company quite as trying.

*

Gil spent the next few days attempting to persuade his brother to view the large, old house he had envisioned as a school, but

Underwood was proving unusually resistant. He did not actually refuse to go, but he did always seem to have something much more pressing to do.

He insisted now that his wife take the waters every morning, luncheon was always taken with Gil at the vicarage, then she was free to pursue her pastime of painting or sketching for a couple of hours. There were so many pretty spots, and places teeming with people that Verity was never at a loss to find an interesting subject to draw. A brisk walk every day after tea filled the time until the evening's entertainment. Both Underwood and Verity were accomplished musicians, so they never tired of the concerts and recitals held in the Assembly rooms, nor missed any new plays shown in one of the several theatres. They explored every portion of Hanbury and as they came to be recognized in the Pump-rooms, they began to receive invitations to teas, dinners, parties and soirees. Verity was enjoying herself far too much to support Gil in his attempts to make Underwood look to his future. She knew, of course, that the holiday must eventually come to an end, and they would have to decide how their living would be made, but this new mood of recklessness in her husband was too precious to be quickly abandoned. The feeling of illness which had dogged her was also fading, much to her relief, though whether this was due to the healing waters, or merely her present happiness, she could not quite decide.

At last, however, Underwood ran out of excuses, and on the first rainy day they had to endure, a carriage was ordered. Verity immediately wished she had been left out of the expedition, for their progress was along one of the steepest roads in the town and she could plainly hear the horse's hooves slithering and sliding as the nag struggled to keep a foothold on the rain-greased cobbles. Her knuckles gleamed white in the dank interior of the vehicle as she clutched desperately at the squabs and straps in her tussle to keep her seat. Bravely she made no demur, but her knees were trembling beneath her when she finally alighted.

She almost scrambled back into the hated carriage when she beheld the place to which they had been brought. Dark grey walls, streaked with rivulets of rain, rose sheer before them, with small windows set deep into the walls. It looked like a prison and Verity shuddered at the very sight of it. She could not believe it had ever been used as a dwelling, and felt Gil must have been mistaken. One glance at her husband told her he was equally unimpressed. She had rarely seen him look so severe. Only Gil was enthusiastic, but even he was having to force himself.

"I know it does not look much now, but a great deal could be done with it."

"Yes, Gil. It could be converted into a prison or a workhouse – if that was not its original use! What possessed you to think I would condemn any child to enter that building?"

"It's very cheap," said Gil, faint, but pursuing.

"It would have to be given away – and I still wouldn't consider it. But wait, I presume too much! I have not asked the opinion of my wife. What say you, Verity? Shall we start a school here?"

She shook her head, the power of speech momentarily taken away from her. She had never seen a building which looked as though several generations of horrible murders had taken place within its walls, but this place fitted the aura perfectly. If Underwood had begged her on bended knees to enter its portals, she would have refused him – for the first time since their wedding.

Gil looked so downcast she could not help but take pity on him, though she was bitterly disappointed. He had evidently been looking at the property from a purely practical point of view and did not quite understand their extreme reaction. For herself, she had been looking forward to making a home in Hanbury, for her heart lay in the Pennines, and she could think of nothing more perfect than working side by side with him in the town she loved. It now seemed the dream was over. When the holiday ended they must return to his mother and think again.

"Never mind, Gil," she said kindly, "You tried, and it was kind of you."

"Ah, well the Lord loves one who tries," said Gil, rallying.

"He must adore you then," muttered Underwood, unkindly. Verity jabbed him sharply in the ribs with her elbow, then smiled sweetly at her brother-in-law, "Do you mind taking the carriage and leaving us to walk home, Gil?"

"I'd walk with you, but I am in rather a hurry," said Gil, consulting his fob in a way which fooled nobody.

"We will meet again at dinner, then," said Underwood, taking Verity's hand and hooking it over his arm in preparation for their walk.

Gil needed no second bidding and presently they were left alone, blinking in a sudden burst of watery sunlight which had managed to break through the leaden clouds.

"I suppose it looks a little better in the sunshine," said Verity grudgingly, glancing upwards one last time.

"Better than what?" asked Underwood tersely, "We have to face it, my love. Gil has a very different idea of this school than ourselves. He sees the whole enterprise as nothing more than a method of earning money, but teaching, to me at least, has always been a vocation – and one which I'm not entirely sure I still wish to follow. I spent nearly twenty years buried in Cambridge and missing out on things I never knew existed. I want life now, not a smaller version of the same deadness."

Verity was swamped by a variety of emotions, each of which clamoured for release. Her delight in his confiding in her was swiftly replaced by panic, excitement and fear.

Her panic was based on the fact that Underwood was peculiarly unsuited for any other form of employment than teaching. Excitement was roused by the knowledge that they were free – free to do whatever they wished.

"But what else is there?" she asked, not in a critical tone of voice, for he knew she trusted him completely, but in a musing sort of way.

As they strolled back into Hanbury, Underwood told her exactly what there was, and she was glad of the support of his arm, for as he talked she grew more and more stunned. She began to feel that she did not know this man she had married, and would never, ever have any real notion of the workings of his mind.

*

He did not ask her not to mention their discussion to Gil, but instinctively she knew that his brother was not yet to be invited to share their vision of the years ahead, so accordingly the talk over dinner was of mundane matters.

Mundane, that is, until the subject of Oliver and Josephine Dunstable arose. Gil, who only became odiously sanctimonious when accused of gossip, had a most interesting tit-bit to disclose.

"Josephine's daughter Leah had arrived in town, dragging her husband and child in her wake. Judging from the scene she caused in the Pump-room yesterday afternoon, she is not best pleased to hear of her mother's marriage."

"Poor Mrs Dunstable," said the soft-hearted Verity, "But was she not invited to the wedding?"

"No, apparently it was a clandestine affair from beginning to end," reported Gil, "And I would not be too concerned for 'poor' Josephine, if I were you. It would seem she gave quite as good as she got, accusing Leah of wanting her money for her wastrel husband."

"And is he a wastrel?" asked Underwood, peeling an apple with precision, a curl of skin falling neatly onto his plate.

"The term describes him well enough, I understand," answered Gil, "But one can only sympathize with his wife, if it is so. Their only child has been a deaf-mute since birth, and is incredibly difficult to control. She has the most appalling fits of anger, due, no doubt, to the frustration of being unable to communicate her wants and desires."

Verity was appalled by this series of misfortunes, "How dreadful! Can nothing be done for the poor child?"

"It would seem not – but Leah is well-cared for, since her mother has always been most generous, even though she knows most of her money goes to financing the husband's indulgences and not helping the child."

"Altogether a charming family," remarked Underwood cynically; "It would appear the child requires as much sympathy for the relatives she possesses as for her disabilities."

Gil and Verity both made a pretence at protesting at this, but neither really disagreed with him.

"How do you come by all this information, Gil?" asked Verity suddenly intrigued by the wealth of detail he could usually muster.

"Afternoon tea can be most instructive," he replied with a smile.

*

Not too many days were to pass before the Underwood family were to meet the Gedneys, and they could judge for themselves how true were the various assessments of their characters.

Verity tried to be Christian, Underwood did not bother, but in the end their notes would have tallied almost perfectly.

Adolphus Gedney was an obnoxious man, but his odium was not immediately apparent, for he was not an unpleasant looking man, being tall, with slightly reddish hair, and a not unhandsome

24

countenance – or at least not when viewed from a distance. Close to it bore all the ravages of the habitual drinker. He was jovial enough at first meeting, but time quickly exposed his true self. He was loud, arrogant, self-opinionated and callous towards his family, especially his afflicted daughter, whom he largely ignored, but when in his cups he was inclined to berate as a poor reflection upon his own manhood. He unashamedly blamed his wife for the fall from perfection. He rarely touched the child, leaving his wife to struggle alone in attending to her wants and needs. Verity could have forgiven him much if he had, just once, spoken kindly to the unfortunate Melissa.

Mrs Gedney, not surprisingly, had a streak of bitterness which was not alleviated by her insistence upon playing the martyr. She haughtily refused all offers of help, then made much of her suffering, of her struggles and misfortunes.

Verity, in particular, had been more than ready to take the woman's side and would gladly have befriended and assisted her, but she was quickly made aware that such an approach would not be welcome. Leah Gedney was vociferous in her condemnation of any who dared to pity her, but at the same time, was amazed and appalled when she failed to win special treatment. She criticized her husband constantly when he was out of earshot, but was vicious in her attacks on anyone else, especially her mother, who had the temerity to join in her tirades against him. She showed no sign of being in love with him, but for some twisted reason of her own, she stood solidly by him. Verity could only surmise that to fail to defend him would in some way expose her own stupidity in ever having married him, for he had been her own choice and not her mother's. On the contrary, Josephine it seemed, had recognized his type from the onset and had done her utmost to dissuade her headstrong daughter from the liaison.

Verity sensibly decided that she was altogether too dangerous a person with whom to become intimate, but still her heart bled for the child. The only consolation seemed to be that the ten-year-old Melissa was unaware of the unhappiness surrounding her – though strangely she did display a deep aversion to her father.

Verity could not help but wonder if either parent ever noticed, or indeed cared, about the effect their behaviour had on their young and deeply troubled offspring. She doubted it; both were entirely self-centred and determined only to feel self-pity for the misfortune Heaven had seen fit to lay upon them. It gave the vicar's daughter quite a jolt to observe all this, for in the past she had always believed that God gave people the strength to cope with whatever cross they might be required to bear. For the first time in her sheltered life she was forced to acknowledge that this might not necessarily be true.

When she sobbed a little on Underwood's shoulder in the dark intimacy of their big, old-fashioned four-poster, and refused to tell him the cause of her tears, he could only hold her in his arms and hope that whatever troubled her would soon pass. He could not know, nor would he have understood, that something fundamental was shaken within her. Some part of her innocence was destroyed forever with the knowledge that people were capable of being so utterly beastly to each other. Tragedy should, she knew, bring a married couple closer together, not give them excuses to revile each other. Such thoughts made her fret about her own relationship with Underwood. She wondered constantly how they would react should some such disaster overtake them. Her health took another sudden plunge, but now she was being physically sick. It took all her ingenuity to hide this from her husband, but Gil was not fooled so easily.

She was mortified when early one morning, about ten days after their arrival in Hanbury, she raised her head from vomiting in a bowl in the kitchen and met the concerned gaze of her brother-in-law, who was standing in the doorway.

He said nothing, merely crossed the room and handed her a cloth to wipe her mouth, then led her solicitously to a chair. She sank listlessly into it, then promptly burst into tears, "Please say you won't tell Cadmus, Gil!"

"But why, Verity? Don't you want him to know you are going to have a child?"

Her head jerked up so swiftly he almost expected to hear the vertebrae crack,

"What!"

"A baby, Verity. That is what all this is about, isn't it?"

To his amazement she broke into even wilder sobs, "Oh, dear God, is that what's wrong with me?"

"Didn't you know?"

"No! I thought I was ill. I never had a mother to tell me about these things. It never occurred to me to think of a baby."

Sudden affection for her clutched at his heart. Bless the girl! She knew nothing at all, of course. Her mother died young and her father

26

was a clergyman – a man hardly likely to sit and explain the facts of life to his daughter.

"Well," he said bracingly, "I'm no expert, and I think you should consult a doctor, but I should be astounded if there were any other explanation."

Her relief was such that she rose to her feet and flung herself at him. After a momentary hesitation he put his arms around her, feeling incredibly uncomfortable, but understanding her need to be held.

It was thus that Underwood, come in search of his missing wife, saw them through the kitchen door. First tears in the night, and now this. With a faint frown creasing his brow, he turned silently away and went back to his rapidly cooling bed.

CHAPTER FOUR

'Odi Et Amo' – I love and I hate at the same time

Verity decided to wait for confirmation from a doctor before she told Underwood their news, but events conspired to prevent her from doing so for quite some time.

Their customary visit to the Pump-rooms the following morning was spoiled for Verity by the presence of one whom she had hoped never to see again.

Her heart began to beat a little faster before she was even conscious of recognizing the bright abundance of chestnut hair visible across the expanse of the room, then the woman turned and Verity knew with sickening certainty that it was none other than Charlotte Wynter – the girl to whom Underwood had been betrothed before Fate had intervened and left him to Verity.

Charlotte had, if anything, grown more lovely with the passing of a year. She had lost the charming girlishness, it is true, the rounded plumpness, the silliness, but in its place there was a woman of poise, grace and a certain dignity which her sorrows had bestowed upon her. Still barely nineteen, she seemed older, and it was that fact alone which struck terror into Verity's heart. In a battle for Underwood's affection, she could have beaten the silly child hollow, but this grave young lady was a different matter entirely.

Charlotte saw them before Underwood noticed her, for he was busy exchanging greetings with various acquaintances and did not look towards her until he heard her voice, "Why, it is Mr Underwood and Verity. I had no idea you were here."

There was something in her voice, and still more in her calm demeanour which suggested to Verity that this statement was untrue and she had known full well of the Underwoods' presence in Hanbury. She managed to force a smile, but her covert glance at her husband told her nothing of his reaction. He certainly was not smiling, and he looked a little paler, perhaps, than usual, but no more than naturally surprised to be thus addressed, "Good Heavens! Miss

Wynter. What brings you to Hanbury?" he asked, after the slightest hesitation.

"The stage, my dear Mr Underwood!" she replied, her gay laughter lifting the gravity of her expression for one compelling moment.

A physical pain stabbed Verity when she saw her husband's face also break into a delighted smile and his hands reached for his erstwhile betrothed, "You look wonderful, Charlotte. I cannot believe you stand in need of the waters."

Charlotte laid her hand in his and he promptly kissed it.

"Thank you, kind sir," she said softly, then added, "Of course you are quite right. The waters are not for my benefit, but for my sister Isobel."

"Oh, is Isobel here too?" asked Verity, glad to have her thoughts distracted by this piece of news. She had been Isobel's governess and had been particularly fond of her young charge.

Charlotte looked down at Verity for the first time, all her attention having previously centred on Underwood, "Good day, Verity. How are you? I hope you are taking the waters. You ought to, you look so pale and thin!" Her smile was supposed to indicate to Underwood that she was sure she must share this opinion with him, and Verity's cheeks became suffused with painful colour at the insult. She knew she was not looking her best, and had no desire for her shortcomings to be paraded before her husband.

"Yes," continued Charlotte, not displeased with the effect her words had had upon Verity, "She is over by the fountain there, dutifully drinking her water with a wry face. Would you be sweet and go over and tell her where I am? I am sure she would be delighted to see you." This apparently ingenuous dismissal gave Verity no choice but to comply and she did so with evident reluctance. She was not much cheered by Isobel's reaction to this piece of folly.

"Good gad, Verity! What are you thinking of, leaving Charlotte alone with Mr Underwood?" she rebuked her old governess, when the barest of greetings had been exchanged, "She only thought of bringing me here for my health when she heard from Ellen Herbert that you were both here."

Verity silently cursed her own stupidity in writing and imparting this information to her friend Ellen. But how could she have guessed Charlotte was still interested in Underwood? She had been given enough chances to marry him, had she so desired, and had rejected him in no uncertain terms. It would seem she was now regretting that decision, but was Underwood?

As she glanced across the room, Verity saw, with a sinking heart, that Underwood was showing every sign of enjoying himself immensely. He was laughing at something Charlotte had said, and she was leaning towards him, her hand resting lightly on his sleeve.

If only she had known it, Underwood was not quite as relaxed as Verity was imagining. As soon as he saw Charlotte's lovely face, he had been painfully reminded of the passion the girl had roused in him, but the emotion was fleeting. Her behaviour from the outset appalled him and he suddenly realized that she was, in fact, not a particularly pleasant girl. The way she first ignored Verity, then spoken dismissively to her, as though she still saw her as a servant and an inferior, and had then obviously enjoyed the visible humiliation Verity had experienced, had killed any possible rekindling of his old affection for her. He knew now, beyond any shadow of doubt, that he had never loved Charlotte, though he had been infatuated with her. As he looked at her, dispassionately examining her, he could forgive himself for that weakness, reflecting that any man would have had his head turned by her. She was a magnificent creature, but her outward appearance hid a young woman who was vain, selfish and more than a little cruel. He silently thanked Providence that he had been saved from himself and her. All that, however, did not quite banish the memory of finding his wife in his brother's arms. He did not really believe they were betraying him, for he felt he knew both their characters well enough to be sure that neither was made for infidelity, but he still wanted to know exactly what was going on between them, and he felt Verity deserved a little punishment until she chose to confide in him. It was for this reason that he did not follow his first instinct and walk away from Charlotte the moment she started being rude to his wife.

Verity, unaware of any of these machinations, could only watch with growing misery as her husband smiled at the gaily-flirting Charlotte.

Isobel, altogether a much nicer and more intuitive creature than her sister, saw at once Verity's distress and set out to take her attention away from the unpleasant scene unfolding before their eyes, whilst silently vowing to castigate her sister later, in the privacy of their rented house.

"Verity, I am so very glad to see you again," she said, beginning to walk and drawing her companion with her. Verity was forced to tear her gaze away from her husband and fall into step beside the younger girl.

"Dear Isobel," she said, realizing what was being attempted and achieved, "how very grown up you have become. You used to be so shy, I feared you would never leave the house again, once I was gone."

Isobel laughed, not in the least perturbed by this plain speaking, "I was a strange little thing, wasn't I? But when Papa died, everything changed. It was as though a great weight had been lifted from me. I had been quite terrified of him, but so accustomed to the sensation that I couldn't imagine any other way of living. I suppose I thought everyone must behave as he did, and all I ever wanted was to become invisible, so that no one would shout at me, as he had always done. It altered my life beyond description when I met you, then Mr Underwood, for suddenly I understood that not everyone in the world was like my father and Harry and my horrid cousin Edwin."

"I suppose he is still at Wynter Court?"

"Oh, yes – and as odious as ever. Did you hear that my sister Maria died, and now he is free to marry again? That is part of the reason why we came away. He proposed to Charlotte and she wants to think about it."

Verity was aghast, "Good God, she is never thinking of accepting him? After the way he treated Maria?"

31

"Well, she loves the house so, and her horses, and as she pointed out, she will have to marry sometime, so why not Edwin? She thinks she will be able to control him in a way poor Maria never could."

Verity, who could think of a thousand 'why not Edwin' answers, could only shake her head in disbelief. She was saved from having to comment further by the sound of Charlotte's laughter echoing across the room, and the pained look which passed over her face prompted Isobel to say, "I had hoped walking about the room a little would cool me, but I am still far too hot. Would you mind if we went out into the fresh air?"

Her companion nodded miserably, too suddenly weary to think of a reason for denying her. Their peregrination led them past the circulating library, and of one accord they entered those august portals. However, once inside, they wandered about in a most desultory manner, neither feeling much inclined to find a book to read. Verity thought Isobel looked most unwell and her growing concern for her young friend made her forget her own troubles for a while.

Strangely enough, Isobel's thoughts were of a similar nature and she wished heartily she had possessed strength enough to have dissuaded Charlotte from this visit. Her own selfish desire to see Verity again had blinded her to the difficulties her sister would inflict on the ex-governess.

"I'm so sorry," she said. Verity glanced at her, rather startled by such vehemence.

"What on earth have you to be sorry for, my dear?"

"For letting Charlotte bring me here. I should have known she meant to cause mischief!"

"Does she mean to do so, Isobel?"

"I fear she does."

Verity looked defeated for a moment, then squared her shoulders as though to prepare them for the load they might be required to carry, "Underwood is a grown man. He must make his own decisions. Only…"

"Only what?"

"There is something my husband should know, but I cannot tell him until he decides whether it is I or Charlotte whom he wants!"

Isobel was about to enquire further into this intriguing statement when their conversation was interrupted by the arrival of a young couple into the almost empty library – a young couple who proceeded to behave very oddly indeed.

Verity and Isobel had found themselves a secluded spot at the very back of the rooms, and had seated themselves on two of the many scattered chairs, placed there for the convenience of browsers. The two newcomers, without noticing their presence, did likewise. There followed a period of love-play which might have entranced the watching Verity had it not been for the fact that the young man was Oliver Dunstable, but the companion who was receiving his kisses with such laughing relish was most certainly not his wife Josephine.

Verity took Isobel by the arm and hissed urgently, "We must get away from here now, and that man mustn't see us! I could not bear the embarrassment if he were to realize what we have just witnessed."

She thought, when she considered the matter later, how very ironic it was that it should have been she, and not the wrongdoers, who had ended the morning by sneaking out of Hanbury Library like a thief!

Isobel, though she had the sense to wait until they were out of earshot, was naturally agog to know what had caused Verity's sudden desire for departure, and was suitably appalled by the duplicity of Mr Dunstable.

"What a cur he is," she exclaimed hotly, "Oh how I hate all men!"

Verity felt she ought to dilute this all-encompassing vitriol a little, "Surely not all men."

"All!" asserted Isobel with passion, "Why, even Underwood, whom I know you consider to be the best of men, is at this moment flirting outrageously with my worthless sister."

"Well, Gil is not!"

"A vicar? I should think he is not. But he hardly counts as a full-blooded male, does he?"

Poor Gil, thought Verity, immeasurably glad he had not been present to hear that epithet.

As they wended their way back to the Pump-rooms, they were met by Gil and Underwood, who had evidently come in search of them. Part of Verity was glad to see her husband, but that was overtaken by a curious feeling of shyness and embarrassment mixed. She was horrified to find herself blushing as she looked at him.

"I wish you had told me you were leaving, my dear. I would naturally have accompanied you."

"There was no need. Isobel and I simply found the Pump-room a little close, and I knew you were delighted to be renewing your acquaintance with Miss Wynter." She tried hard to keep any hint of sarcasm out of her voice, and almost succeeded.

Underwood, far from being annoyed by this sally, merely smiled, "If I did not know you better, I'd swear you were jealous," he joked, with his usual lack of tact.

She eyed him steadily, no answering smile adorning her lips; "Perhaps you ought to tell me if I have need to be jealous? You are, after all, more experienced at the game of love than I."

"Hardly!" he commented brusquely, mildly irritated that she should choose the street and two interested witnesses for this display of moodiness, "Shall we return to the Pump-rooms?"

"You do so, by all means. I'm feeling a little tired and will go back to the vicarage."

"Then I shall bear you company."

"Pray do not put yourself to the bother."

"I have said I will come with you," he answered firmly, "Gil, I trust you will see Miss Isobel back to her sister?"

"Certainly, certainly," said Gil, quickly coming to his senses, for he had been watching this exchange with rising disquiet. He was beginning to find this situation extremely trying, for with their relationship at such a delicate stage, the last thing the Underwoods needed was the presence of Charlotte Wynter. He took Isobel's arm and they walked away, leaving Verity and Underwood alone on the street.

"Shall we go?" Verity nodded unhappily and obediently fell into step beside him, though she made no attempt to take his arm. They said nothing for a few minutes, then Underwood said gently, "I wish you would tell me what is troubling you, my dear."

She wanted to tell him everything, but found she could not, so instead she told him of seeing Oliver Dunstable in the library with his mistress.

"Has that caused you to think all men are alike?" he inquired tersely.

"What do you mean?"

"Just because Oliver Dunstable is being untrue to his wife, it does not follow that I have been behaving in the same way."

"I know that."

"I sincerely hope you do!"

*

Verity spent the afternoon sleeping on a sofa in the vicarage parlour, quite worn out by the events of the morning. Underwood found her there and gently covered her with a silk shawl, then sat quietly with a book until she woke just before tea, much refreshed and ravenously hungry. She was surprised to find him beside her and said so, at which he smiled and replied that he had set himself as guard-dog to drive away the procession of callers who had been determined to disturb her rest.

"Have I had callers?" she asked, quite astounded.

"Why the surprise?" he responded, "You have made many friends here. Lady Hartley-Wells sent Miss Cromer to ask after your health. She had noticed you looked a little pale this morning and was concerned. Isobel Wynter came whilst Charlotte was out riding. And Josephine Dunstable also called."

At the mention of this last name Verity's face drained of all colour, "Thank Heavens I did not have to face Mrs Dunstable! I could not have looked her in the eyes after this morning. How awful it is to know something so dreadful about someone else's husband."

Underwood looked gravely at her, "You must not think of telling her, Verity, you know that, don't you?" she met his glance with troubled eyes, "You think not?"

"I know not. For God's sake, my dear, do not become embroiled in this. I know you are sure of what you saw, but there could be a perfectly reasonable explanation for Dunstable's behaviour, and untold trouble would be caused if you had your facts wrong. Let the Dunstables sort out their own affairs – after all, there could be many reasons for a man to embrace a woman who is not his wife."

The pointed way he said these words made Verity look sharply at him, but he gave her no clue as to his meaning. She had entirely forgotten her own embrace with Gil, for it had meant nothing to her beyond brotherly comfort, therefore she foolishly imagined he was making some feeble excuse lest she later be told that he himself had been caught embracing Charlotte Wynter. The blood rushed back into her cheeks and she said bitterly, "I can think of no innocent explanation for such behaviour!"

"I'm sorry to hear you say so," he replied evenly, "Now, do we dine with Lady Hartley-Wells?"

"Whatever you wish, I don't care!"

"Then since she keeps an excellent cellar, I shall gladly accept."

*

Verity very nearly turned tail and ran when she realized that the Dunstables were also guests of Lady Hartley-Wells, but quickly recovered her equanimity – after all, she was going to have to meet Oliver Dunstable and his wife sooner or later – and he had no idea she had witnessed his assignation.

Surprisingly the meal was a merry affair, for it seemed that Mrs Dunstable and Lady Hartley-Wells were old friends who had many amusing anecdotes to relate. Of course Gil and Underwood were always at their best when entertaining elderly ladies, since they were able to relax and not imagine themselves pursued – something which

36

they both professed to abhor, but neither of whom seemed to run very speedily in the opposite direction.

The only sour note to the evening was the excessive attention poured upon Josephine by the detestable Oliver. No one ever found his fawning and gross flattery of his aged wife particularly pleasant at the best of times, but with the knowledge they now possessed, his behaviour was frankly nauseating.

They would have found it much, much worse had they known what the next few days were to bring.

CHAPTER FIVE

'Altissima Quaeque Flumina Minimo Sono Labi' – Literally, the deepest rivers flow with the least sound – Still waters run deep

Verity had slept badly, woken early to be sick, and now sat, heavy eyed and lethargic, waiting for her husband to bring her the customary cup of healing waters. She was beginning to find the Pump-rooms intolerably dull and had she been able to summon the energy, she might have put her mind to thinking of other things she and Underwood might be doing with their mornings. She refused to acknowledge that this sudden dislike of Hanbury water might be in any way connected with the fact that the two Misses Wynter also frequented the Pump-rooms every day.

She also knew she ought to be encouraging Underwood to consider their position as guests at the vicarage. It was time they found a home of their own and decided exactly how Underwood was going to earn his living, but she felt curiously protected beneath Gil's roof and was loath, for the moment, to face the harsher realities of life.

Underwood exchanged a brief greeting with Oliver Dunstable at the water fountain, as they both filled their respective wives cups – though Mrs Dunstable had a silver goblet, and not a mere glass like Verity. Underwood then returned to his wife, handing her the water and smiling at her, "Feeling any better?" he asked.

She took the glass from him, carefully avoiding any contact between their fingers, "I have not complained of feeling anything other than perfect well," she answered irritably.

"No, you have not, but I am neither deaf nor blind…" She never discovered how this sentence was destined to end for at that moment a piercing scream sliced through the usual low hum of conversation, followed by another and yet another. Verity – and several other ladies – started so violently that their cups and glasses fell from their hands and general pandemonium broke out as a mass of people surged forward towards the sounds.

Underwood and Verity were near enough to see that the screams were issuing from the lips of Josephine Dunstable's daughter Leah, and that Josephine herself had slid from her accustomed seat and was now writhing upon the floor in a series of jerks and contortions which were horrific and frightening to witness. Flecks of bubbling spittle were dribbling from the side of her mouth and the stiff, puppet-like movements of her arms and legs had caused the hem of her already too-short dress to rise above her arthritically bulbous knees, exposing thin and shrivelled calves clad in the finest silk stockings. Oliver was staring down at her in horrified fascination; Leah was giving voice to louder and more frenzied shrieks. Since it was painfully evident no one was doing anything to aid the unfortunate Josephine, Underwood thrust his way past the crowd which had rapidly gathered about the scene, and was on his knees by the woman in seconds. He managed to catch the wildly flailing arms and perform the dual action of taking her pulse and preventing her from injuring herself any further. He hoisted her up into his arms and tried to speak to her, to calm her and find out, if possible, what exactly ailed her, but he was too late. Her head flew violently backward and with a sickening gurgle, she breathed her last.

Someone, the Underwoods never discovered whom, dealt Leah a resounding slap and the ensuing, shocked silence was more blood freezing than the previous chaos.

Oliver Dunstable was the first to speak, "Dear God, she is dead, isn't she?"

Underwood glanced up at him, then slid Josephine gently out of his arms and back onto the marbled floor, "I'm afraid she is."

"What was it? A heart attack? Some sort of seizure or fit?"

Underwood rose, but his gaze remained firmly fixed on the recumbent figure at his feet, "I think we should have a doctor here – and the Constable. In my, admittedly limited, experience, we have just witnessed the symptoms of the administration of some sort of toxin."

"Poison?" Leah seemed to suddenly come to life, from a gibbering wreck only seconds before, she became lucid and vengeful, "Give me her cup!" Someone handed it to her from the floor whence it had been cast in Josephine's first agony, and she raised it to her nose and sniffed suspiciously. A look of triumph crossed her face, "He is right. This cup contained more than plain water. My mother was murdered!" She pointed a trembling finger at the white-faced Dunstable; "He was the one who fetched the water. I want him arrested and hanged. God grant my mother revenge for this most foul deed!"

Dunstable and Verity both fainted at almost the same moment.

*

When Verity recovered her senses, she found it was Gil who was by her side as she lay on one of the hard benches at the far end of the Pump-room. In the few seconds it took her to recall the events of the past few minutes, she first noticed Underwood's absence, and the knowledge of his desertion pierced her heart. She tried to sit up but was prevented by a wave of nausea, so she lay back and re-closed her eyes, saying as she did so, "I see that your brother had more important things to attend to other than his own wife."

She felt Gil firmly clasp her wrist, "No, no, my dear. You have him wrong. When you swooned, his anxiety was such that he felt he could not be of any use to you. I have his strict instructions to call him the moment you regained your senses."

Verity drew in a deep breath and with a great effort, she pulled herself back from the brink of another faint. She had no idea whether Gil was speaking the truth, or merely calming her with kind lies and strangely, she found she hardly cared. A curious lethargy was afflicting her, and when she spoke it was slowly and with cold monotony, "You need not trouble to call him. I shall get up in a moment."

"Would you like a drink of water," asked Gil solicitously, then wished he could unsay the words as her startled glance flew to his face and she exclaimed in horror, "Good God, no!"

He had not been present when Mrs Dunstable had died, having arrived just in time to take the insensible Verity from his brother's arms, but he knew all about the accusations of poisoned water, since Leah Gedney had been vociferous in attacking the young man who was her step-father. Gil was made painfully aware by her reaction how very thoughtless it was of him to offer 'water' at that time and in that place.

Verity gave herself a few more minutes, then rose unsteadily to her feet and rejoined the group, now much smaller, which was still gathered about the prone form of the dead woman.

Underwood had evidently taken charge, and with the help of the Pump-room caretaker, he had arranged for all but the main witnesses to be expelled into another room. He had removed his own frock coat and used it to cover the face of Mrs Dunstable, and he now stood, in his shirt sleeves, waistcoat and breeches, apparently deep in conversation with Mr Gedney. For all that had happened, Verity could still not see her husband without the breath catching in her throat. He looked strangely attractive arrayed thus, and when compared to the other men. She realized in that fleeting second that for all his faults, there could be no other for her. With a sensation of plunging misery, she wished it could have been the same for him with her.

As he caught sight of her out of the corner of his eye, he swiftly excused himself and walked across to her, taking her hand and quickly kissing it, his only concession to a public display of affection and concern, "You are fully recovered?" he asked anxiously. She nodded and he added, "Thank God! Please don't do that any too often, my dear."

"I'll try not. It wasn't altogether pleasant for me, either."

"No, I imagine not. You did not hurt yourself when you fell? You seemed to hit the floor with a terrible crash?"

"I don't think so. To be honest I haven't had time to assess the damage."

"I'm so sorry you had to witness this," he said suddenly, "Would you like me to ask Gil to take you home?"

"No, I want to stay here with you."

She was surprised he didn't argue, but took her hand again and pressed it warmly before saying, "Very well, but be sure to let me know if you change your mind."

There was no time for any further conversation for a rustle of interest in the assembled company heralded the arrival of the town's Constable, a bucolic little man, shorter than Verity, with a very red face and neck, who looked frankly terrified of the task which lay before him. Verity thought how ridiculous it was that a man should be plunged into the unenviable position of finding a possible murderer, when his only entitlement to the task was a few votes by his friends on the town magisterial bench.

With an unmistakable tremor in his voice George Gratten asked, "Who can tell me what has occurred here?"

All eyes turned to Underwood, and having thus been tacitly elected spokesman, he began, "Mrs Dunstable appeared to fall into some sort of seizure. I held her in my arms as she was dying and managed, with no great ease, to very briefly feel her pulse and examine her other symptoms at close range. Having made a minor study of the subject, I would strongly suspect the presence of some kind of poison in her system."

Some of Mr Gratten's high colour faded, and his eyes bulged slightly, "Are you quite sure of this?" he gasped, obviously deeply shocked.

"Well, naturally I would prefer to have my suspicions confirmed by a doctor, but I fear I shall be proved right."

"Do you have any idea of the sort of poison?"

Here Leah Gedney stepped forward and thrust her mother's cup into the hands of the startled Gratten, "It is tansy. I recognize the smell, faint, but unmistakable."

"And you are?" asked Gratten rather coldly. He did not like her attitude towards him. He was a man very conscious of his dignity and he expected for people to wait until they were addressed before thrusting themselves into his notice.

"I am her daughter," Leah nodded towards the body, apparently quite recovered from her hysterical shock and distress and now only intent upon revenge, "And I demand justice in her name. He is the man who killed her. He filled the cup and gave it to her. An easy matter for him to have slipped the poison into her water." A finger, now without a trace of a tremble, pointed directly at the now conscious, but still ashen Dunstable.

He staggered slightly as he backed away from her, his whole body shaking, "No ... no." he mumbled, "It isn't true..."

Mr Gratten, sensibly, discounted much of this, determined not to be swayed by the raw passion which coloured much of the scene. He returned his attention back to Underwood, sensing his calm detachment. Here was a man who would tell the facts as he saw them, not as some hysterical woman wanted them to seem, "What is your opinion, sir?"

"The symptoms do concur with a dramatic overdose of tansy oil, but that generally takes a few hours to work its way through the system. Very few vegetable-based toxins kill instantly. I really don't see how poisoned Spa water could have killed Mrs Dunstable so swiftly. She was dead within minutes of falling ill."

"Nonsense! She was an old woman. Any poison would have killed one of her weak constitution in moments," intercepted Leah Gedney, throwing a darkling look at Underwood.

"Do you agree with that assessment?" asked Gratten of Underwood, who was forced, from honesty, to admit that he had no idea, "As I said, I would prefer a competent doctor to be called in."

"That is all being dealt with," said Gratten, with an impatient wave of his hand, "Now, did anyone actually see – what was the woman's name?"

Underwood supplied the required information when Leah Gedney determinedly closed her lips, as though refusing to sully her lips with the name of the man whom she considered to be her mother's murderer.

"Did anyone see Mrs Dunstable drink the water?" asked Gratten.

A thin girl stepped forward, "I did, sir."

"And you are?"

"Rachael Collinson, sir. Mrs Dunstable was my employer."

"In what capacity?"

"Ladies' maid, sir."

"Did anyone see…?" Gratten gestured towards the cowering Dunstable, who had been given a chair by Gil, since it was evident he could barely stand, "Who are you, my man?"

"Oliver Dunstable," was the muttered reply.

"Her son?" asked the astounded Gratten. The response stunned him even more.

"Her husband." Gratten was rendered speechless by this unexpected development, but swiftly recovered himself; "Did anyone see Mr Dunstable filling the goblet at the water fountain?" He held aloft the silver vessel which Leah Gedney had so triumphantly produced.

"I did," said Underwood quietly. He was oddly disinclined to give any assistance to Leah's accusation, but he was always relentlessly truthful, no matter what the outcome.

Gratten looked about the assembled company, all of whom had fallen silent, waiting for his judgement.

"I don't think there is any purpose to be served by standing about her any longer. I shall require names, addresses and occupations of all here present, and would ask you all to write a statement of your own experience of the tragedy whilst it is still fresh in our minds. No one may leave Hanbury without the prior permission of myself or the local magistrate."

There was a short pause, then Leah Gedney burst forth with a torrent of invective, "What of that beast? You cannot mean to leave him free to wander the streets after what he has done to my mother. I want him jailed!"

Gratten hesitated, unsure of his position in this matter, for the truth was he had never had a suspicious death occur during his time as Constable. The title had been a courtesy one only until this moment. He had been hoping to slip away and consult with his magistrate friends before committing himself to any action.

"I ... I doubt we have enough proof to perform an arrest, madam," he ventured.

"My mother lies dead, poisoned with water from a cup filled by that man – what further proof do you need?"

Gratten glanced helplessly at the impassive Underwood.

"We have no evidence Mrs Dunstable was actually poisoned, Mrs Gedney, merely a suspicion. Perhaps if Mr Dunstable were to agree to stay with, shall we say, the vicar, and he were to agree to stand guarantor for his continued presence in Hanbury, until a *post mortem* has been performed..." Underwood gently suggested. Verity knew immediately that there was method in his offer of shelter. He intended to solve the mystery of Josephine Dunstable's death, and having the accused under his eye was the first step.

Gratten looked intensely relieved, "A very sensible suggestion, sir, if I may say so, and one that should satisfy all parties."

He glared about him, daring anyone to disagree. Leah Gedney looked mutinous, but her husband's restraining hand stayed any further protest. It occurred to Underwood to be surprised that the usually belligerent and opinionated Gedney had been so uncharacteristically quiet through all this.

"Due to the nature of the accusation, Mr Dunstable, I have no choice but to order the immediate sealing of the dead woman's home, until any remains of food or drink she may have consumed can be examined by the doctor. I'm afraid I cannot allow you to return to your lodgings, so you will have to borrow or buy anything you require in the way of night-attire and so forth."

Dunstable seemed past caring. Still shocked and stumbling, he allowed himself to be led away by Gil, whilst Underwood took Verity's arm. It was a very subdued party who returned to Hanbury vicarage that afternoon.

CHAPTER SIX

'Mendacem Memorem Esse Oportet' – Liars should have good memories

Though Verity entirely understood Underwood's reasons for bringing Oliver Dunstable to the vicarage, she was nevertheless deeply unhappy that he should have done so.

The quarrel, for a quarrel it turned out to be, was conducted in the vicar's study, of necessity in heated undertones, neither of them wishing to embarrass the unwilling and unwanted guest with the knowledge of the dissent he had unwittingly caused.

"How do you expect me to face that man every day, knowing what I do know about his behaviour?" hissed Verity with no preamble. Underwood began very calmly, but it was not long before his extreme irritation broke through the façade of stoicism.

"You know nothing about the man," he answered quietly.

"I know what I saw in the Circulating Library."

"What you *think* you saw," he corrected, but the note of condescension in his voice was just the provocation Verity needed to make her lose her temper.

"Are you suggesting that, as a *mere* woman, my eyes and ears are not to be trusted? If Gil had seen Oliver Dunstable petting his mistress, you would never dream of doubting his word!"

"I never suggested I was doubting your word. That wasn't what I said at all."

"Then what did you say, Mr Underwood? That it is quite acceptable for any man to clandestinely meet a girl young enough to be his daughter and flirt outrageously with her, whilst his wife waits patiently by?"

"Young enough to be his daughter? The young lady must have been young indeed then," said Underwood sarcastically, knowing full well that Verity had been referring not to Dunstable but to himself and Charlotte Wynter.

"You know exactly what I meant," she returned furiously.

"I did, and I tell you now, do not tread this path," he said warningly.

"Should I not?" she retorted, "What are you afraid of being exposed?"

He gave her a look of contempt, "I think we had better say nothing more until we have both calmed a little. Mr Dunstable stays and there's an end to it. He did not murder his wife, of that I am convinced. His private affairs have nothing to do with the matter, and I'm certainly not going to stand by and watch the poor man hanged simply because you do not approve of his morals."

This harsh comment drew a gasp of shock from his wife, the horror at his opinion of her motives showing plainly on her face, "I cannot believe you think so little of my character! I do not know if he is innocent or guilty, for it is not given to us all to be so sure of everything as *you* plainly are. I do not care if he has a mistress or not, I simply cannot bear to bide under the same roof whilst knowing I have witnessed him in an indelicate situation."

"Then I suggest we tell him, and allow him to give you his explanation. Will that satisfy you?"

He walked out of the room before she could stop him, and her cheeks burned with utter mortification at the whole unsavoury situation. She had never felt herself so much at a disadvantage. She had lowered herself in the eyes of her husband and must, in addition, listen to the sordid confessions of a man she did not particularly like. The day was growing worse by the minute.

Dunstable made no attempt to hide anything from them, and Verity could not decide if this attitude were not almost worse than if he had lied through his teeth in denying the existence of another woman besides his wife in his life.

Looking at his still pallid face and haunted eyes, she guessed it must be the shock of his recent experiences which had stripped him briefly of the desire to keep his affair a secret. She knew he must be aware that his situation was desperate and Underwood was probably the only man who believed in his innocence and who could save him from the gallows. In such circumstances it was only sensible to keep nothing back.

Underwood was his usual straightforward self; Verity had never known him employ diplomacy when he wished urgently to acquire information, and this was no exception, "Mr Dunstable, my wife says she saw you in a compromising position with a young lady not of her acquaintance, and naturally feels you ought to know of this if you are to remain under my brother's roof."

At least he had the grace to look sheepish before admitting ruefully, "I hold up my hands, Underwood. Your wife was not mistaken. I do have a young friend – of whose existence my wife had no idea – but that does not mean I did not view Josie with the greatest respect and affection. The truth of the matter is, my wife was elderly and often unwell and – well, I am a man after all, and many men have mistresses!"

Verity grew scarlet to the roots of her hair, but Underwood accepted the confession with equanimity, "Thank you for your candour, Mr Dunstable. I realize that this concerns us in no way at all and you would have been quite within your rights to tell us to go to perdition."

"Not at all," protested the young man, "Do you think I am not signally aware of the help you have already given me, and the future aid I trust you will offer? I consider you have the right to ask me anything at all, if it will help convince you both of my innocence. God! My poor Josie. I've scarcely had time to think of her in all this, so fearful have I been for my own safety. Underwood, I swear the Gedneys mean to see me hang, I know it. What shall I do?" This last cry of despair moved even Verity, who had been trying to remain impartial, but was swayed by her dislike of the man.

His head sank into his open hands and his shoulders shook with barely restrained sobs. Verity and Underwood exchanged a glance over his bowed head, and Verity slowly nodded. Underwood took this gesture to mean that she was now prepared to allow Dunstable at least the benefit of the doubt. He would stay at the vicarage, for the present.

Underwood considered his next move. He felt very strongly that he needed a doctor he could trust to perform the *post mortem* examination. He certainly did not intend to accept any choice of medic by the Gedneys. It was with this in mind that he wrote a short missive to the Constable, asking that the Coroner's inquest, which was to be held next day, should immediately adjourn until further evidence of foul play could be gathered, and naming Francis Herbert as an excellent and trustworthy professional.

Had she been aware of this move, Verity might well have pointed out that Francis might not wish to travel a distance of some twenty miles to perform an autopsy merely to oblige Underwood, but she was not consulted and knew nothing of Dr Herbert's involvement until he arrived two days later, bringing his wife and young son with him.

To say that Verity was pleased to see her old friend would be to much understate the matter. She was not only delighted, but secretly rather relieved. She had been wanting to seek the advice of a doctor, but had not been able to do so without her husband knowing. More than ever now, she wanted to be sure of Underwood's feelings for her before she told him of her condition, for she could foresee no greater misery than for them to be bound together by a child, in a loveless marriage. She had been almost convinced of his devotion before Charlotte's arrival in Hanbury, but her insecurity, coupled with feeling constantly unwell had eroded all her self-confidence and she was less sure of him than she had ever been before.

Francis gladly examined her and confirmed her pregnancy, but was rather concerned when she insisted upon confidentiality, even from Ellen. He tried to convince her that her worries about Underwood and Charlotte were unfounded, but failed miserably and decided in the end that he had no choice but to follow her wishes. His own experience with his wife had taught him that women could be infernally emotional at such times in their lives and were best humoured. If either Verity or Ellen had read his thoughts, he would have been soundly trounced!

In the three days which had passed since Mrs Dunstable's death, Underwood had not been idle. He had consulted several books on the subject of poisons and poisonings and confirmed his original theory that the oil of tansy which Leah Gedney had named as culprit did indeed need a fairly large overdose and several hours to take effect – though the effect on the elderly or infirm was not stated with any degree of certainty. It was commonly used in the countryside to kill intestinal worms or to induce abortion or menstruation and it was therefore possible Mrs Dunstable had dosed herself, either with oil, or with tea made from steeped leaves. Because of her advanced age, it would have been unlikely to be for the latter reasons, and the doctor would know if it were for the former. He also discovered the plant itself grew in peat based soil, so it was very possibly available in the Pennines.

He now needed to interview the servant, Rachael Collinson, who would be the most likely to know the movements of all those concerned on the day and night before the death.

Of course, what he really needed to know was that Mrs Dunstable had actually been murdered and was not merely the victim of a seizure, and for that he urgently needed the result of the doctor's examination.

*

48

The Pump-rooms were closed for the day following the unfortunate demise of one of its patrons, partly due to the fact that most of the inhabitants were crushed into the White Boar for the Coroner's hearing, which was disappointingly short, the Constable having taken Underwood's advice and arranged an adjournment until proof of foul play had been found or dismissed; but mostly, since the precious waters had been placed under suspicion, that day was filled with panic-stricken investigations into the purity of the water by various medical and scientific experts hastily brought to the town by the authorities. The result was greeted with huge relief. Hanbury water was found to be as clean and clear as ever. Any hint of such a scandal could have ruined forever the town's reputation, and destroyed its most lucrative of products.

After that, however, everything returned to normal. Verity could not help but feel a little sad and guilty that she should still be enjoying life when Mrs Dunstable lay dead in the morgue.

Not one of the concerts or balls were postponed and within twenty-four hours, one would never have known that Josephine had ever existed.

Charlotte, furious that she had been absent from the Pump-rooms on the fateful day, and had missed all the excitement, lost no time at all in pursuing Mr Underwood on the pretext of asking him to tell her all about the disaster.

Her opportunity came on the day of the *post mortem*, for Underwood had no intention of attending anything so sordid. He did the brainwork, let others wallow in the gore, was his opinion. Dr Herbert was busy with the body, Verity and Ellen had seized the chance to shop and catch up on all the gossip. Underwood had excused himself from this and was browsing in the library. It did not take the determined Charlotte long to run him to ground, and to insist that he accompany her to partake of coffee in the private parlour of the Bull Inn.

When the tray was laid before her, Charlotte removed her hat, aware that it hid her face from the still-standing Mr Underwood.

She poured the coffee from the silver pot, remembering that he liked cream and sugar, then bestowed her most dazzling smile upon him as she handed him his cup, "Will you not be seated, Mr Underwood?"

"I prefer to stand, thank you," he replied as he took it from her, but he smiled in return.

She took a sip, eyeing him cautiously over the rim of the cup, "I had quite forgotten…" she murmured after a pause, almost as though she had not meant to speak aloud.

"Forgotten what?"

"How very handsome you are," her voice sank lower still, and there was a yearning in it which made Underwood look thoroughly startled, "Miss Wynter…"

She set her cup down, rose to her feet and joined him before the empty fireplace, "Please, don't say anything. How I would hate to hear conventional little platitudes from your lips. After all there has been between us…"

"'Was' is correct, Miss Wynter!" he said tersely, recovering his equanimity, and stepping hastily backwards, almost falling over the fire irons as he did so, "I am a married man…"

"Are you going to hide behind Verity's skirts then?" she asked scornfully, advancing on him.

"I'll gladly hide behind anything I need to, Miss, to save myself and you from this hideous embarrassment!" he retorted, skilfully putting the table between them and replacing his own unfinished coffee on the tray, lest he should need to make a hasty retreat.

"Am I an embarrassment, then?" she asked mournfully, raising sad eyes to his.

"Yes!" he said brutally, aware that her unshed, but very evident tears were supposed to call upon every ounce of chivalry he possessed, but which, unfortunately for her, did no such thing. He desired nothing more than to escape, but was suddenly conscious of the need to end this situation once and for all. Charlotte must leave the Bull knowing he cared nothing for her and that she would never be alone with him again.

"I am still in love with you," she said huskily.

"You are not. You are a prodigiously silly girl, who only wants what she cannot have. And I do assure you, Miss Wynter, you *cannot* have me!"

She sank back onto the sofa and began to sob helplessly, "How can you be so cruel?"

"How can you?" he responded severely, "Have you no affection or respect for Verity that you can speak thus to me? I'm sorry if you were hurt, but you have none but yourself to blame!"

"Have I not?" she shot back, more angry than upset, "But you came here with me. No one forced you, yet you encouraged me to think there was something to hope for by being here."

"I came here in a spirit of friendliness and because I had no notion you were going to rake up a past which is dead. Fool that I am, it did not occur to me that you would so far forget yourself as to say such things. But since you have done so, I will repeat exactly what I have said, in private, that you might be spared the humiliation of a more public rejection. I am married to Verity now let that be an end to it!"

"So, you care nothing for me, and never have!"

"If it pleases you to think so. Now, I am leaving, do you wish me to escort you back to your lodgings?"

She looked up at him, appearing, he could not help but notice, more lovely than ever, her green eyes swimming with tears, her hair clinging in tiny tendrils to her hot forehead, "Have I completely forfeited your friendship?" she asked humbly, holding out her hand to him.

He hesitated before he clasped it lightly and briefly, "Not if you behave yourself from this moment on," he said with mock severity.

"I cannot help it if I wish things had been different," she murmured.

"That is your misfortune, my dear. For myself, I am more than happy that events ended just as they did. Verity is a good wife and we suit each other well."

"So you are no longer in love with me, but love only her?"

"My feelings for my wife are entirely my own affair, Miss!" He was not about to be drawn on a subject which he had not even discussed with Verity. He found most strong emotions embarrassing and difficult to voice, "Suffice it to say I regret you have been hurt. That was never my intention."

"Then I must learn to live with my regrets, and it only remains for me to beg your pardon for having subjected you to a display of unseemly behaviour."

"There is no need," he spoke brusquely, desiring nothing more than to be away from her, and tossing his handkerchief into her lap he added rather callously, "Now mop up your tears and let us go."

*

When he entered the vicarage, rather drained and tired, he found that Ellen and Verity were still out, and the doctor had completed his survey.

"What news, Francis?" asked Underwood eagerly, banishing all thoughts of Charlotte from his mind with an ease which would have vastly offended her had she known of it.

"It looks as though the daughter was correct. There were traces of tansy in the contents of the stomach – but I only found it because I knew what I was looking for. There is, as yet, no scientific way of testing for herbal poisoning. If Mrs Gedney had not told us of her suspicions, Mrs Dunstable's death would probably have been put down to natural causes."

"Any idea how and when she ingested it?"

"I would imagine the night before, possibly in food, but I could not discount the idea that she simply took it straight."

Underwood looked thoughtful; "Do you think she took it herself?"

"It's not impossible, but I would have thought it unlikely. Judging from the amount still undigested, I would say she had quite a lot, much more than would be required for the worst case of worms, for example."

"Was there any evidence she was suffering from that particular affliction?"

"None at all, but it is not uncommon for people to take remedies as a preventative rather than a cure."

"Could it have been in the water her husband gave her?"

"Not without her tasting it, I would think. Besides she cannot have had much more than a sip, there was very little in her stomach. It can only have been mere coincidence that she collapsed after taking it."

"So, we are looking at murder?"

"Or suicide – but that I doubt. There are other poisons which cause less discomfort. Tansy is not something I would choose to swallow in large amounts. So, unless it becomes apparent the lady was in the habit of dosing herself with vast amounts of the stuff…"

"Did anything in the house show traces of poison?"

"No. The whole house was spotlessly clean – suspiciously so. Even the empty wine bottles had been rinsed. Either Mrs Dunstable ran a very tight ship, or someone in the household had something to hide!"

"The personal maid must be questioned as a matter of urgency."

"I agree that she should be first, followed by the husband and daughter."

"Then there is no time to be wasted."

"Do I take that to mean you intend to involve yourself in this?"

"If I do not, an innocent man might be hanged."

Dr Herbert closed his eyes and shook his head, as if incredulous and long-suffering, "Will you never learn, Underwood?"

"I don't pretend to understand what you mean by that," was the swift and not very convincing reply.

"You know exactly what I mean by it. But nothing I can say will stop you."

Underwood smiled grimly, "You are a very wise man to realize it."

*

Isobel Wynter eyed her sister suspiciously as she drifted into the drawing room of their rented house, humming softly under her breath, "You look very happy."

"I am."

"I hope that means you have found some other gentleman into whom you may legitimately sink your claws, instead of trying to steal Mr Underwood from under Verity's nose!"

Charlotte raised her brows and threw her sister an arch look; "You have an abominably offensive way with words, dear sister. For your enlightenment, I shall tell you that I have just taken coffee alone with Mr Underwood in the private parlour of an inn. Does that sound as though I am having to 'steal' him from anyone?"

"Alone?" Isobel was astounded, but quickly recovered herself; "I don't believe you."

"Then ask the landlord, sweet sister. Believe me, it will not be long before Underwood and I are making plans to run away to Italy together."

She ostentatiously waved Underwood's monogrammed handkerchief before her sister's appalled eyes, the careful embroidery of Verity being plainly recognizable to the ever fond Isobel; "You are more of a cat than I ever imagined, Lottie!"

"Nonsense! As someone said – I misremember who, 'all's fair in love and war'. If Verity cannot hold his interest, that is hardly my fault, is it?"

53

Isobel writhed with impotent fury, despising not just her sister and her ignorance, but Underwood too, and all his breed.

How she hated all men! Not one of them could be trusted.

CHAPTER SEVEN

'Experientia Docet' – Experience teaches

Rachael Collinson was not a prepossessing person. There was a sly look about her which rather chilled Verity, who felt that she was not in the least sorry that her mistress had died under such distressing circumstances, and that she desired merely to get the most she could out of any situation in which she found herself. She made it quite clear to Underwood she expected to be paid for any information she imparted. Verity was infuriated by her impertinence, but Underwood merely smiled, not unkindly, but not with his usual warmth.

"I can appreciate your fears for the future, Miss Collinson, but this is hardly the time to look to your fiscal security."

"My what?" she demanded rudely.

"Money," explained Verity tersely, "Surely you cared more about Mrs Dunstable than a few miserable shillings?"

"Not really," said the girl, with a shrug of her thin shoulders, "Why should I? I worked for her, she paid me; there was nothing more to it than that. Why should I like her or she me?"

Verity had no response to offer, but she felt more sympathy than ever for the deceased. Poor woman to have been surrounded by such dregs of humanity as these. A faithless husband, a disloyal servant, a money-grabbing daughter and an odious son-in-law. She was almost fortunate to be dead. Perhaps she had taken the tansy oil herself. Who could blame her, if she had?

"If you have been a good servant, Miss," continued Underwood smoothly, "I have no doubt you will be remembered with a sizeable bequest."

The sarcasm was not lost on Collinson, who flushed painfully and threw him a poisonous glance, "No doubt!"

"Now, I should like you to tell me exactly how Mrs Dunstable spent her last day, including who she saw, what she ate and where she went."

The lady's maid was aware that she had very little choice and it was with obvious reluctance that she complied.

"She woke at seven as usual and drank hot chocolate."

"Prepared in the kitchen by her own staff?"

"No, I always made that. She said I had the knack of getting it just right."

"Then?"

"She bathed as she always did – I brought up the hot water. At about ten, after dressing and applying her face paint, she came down to breakfast with her husband – he also rises at seven, but goes riding – at least that's where he says he goes, and he does take a horse out, but it's never very lathered when he gets back, and it's the fattest horse I've ever seen that is getting regular exercise!"

Underwood resisted the temptation to meet Verity's eyes at this and hastily drew her away from the subject of Oliver Dunstable; "We'll come to Mr Dunstable later, let us concentrate on the lady of the house for the moment. What was served for breakfast?"

"That morning, cold beef and ham, bread and butter and China tea."

"And Mr Dunstable ate with his wife?"

"Oh yes, giggling and laughing the whole time! They even fed each other. It was disgusting, carrying on over the table!"

Underwood chose to disregard this comment and continued, "After breakfast?"

"To the Pump-rooms. Mr Dunstable always fetches – always fetched – her water, sits with her for an hour or so, then goes to the Circulating Library for her books, whilst she sits – sat – with her cronies."

Verity thought wryly that she knew all about his trips to the library. Underwood again refused to meet the challenge in her glance.

"At three they went home for a meal."

"Did they both take every dish?"

"I think so. Mr Dunstable took everything anyway. He always does. She only orders – ordered – what he likes."

"How was the rest of the afternoon spent?"

"Same as always, either she goes to visit her friends, or they come to her, and they play cards and gossip, taking tea together later. On that day her friends came to her."

"Who are these friends?"

"Lady Hartley-Wells, Mrs Arbuthnot, Mrs Wolstencroft and her niece Miss Beresford."

"And they all took tea?"

"Yes. Mr Dunstable goes to his club, to gamble with his friends, or if the weather is fine, he might go to the races or to a mill or a cockfight. He said he was in Braxton that day. After tea Mrs Dunstable always rested for an hour or so in her room, to refresh her for the evening's entertainment. They would go to a ball at the Assembly Rooms, or a concert or play at the theatre. Usually they dined at home, but sometimes out with friends. That night they dined at home, but Mrs Gedney was there with her husband. Young Melissa stayed at their house with her nursemaid."

"Why did the Gedneys not stay with the Dunstables? The house they have hired is certainly large enough to contain them all comfortably."

"Mrs Dunstable will not stay under the same roof as Mr Gedney. Even though she pays for the hire of their house, she would rather pay the extra than have him near her – I mean she used to…"

"Did everyone partake of everything at the dinner?"

"Yes, but Mrs Dunstable always drank a full bottle of claret to herself. Mr Dunstable insisted, because she often had trouble sleeping. No one shared that, nor the box of bon-bons which were a gift from Mrs Gedney. They all knew they were Mrs Dunstable's weakness, so refused when offered. She would have finished the lot by bedtime."

"Was the claret decanted?"

"No. Mr Dunstable always uncorked it and left it to breathe, but he didn't decant it, so there could be no error as to who received it. I understand it was very expensive wine."

"Was Mrs Dunstable in the habit of taking any medication?"

"She had lots of things, tonic, physics; liniments for rubbing and vapours for inhaling. Bottles and bottles of the stuff."

"Did she ever use tansy oil?"

"Tansy oil!" Collinson evidently knew of only one use for the herb for she snorted contemptuously, "At her age? I should think she would have welcomed the miracle of a child, not tried to get rid of it."

"It has other uses," said Underwood curtly, "But you say she never had any?"

"Not to my knowledge."

"Thank you, Miss Collinson. You have been most helpful."

"Think nothing of it, Mr Underwood," was the sardonic reply.

When they were alone again, Underwood spoke thoughtfully to Verity, "I suggest that gives us two possible methods of administering the poison – though of course, if Collinson did it herself, she would hardly tell us how she accomplished the deed."

"The wine and the bon-bons," mused Verity, "That gives us Mrs Gedney and Oliver Dunstable."

"Amongst others. The wine would probably be left unattended on the sideboard for an hour or more – anyone with access to the house could thus adulterate it. The same applies to the bon-bons, unless the box was somehow sealed. I also forgot to ask Collinson if Mrs Dunstable had a night time drink before retiring, but that will do another time. We have plenty to work on for now. It is a pity we could not have been sure Mrs Dunstable was poisoned sooner, we have given the culprit ample time to dispose of any bottles, boxes, plates and glasses which might have contained traces of poison and shown us how and when it was administered."

"Do you really suspect Collinson?"

"Not unless she proves to benefit financially from her mistress' death. That young woman is interested only in money, and it would be her only temptation to murder, I think. A look at Mrs Dunstable's Will would be most instructive. I must see George Gratten about arranging it."

"It's horrible to think she was killed for her money."

"Horrible, I agree, but unfortunately, the most likely explanation. Dunstable had no reason to kill her in order to be with his mistress, for it seems he was given complete freedom to indulge himself as much as he wished, and he knew his wife was in poor health. He needed only to wait for nature to take its course and he would be free without risking his own neck. It makes me quite grateful I don't possess great wealth."

"What a strange thing to say," snapped Verity, cut to the quick by the remark which she considered was directed solely at her, "Do you suspect that I might poison you for your riches?"

Underwood, who had been attempting to lighten a dark moment with a joke, suddenly felt very old. It seemed he could say nothing to his wife without offence being taken where none was intended, "In your present mood, you'll be the death of me anyway," he said wearily, "Can I not make the lightest of light hearted remarks without you tearing at me?"

Verity burst into tears and ran from the room.

"Good God Almighty!" roared the suddenly frustrated husband, "What the devil have I said NOW?"

*

George Gratten was only too willing for Underwood to take over the investigation into the death of Mrs Dunstable, and would have agreed to almost anything the gentleman might ask of him. The request that Underwood, Dr Herbert and himself should all go to the Dunstable home and search it together met with his complete approval. He had never before been faced with a murder to solve, but his pomposity and vanity demanded that he bring the culprit to justice without recourse to the local Magistrate, with whom he had a long-standing and rather vitriolic feud. It would have been a bitter gall for Gratten to swallow, had he been forced to ask the help of Sir Alfred Dorrington. The Magistrate with whom he was friendly, and who he had hoped to consult, was unfortunately away from home and not due back for several days.

The house was cold and clammy after its swift desertion and careful sealing, for not a window had been left open, nor door unbarred.

The three men began a systematic round of the house, and very business-like they seemed, though only Underwood had any clear idea of what exactly they were seeking. After setting his two companions various tasks involving opening cupboards and drawers, he started his own self-imposed task of going through the contents of the lady's desk and box of private papers.

He found a copy of her Will, which was precisely what he wanted, and quickly scanned it with great interest until he was recalled to the present by a shout of triumph from Dr Herbert.

He ran down the stairs two at a time and joined the other two in the dining room, whence had come the voice of the doctor.

"The glasses in this cupboard reek of tansy, Underwood. It looks as though the entire household was under threat of death!"

Underwood took one of the proffered glasses from the doctor's excitedly shaking hand and sniffed at it, "Undoubtedly tansy, but not placed there for the reason you imagine, Francis."

"How do you know?"

"Because a meagre smear would not kill anyone – it would not even hurt them. Don't forget it is used as a medicine in smaller doses. It takes rather a lot before it proves fatal."

"Then why have the glasses been tampered with? I don't understand it."

"Because this plot has been carefully planned and callously executed. We are not just dealing with one murder here, but also attempted murder. Whoever killed Mrs Dunstable was quite determined that Oliver Dunstable would be hanged for the crime."

"But how was that to be achieved? No one could be sure Oliver would be on hand to take the blame. You said yourself that tansy oil can take several hours to kill." George Gratten had his suspect and was loath to lose him, even though he was allowing Underwood to investigate the matter, it was more through a sense of fair play than any belief in Oliver's innocence. When he got his conviction, he wanted it to stand.

"That is why these glasses have been soaked in the oil – wherever Mrs Dunstable was when she met her end, someone was going to be able to take a vessel from her hand and scream the accusation of poison. If she had collapsed here and not in the Pump-rooms, she would still have a glass in her hand which would have been placed there by the unfortunate Oliver. He always ate in her company, you see, no matter where else he might be in between times."

"But of course, he could have done all this himself, in the hope that someone such as yourself would have leaped to the same conclusion," argued the incorrigible Gratten, "After all, everything else the old lady used has been cleaned with the exception of these glasses."

"Very true," conceded Underwood, "But things moved very quickly once she was dead, it would have been remarkably difficult to get back into the house, and incredibly suspicious behaviour if one had been caught washing what were, in theory, clean glasses. I think our suspect was forced to leave them and hope that the smell had faded by the time they were, if ever, found. Thanks to our ever-vigilant doctor, that was a vain hope. Unfortunately, it does not bring us much closer to finding the culprit, for even though Mrs Gedney was the one who sent up the cry of murder by poison, we have no proof that it was not mere coincidence and luck that she recognized the aroma of tansy."

Dr Herbert looked at his friend, his brow furrowed, "Do you think it a coincidence, Underwood?"

"What I think is of no consequence. If I want to save Oliver Dunstable from the gallows, I must have solid proof, not mere conjecture."

Mr Gratten grunted his acceptance of this fact, "Damned fishy, though, all the same. Well, Underwood, are we to continue our search, or have you found what you wanted?"

"I think our work here is done, Mr Gratten, but I would ask your permission to take away the private papers of the lady of the house. There seems to be a copy of her will, which requires greater scrutiny than I have yet been able to manage."

"I see no reason why not, but don't, for God's sake, lose any of them."

"I shall guard them with my life," Underwood assured him gravely, "But in return, I would ask you both to refrain from mentioning to anyone that they are in my possession, for the present at least."

Having been given the word of both gentlemen, Underwood suggested they reseal the house and go to their respective homes to write a report of the day's labours.

*

Reluctant as he was to associate with the unpleasant Gedneys, Underwood knew he could not much longer delay the inevitable interview, so he set his steps in their direction the next morning.

The maid showed him into the drawing room and left him whilst she went to find her mistress. He glanced about him, noting the overly fussy décor, typical of the Spa's rented houses. Hanbury was trying very hard to become fashionable and aped its rival resorts of Bath and Harrogate in trying to outdo themselves in gentility and opulence. One could almost be in the drawing room of a Duchess, such was the number and variation of spindle-legged chairs, china ornaments and decorative swirls and festoons of plaster and gilded carving.

He was joined very swiftly by Mr Gedney who burst into the room and not bothering with the niceties of a greeting demanded, "You asked to see my wife? May I ask why?"

"I did," agreed Underwood amiably, taking his snuffbox from his pocket and helping himself to a generous pinch. He offered the box to the glowering Gedney, who impatiently brushed it aside.

"I don't know what the devil you want with her, but you are out of luck. She has been devastated by her mother's death and has taken to her bed."

"I am sorry to hear it, but it is of no consequence. You may just as well answer my questions."

Gedney looked first stunned, then grew red and began to bluster angrily, "Be damned to you! By what right do you come here, prying into our private affairs?"

"I am here at the personal request of Mr Gratten, the Constable of Hanbury. We are investigating the death of your mother-in-law, Mrs Dunstable."

"I don't see what there is to investigate. That sneaking little runt of a husband did it."

"Did what?" asked Underwood reasonably.

"Murdered her, of course!"

"Who told you she was murdered?"

Gedney was lost for words for a moment, then began a furious tirade, "What the hell do you mean by that? Of course she was murdered. You said so yourself on the day she died. I heard you talk of poison with my own ears."

"You may well have done so, but that does not necessarily mean she was murdered. She might have taken the poison herself."

Gedney grinned suddenly, but it was neither a pleasant nor friendly expression, "So that is your game, is it? You are going to get your little friend off by claiming suicide. Well, it won't work. I'll see that rat in a gibbet or my name isn't Adolphus Gedney."

"You seem passionately set on revenge, Mr Gedney. I was told that you did not hold Mrs Dunstable in any particular affection, nor she you, so I fail to understand this sudden desire to avenge her death."

"What? And let that rogue Dunstable walk off with her money? You must be out of your mind!"

"Ah, everything becomes clear. But does Dunstable inherit? You seem very sure of that fact."

"I've not seen the Will with my own eyes, if that is what you are hinting at, but it does not take a genius to work out that he'll get the bulk of her money – money that should, by rights, go to her daughter."

"And thence her son-in-law," murmured Underwood, not bothering to keep the contempt out of his voice, "Tell me, Gedney, did you and your wife have free access to Mrs Dunstable's house?"

"I see no reason to lie about it, yes we did."

Underwood surveyed the man before him for a few seconds in silence, then said mildly, "One more question, then I shall leave you in peace – for the moment. Have you always suffered from that rash on your hands?"

Gedney glanced down at the reddened, swollen patches on both his hands, before thrusting them behind his back, "No, I haven't. Perhaps the water here doesn't agree with me either!" He laughed coarsely and Underwood walked past him and out of the door, appalled that he could make so tasteless a joke about the death of his mother-in-law – a death which he as well as Underwood had witnessed, and which he must have known was agonizing for the woman.

Gedney might be a thoroughly obnoxious individual, but unfortunately that did not prove him to be a murderer.

Underwood went home, disheartened, but not yet beaten.

CHAPTER EIGHT

'Facilis Est Decensus Averni' – The road to Hell is an easy one

Lady Hartley-Wells was delighted to see her visitors and immediately ordered tea, "Underwood and dearest Verity. I hope we are to see you at the Ball this evening in the Assembly Rooms?" Lady Hartley-Wells was a great supporter of the Charity Balls which were held monthly in Hanbury, though she did not ever dance herself. Gil usually partnered her, though his evening would be spent playing whist or backgammon.

Underwood had been doing his utmost to avoid this gathering, but Verity was eager to attend, so a recommendation – which almost amounted to an order – from the elderly tyrant, was most welcome. Verity smiled her sweetest and replied, "We would not miss it for the world!" Underwood was betrayed into the slightest of scowls, but made no demur. He placed himself squarely before the unlit fire and accepted a tiny, delicate cup of tea from his hostess' footman. "Certainly, certainly," he said gruffly, "But we did not come here to discuss the dance, but the death of Mrs Dunstable."

Lady Hartley-Wells regarded him steadily then said, "If you are going to tell me there was 'foul-play' as I believe the expression runs, then I cannot honestly say I am surprised."

Underwood raised one brow, as was his habit when he was faced with something unexpected, "Would you like to expand on that comment?"

"Josie was a wealthy woman – and her second marriage was not the most popular move she ever made."

"Not popular with whom? Her family?"

He found himself the subject of her intense scrutiny for several seconds before she seemed to make a decision and speak again, "I shall not hide anything from you, Underwood, for two reasons. One is that I know nothing I say can hurt my old friend now; the second is that I believe you to be a gentleman and you will treat whatever I have to tell you with discretion."

"You may have my word upon that," he replied rather pompously, but Lady Hartley-Wells merely laughed.

"Lord bless you my dear, I know it! A girl of Verity's sensibility would never have married you otherwise."

Verity blushed rosily at the compliment, but Underwood was, for once, rendered speechless. It had never occurred to him that he might be judged on the strength of his wife's character. There would be no more evidence of an over-blown ego from him that afternoon – or indeed for some considerable time thereafter.

"To return to the subject," he interjected hastily, "You have some information about Mrs Dunstable?"

"I have a great deal – none of which you would have heard from my lips had she not died under such dreadful circumstances. But let me begin by warning you that you would be very wrong to imagine that no one but her family might wish her dead?"

"Are you saying she had enemies?"

The old lady laughed humourlessly, "More than you could shake a stick at, my dear."

"Good grief! What had she done to deserve that?"

"The trouble with you young people," observed the aged one grumpily, "is that you look at we old folk and imagine we have always been ancient and decrepit. We all have pasts, Underwood, and Josie's was more colourful than most."

Underwood and his wife exchanged a glance which confirmed exactly what their elderly hostess had surmised. They had indeed both been seeing Josephine Dunstable as a wealthy, sweet little white-haired old lady, somewhat eccentric and gaudy, but harmless, nonetheless. It had not occurred to either of them that they ought to delve into her more distant past for a reason to explain her untimely and violent passing.

"Tell us," said Underwood simply and Lady Hartley-Wells continued.

"You have heard, I imagine, of 'baby farmers'?"

Naturally they had, though Underwood's knowledge was a little sketchy, to say the least. He had led rather a sheltered life within the confines of his university prior to his marriage, and though he congratulated himself upon keeping abreast of life outside, there were large gaps in his education. He therefore nodded, but still looked blank and Verity, coming to his rescue, hastily explained, "They are women who take in unwanted children – for financial remuneration."

"That is surely laudable, is it not?" asked Underwood, imagining happy families, with maternal ladies and rosy-cheeked cherubs, "And what do you mean by 'unwanted'" he added, still not quite clear.

"Illegitimate!" supplied Lady Hartley-Wells tersely, "As to laudable – that rather depends … The money is more to pay for secrecy than the upkeep of the child – and it is often not perceived as particularly tragic by either party if the child never reaches maturity."

"Do you mean to say that these children are killed?" The truth was beginning to filter through Underwood's naiveté.

"Well, no one exactly smothers them – at least not often, for it would be a criminal offence, if discovered! But neither are most of them nurtured sympathetically, and once they are old enough to fend for themselves, they are usually cast out into the streets to do just that – or set to earn for their fosterer."

"How?"

"Factories, sweat-shops, prostitution…"

"Good God! And Mrs Dunstable was one of these … baby farmers?"

"She was – and not only that. She had a very profitable side-line in blackmail and extortion. Some of the ladies who brought their children to her were very eager to ensure their husbands' or families' continuing ignorance of their little indiscretions."

"I had no idea…" he murmured, still shocked to the core.

Verity reassured him hastily, "Not all are like that, Underwood. Some raise the children as their own for very little recompense, but there are always going to be those who feed like vultures upon the misfortunes of others."

"I suppose so," he pulled himself together with a visible effort, "I do beg your pardon, ladies. No sooner do I convince myself that mankind can no longer surprise or disgust me with the depths to which they are prepared to plunge, than yet another vice rears up before me."

Lady Hartley-Wells shrugged eloquently, seeming not to notice the melancholy edge to his tone, "I have long ago given up being shocked or appalled, Underwood," she said briskly, "If there is one thing I have learned about life it is there is no limit to man's inhumanity to man. That pit is definitely bottomless."

"Do you mind if I ask why you chose to associate with Mrs Dunstable, if you knew of her past? Surely there must be more pleasant companions?"

"Fewer and fewer when you get to my age, young man," she said tartly. "Besides I became friends with her before I knew any of this stuff, and strange as it may seem, Josie was a kind and humorous woman – I can only think she had the capability of being able to view those children as business and nothing more, just a commodity. It is hard to understand I know, but she seriously believed she was doing the Lord's work. The women she blackmailed deserved punishment for their sins, the children were a product of that sin and therefore tainted. As for myself; I have long ago ceased to presume to judge others. And Josie was punished by God, if one believes in that concept, by the birth of young Melissa. She was truly devastated by that – and by the misery inflicted on her daughter by that rogue Gedney. Josie suffered, take my word upon it."

"From what you have told us, there could be literally dozens of people who wanted Mrs Dunstable to die in agony – revenge being the motive."

"I'm not saying that exactly, Underwood, I just want you to be aware that you would be making a very grave error indeed not to consider the possibility."

As Verity and Underwood walked down the flight of stone steps which ran from the path to the imposing front door, the former remarked forlornly, "With the thought of all those poor, suffering little children, I really don't feel much like dancing this evening, do you?"

"I never did feel much like dancing," returned Underwood forcefully, "But I understand your meaning, and the answer is no."

*

When Verity arrived back at the vicarage, it was to find a note from Isobel waiting for her, asking for a meeting at the Pump-rooms, without delay. She was inclined to refuse, feeling, as she did, rather tired and low, but Ellen persuaded her otherwise, "I should love to see the spa – and Isobel," she said heartily, determined to shake her friend out of her lethargy. As they were leaving, Gil offered to accompany them, since Francis and Underwood were once more closeted in his study, effectively barring him from his own belongings, exchanging theories and notes on the murder.

Verity's attention was centred on her companions when they came into the Pump-rooms, so it was several seconds before she noticed Gil standing motionless beside her, staring across the room as though transfixed. She followed the direction of his glance and saw that he was looking at a young woman, standing by the water fountain, dressed in black from head to toe, a small boy in a bath chair at her side. She was smiling down at him as she handed him a full cup, but there was an aura of sadness about her which even the warmly tender smile could not dispel. Verity spoke twice to Gil, but he did not seem to hear her, so she tugged at his sleeve, "Who is that, Gil? Do you know her?"

Gil dragged his gaze from the woman and looked down at his sister-in-law, "What? I beg your pardon, Verity. Did you say something?"

Verity did not trouble to hide her amusement, "I asked if you knew the young lady."

Gil was so smitten he did not even attempt to be coy; there were no protestations of misunderstanding. Sounding remarkably like the red-blooded male Isobel had so recently declared him not to be, he said, "No, but I fully intend to,"

Verity laughed out loud, "Why, Gil, I have never seen you like this. I thought you weren't interested in women."

"Great Heavens! Whatever gave you that idea?"

"Well, you resist your mother's match-making so strongly..."

"My mother has a strange notion as to what would make a good vicar's wife. And she has never presented me with a gem such as she," answered Gil with emphasis, "Pray excuse me, my dear. I must fetch you some water."

"But I don't want..." she trailed off since Gil was already half way across the room. She smiled indulgently as she watched him engage the young woman in conversation, then turned her attention back to her friends.

Gil, meanwhile, was giving himself no time for second thoughts, for he knew he would lose all his courage if he did so. Almost before he knew what he was about, he was holding out his hand and introducing himself to the bemused newcomer. She looked a little startled by this approach, but politely accepted both the handshake and the introduction, "How do you do, Mr Underwood, did you say?"

"Reverend Gilbert Underwood," he amended, "I am vicar here in Hanbury. I could not help noticing a new face and thought I would presume to bid you welcome."

"That was kind. My name is Catherine Pennington and this is my son Alistair."

Her son. Gil began to realize he had assumed a great deal. He had imagined the child was her charge – had wanted to believe so, if the truth were told – for the boy's obvious frailty made it seem she must be a nurse of governess.

He recovered swiftly, "Is your husband in Hanbury with you?" It was not the sort of personal question he usually asked, but desperate times called for desperate measures!

"I'm afraid my husband died two years ago, Mr Underwood," she replied quietly.

"Please accept my deepest apologies, Madam. How incredibly tactless you must think me." He had the sinking feeling of a man who has not only made a complete fool of himself, but who has also ruined any chance of furthering a friendship. He was about to make his excuses and leave her when his eye caught hers and he saw a soul which twinned his own in loneliness and despair.

"Pray do not say so. You could not possibly have known."

He dragged his gaze from hers, suddenly becoming aware that they were being scrutinized by the solemn little boy, whom he had not yet greeted. He detested people who ignored children, treating them as barely human until they reached adulthood. He squatted so that his face was on a level with the child's. "Hello, Alistair, are you enjoying your stay in Hanbury?"

The boy smiled, but even that seemed to take a strength he barely possessed. His eyes were enormous in his tiny, pale face, his cheeks hollow, his frame painfully thin, "I like the hills, but I don't much care for the waters," he said. Gil thought he must be around nine or ten, but he was so pathetically small, one would never know it until he spoke.

"Well, it is because of the hills that we have the water. Rain falls on the hilltops, then filters down through the ground until it flows out at the bottom, but it takes thousands of years. The water we are drinking now probably fell as rain before Christ was born."

This apparently appealed to the young gentleman, for his little face was lit with enthusiasm and he looked at his cup with renewed interest, "It doesn't taste too badly for such *old* water, does it?"

"Not too badly at all," Gil smiled and when he raised his eyes to Catherine Pennington, he saw that she was smiling too, a smile which encompassed him in its warmth, in gratitude for making this precious child happy. Because Alistair was not looking at her, her face also held an expression which told Gil she did not think her boy was destined to reach manhood. If Gil had been brought to her side by her beauty, it was her courage and tender love for her child which held him there.

"There are underground lakes and streams in the caverns high up in the hills, perhaps when Alistair is a little better, we could take him up there to see for himself?"

"Oh yes!" exclaimed the boy, "I have never seen water underground. We may, mayn't we Mama?"

"I don't know how we would manage your chair, dearest."

"I would gladly help," offered Gil and was rewarded with another of those all too fleeting smiles.

"You are so kind, Mr Underwood. Alistair and I will look forward to it."

"In the meantime, shall I see you in church on Sunday?"

"I'm afraid not. Alistair and I do not attend your church. Our devotions must necessarily be of a private nature."

This was a stunning blow and Gil's face showed the depth of his disappointment, "You are Roman Catholics?" he asked, almost beneath his breath.

She knew then that it was over before it had even begun. Her brown eyes were hurt, but full of patient understanding, "Yes, we are. Thank you for your kind welcome, Mr Underwood."

He tried to recover himself; "Shall you be here tomorrow?"

"I imagine so."

"Perhaps I shall see you then?"

"Perhaps. Goodbye."

Gil made his way back to Verity through the crowds of people, barely seeing them as he wove between them, and he also failed to notice that Verity too looked as though she had received her own share of bad news. When she whispered, "Take me home, Gil." He was only too eager to comply. He wanted to be alone, in his church, to think.

CHAPTER NINE

'Cacoethes Carpendi' – A mania for finding fault

Back at the vicarage Gilbert, completely unaware of any fraught feelings but his own, left the two women and went immediately to the church. Ellen led Verity into the garden, where she knew they would not be overheard by Underwood or Francis, who were still closeted in the study.

There was a mossy old stone bench beneath the shade of the trees and it was here the two sat, Verity, white faced and shocked, twisting her handkerchief between trembling fingers; Ellen fighting the emotions of fury at Underwood's thoughtlessness, and deep pity for her troubled friend.

"I'm sure Isobel must be wrong, my dear. Underwood may be many things, but he is no rake. Philandering is in the blood, and he's never shown any inclination towards it before."

"Still being in love with Charlotte is not philandering. It is something he has no power to fight. And who can blame him? She is so beautiful, so lively and I…"

Ellen embraced her friend so fiercely that she was almost deprived of the ability to breathe, "If he cannot see beyond a pretty face, then he is an idiot as well as a rogue. And who says you are not as pretty as that little hussy?"

"My mirror," answered Verity mournfully.

"Oh, Verity! What is the matter with you? I have never known you to be a defeatist. You have qualities far richer than Charlotte Wynter's prettiness. Are you going to give in without a fight and leave the field clear for that horrid little flirt? Do you not love Underwood enough to fight for him?"

"I love him dreadfully," protested Verity, "That is why I want his happiness above my own."

"If you think he will be happier with Charlotte Wynter than with you, you much mistake the matter. How long do you think it would be before she tires of him and casts him aside for a new and more exciting lover?"

Since Verity could not envision any woman growing tired of her beloved husband, this remark had very little effect on her misery.

"You do not understand, Ellen. I think Charlotte truly loves him."

"If that is true, then let it be her problem and not yours. There is a baby to think about now."

Verity was aghast, "Oh! How could Francis betray me? I begged him not to tell anyone."

Ellen smiled at her naiveté, "Calm yourself. Francis did not tell me. I knew without his help, I assure you. Remember I am a mother myself and recognized the signs."

She found her arm being clutched by the panic-stricken Verity, "You do not think Underwood has noticed too?"

"I very much doubt it. Underwood may be very astute when it comes to solving crimes, but like every other man, he is incredibly obtuse when it comes to women. In three months' time he will be complaining you are putting on weight."

"Thank God!" said Verity fervently.

"But why don't you tell him? Surely he has a right to know?"

"No," answered Verity, suddenly adamant, "If Underwood stays with me, it will be me and not his child which binds him."

"You are a fool, Verity. You have the ammunition to blow Charlotte right out of the water, and you will not use it. You are like Nelson, but you have spotted the sniper in the rigging and could save yourself from the fatal shot. For goodness sake, tell him."

"No, I will not! If Underwood chooses Charlotte, then he will never know about this child. The day he leaves me for her, is the day I take the first coach out of Hanbury – leaving him no forwarding address."

Ellen was very much afraid she meant every word.

*

Underwood, blissfully unaware of all these machinations, had spent the afternoon sifting through the prettily inlaid wooden box which contained the private papers of Josephine Dunstable.

The will was much as he expected – and proved beyond doubt that Oliver Dunstable would have been much better off had his wife lived rather than died when she did. Admittedly he was left a handsome sum, but the bulk of the estate went to Melissa, in trust until she came of age. The important codicil stated that Mrs Gedney could use any interest accrued solely for the benefit of her child, but she alone was entitled to decide how the money was used. Mrs Dunstable had tried to keep the money out of the hands of her worthless son-in-law, but at the last moment had weakened, probably at the thought of the penury she was inflicting on her beloved child.

The evidence was not strong enough to convict the Gedneys, but it was sufficient to clear Oliver Dunstable, in Underwood's opinion, at least. If Oliver had been interested only in the money, he would have been much wiser to have milked Mrs Dunstable prior to her death, rather than kill her for his inheritance.

Of course, none of this would carry any weight with a court, for there was no proof Dunstable knew what was in the document – or indeed that the Gedneys were privy to its contents either.

He put the will aside and continued his search. He was at last rewarded when he found, right at the bottom of the box, a small leather-bound note book, very old and worn, which contained numerous lists of names, besides which were written various sums of money. Mrs Dunstable was nothing if not thorough. Had he not spoken to Lady Hartley-Wells on the subject, this book would probably have meant nothing to him, and been cast aside as worthless and indecipherable – but now Underwood thought he knew what it meant and he studied it with great interest.

By the time his brother called him for tea, Underwood had the names of three persons who were listed in the book and who were presently residing in the spa town of Hanbury.

*

Underwood longed to discuss his discoveries with Verity, knowing her sense and intelligence would have been of inestimable aid to his own thought processes, but her mood was such that he felt he could not approach her. He was deeply disturbed by her very apparent unhappiness and his own inability to comfort her. He had never in his life felt quite so helpless and inadequate. He wanted nothing more than to take her in his arms and assure her that everything was going to be all right, but there was something daunting in her tragic eyes which sent him scurrying from the room.

The notion of spending the evening at a ball was appalling, but the thought of telling Verity he did not wish to accompany her was worse. He felt sure any attempt to cancel the event would be met with accusations of being ashamed to be seen in her company, or, more annoyingly, suspicions that he had arranged an assignation with Charlotte, and therefore wanted his wife out of the way. He was beginning to feel that no matter which way he turned, he really could not win.

Ellen was determined to force her friend to fight for her husband's attention, so it was with resolve that she went to Verity's room to help her choose her gown for their evening out, and to dress her hair for her.

She was delighted, and secretly immensely relieved, to find Verity had been taken in hand by her new Mama-in-law, and had a wide selection of lovely evening clothes. She was even more pleased to hear Underwood had not seen any of them.

"Perfect!" she exclaimed, with great good humour, "We shall make that husband of yours realize just what a gem he possesses. Charlotte will look the silly chit she is, when compared to your elegance. I must say Underwood's mother has wonderful taste."

"I think she enjoyed helping me. She confided that not having a daughter had been her one sorrow in life."

Soon the bed was spread with Verity's rejected gowns and Ellen was silently despairing. There was a beautiful jade-green silk, but Verity's paleness had reflected the colour and it made her look ghastly. The white satin played the same trick. Black was too dark, red too garish, pink to girlish, pale blue too insipid.

The last dress in the trunk was midnight blue with a fine silver thread stripe. It was ideal and Ellen's pleasure was not feigned when she saw Verity in it. She knew her friend had never looked lovelier. Her white complexion looked fashionably pale instead of sickly and the colour of the gown gave the illusion of added height. The low cut bodice exposed more of her breast than she had ever shown before, and the high waist hid the beginnings of her bulging stomach. Verity blushed when she saw her reflection, "Ellen, don't you think…" Ellen followed the direction of her gaze and laughed, "No, I don't think! The gown is perfect in every way."

When Ellen's expert fingers had teased her locks into becoming ringlets, the picture was complete, "Now, Verity, I want you to listen to me and believe every word I say, because I speak nothing but the truth. You look beautiful! There will not be another woman tonight who approaches you. Hear it and know it to be true."

Verity smiled at the impassioned sincerity in her friend's voice; "Do you think Underwood will agree with you?"

"Underwood!" snorted Ellen contemptuously, "What would he know? If you don't believe me, just glance at the other men. If their admiration isn't plain to you, then you are beyond all hope."

Verity understood what she meant when she glided gracefully down the stairs. The household were all gathered in the hall, only awaiting her arrival so they could leave. Underwood, Gil and Francis all glanced up as they heard her coming and all three mouths dropped open in astonishment. Verity could scarcely prevent herself laughing aloud, so comic was their joint surprise. Underwood thrust aside his brother and his friend, climbed the stairs two at a time and held out his hand to her, "You look magnificent!" She accepted his assistance and his compliment with a slight smile.

"Good gad! Verity, I hardly recognized you." exclaimed Francis, only to be rapped sharply across the knuckles by his wife's fan.

Gil merely smiled at her, "I don't usually dance, Verity, but I don't think I could miss treading a measure with the belle of the ball."

"I suspect you will have to fight for the privilege, Gil," murmured Ellen warningly, "There is going to be quite a queue forming when Verity enters the Assembly Rooms."

Ellen's prediction was entirely accurate, for there was a quality greater than beauty about Verity that night. She did indeed look attractive, and her early pregnancy had given her figure unaccustomed curves, but more than that she was enjoying herself and she was a woman whose face would always reflect her inner emotions. Her happiness shone in her eyes, drawing people to her though they did not know the reason. Young and old, male and female, they looked at her and found themselves more content for the experience.

She had never danced so much in her life before, nor had so many elaborate compliments paid to her. Charlotte, over-dressed as usual in white silk, too fussily decorated with paste and pearls, could only fume by the window, cooling her hot cheeks with a furiously wafted fan and knowing, for once, how the wall-flowers felt. The prevailing fashion meant that all the younger ladies were attired in the very palest colours, if not white, then pastels. Verity's gown stood out as the ultimate in style and elegance.

Underwood watched her indulgently for quite a while before he grew weary of playing second fiddle, then he fended off his rivals and breaking the rule of a lifetime about not making a fool of himself by prancing about a ballroom, he lead his wife into a waltz. He was spurred into such drastic action by the thought of allowing any arms but his own to encircle his wife's waist. Charlotte had been determined that the waltz should be danced by herself and Underwood and her ire was plain to see – or would have been had anyone glanced her way. The room was too busy admiring the graceful way in which Verity was leading her husband, expertly covering his many errors, and so clearly wearing her heart upon her sleeve that the whole company was completely entranced. It was rare indeed in this age of arranged marriages for a husband and wife to be in love, and rarer still for them to make a public display of that affection. The last demonstrative pair who had been witnessed by Hanbury society had been the Dunstables, and unfortunately they had only succeeded in embarrassing everyone.

Once Underwood felt sufficiently at ease with the steps to stop looking at his feet, he managed to smile at his wife, "Gad, sweetheart, I haven't danced for years – and believe it or not, I never learned to waltz."

Verity could quite easily believe it, for her bruised toes bore silent testimony to his ineptitude, but she kindly refrained from pointing this out.

"It is very nice to see you looking so happy," he added carefully, hoping against hope he was not about to ruin the evening by speaking words which could be taken the wrong way and brooded over – he felt that had been happening to him with monotonous regularity recently.

"Tonight, I am happy," she said, "Are you?"

"No man is ever happy making a fool of himself on a dance floor, but I am not unhappy," he told her with a wry grin.   Verity laughed. She loved that particular smile of his, half amused, half embarrassed. It was one of the few times he seemed wholly human. She thought of all the extravagant gallantries to which she had been subjected all evening, comparing them, not unfavourably, with her husband's candour, "Oh Cadmus!" she chided him, "Has it never occurred to you to occasionally lie in order to please your listener?"

He looked amazed at the very thought, "Good gad! Don't tell me that you are one of those empty-headed females who would rather hear pretty lies than the truth?"

"I'm a woman, Cadmus. Sometimes I think you forget it."

"Don't be ridiculous. How could I forget?"

She smiled mysteriously and refused to answer.

"By the bye, if you have nothing arranged for tomorrow, I would be grateful for an hour or two of your time. I want to discuss the case with you – if you want to be involved, that is?" There was a hesitation in his tone which told her how very unsure of her support he had become, and she was sorry for it. She suddenly realized that here was something she shared with her husband which Charlotte Wynter could never hope to equal. He knew her mind was very nearly as sharp as his own and far from resenting it, as most men would, he delighted in her intelligence and encouraged her to offer her own thoughts and ideas.

"Certainly," she assured him warmly, "I should be most interested to hear what you have discovered."

The dance ended and Underwood led her off towards a convenient seat. Once there he made a gesture which at once delighted and embarrassed her. He drew his snuffbox from his pocket and took a pinch. The box was returned to his pocket, but instead of simply inhaling the mixture, he took her hand, palm upward, and sprinkled the dark powder on the white skin of her inner wrist, then, bowing low over her hand, he inhaled. Once the snuff was gone, he turned her hand over and kissed her fingers in one graceful and fluid movement. Verity grew a little pink of cheek and smiled softly at him. It was as much as those observing them could do not to heave a collective sigh of satisfaction at so romantic a moment. Underwood, aware that he had caused a stir, but determined to maintain his calm demeanour, simply said, "I pray you will feel free to enjoy yourself for the rest of the evening, Verity and I have only one favour to beg in return – don't expect me to dance again – and don't waltz with anyone else."

"At my count, that amounts to two favours, but I will grant them both."

*

"I can scarcely believe it, Cadmus," exclaimed his wife the following morning, having risen late and joined him in the vicarage study for their promised consultation, "Are you really sure of this?"

"As sure as I can. Mrs Dunstable's book says Kitty Wolstencroft is not Adeline Beresford's aunt, but her mother. Mrs Dunstable raised the girl, but Mrs Wolstencroft claimed back her child when her husband died. Grace Arbuthnot is the other name mentioned in the book, but no mention of what happened to her child appears therein."

"But they all seem to be on such friendly terms. Can they really have forgiven her for the past?"

"Perhaps not. It may be the pretence of friendship has given them the necessary access to Mrs Dunstable."

"You think one of them could be the murderer?"

"Undoubtedly possible – it may even be all of them in a murderous conspiracy."

"I suppose so," Verity looked thoughtful, "Another notion has occurred to me, Cadmus. I cannot help but feel we have been altogether too trusting of Oliver Dunstable."

By that she meant he had, but neither of them laboured the point, he merely asked, "In what way?"

"We have never demanded to know the name of his mistress. We should see her. Just because Dunstable was quite happy to maintain the *status quo*, and let's face it, which man isn't? It does not follow that she feels the same way."

"I had not thought of that. I was assuming he spoke for them both, but you are quite correct. I shall right that wrong now."

"I think the day had better be spent doing a round of visits, and asking some very pertinent questions."

CHAPTER TEN

'Abyssus Aybssum Invocat' – One false step leads to another

Grace Arbuthnot was a tall woman; almost as tall as Underwood himself, grey-haired and with a face lined beyond her years. She could not have been much more than forty, but she looked fifty, and even that estimate rose alarmingly when Underwood told her the purpose of his visit; she looked so shocked Verity could not help but wish her husband had couched their errand in subtler terms than those he employed.

Whether it was shock at being found out, or that she was a naturally honest person anyway, Verity never knew, but once she had invited them in and offered seats and refreshments, Mrs Arbuthnot appeared to keep nothing from them.

"Josie Dunstable did take my boy in for me, many years ago now, but I have never felt anything but gratitude towards her. I was not married and my life would have been ruined had any word of my trouble leaked out. I made a childish mistake and Josie helped me recover from it."

"How came you to meet up with her again?"

"I didn't 'meet her again', as you phrase it. I never lost touch with her. I saw my son once a month all through my marriage. He is married himself now and thinks of … thought of … Josie as his mother. I act the part of godmother and we are all happy with that. I never had any children by my husband, so Geoffrey is all I have in the world. Not for anything would I risk our relationship. He will be here for Josie's funeral, but I must ask you not to make any movement towards him which will alert his wife to our true status. I know I did him a great disservice by bringing him into the world so encumbered, pray do not compound my error by spoiling his life now."

"Naturally we shall do no such thing. Thank you for being so frank, Mrs Arbuthnot."

"I have nothing to hide, but my youthful folly, so I think I have no need to ask that it remain confidential?"

"You have my word, dear lady, that once this case is over, I shall personally see to it Mrs Dunstable's notebook is burned."

"Thank you."

They waited until they had reached the end of the street before Verity asked Underwood, "Do you believe her?"

"Until I have further information, there is no reason not to. The story sounds credible enough – and quite honestly, it would be a relief to hear of at least one child who was treated well by Mrs Dunstable."

"Do we see Mrs Wolstencroft next?" she enquired, and he nodded in reply.

The two women who were the Underwoods' next subjects were a vastly different proposition. The stoic stance told Underwood that his visit had not been entirely unexpected, and was certainly not welcome.

It took all his charm to get across the threshold, for both women came to the door together when his card was presented and did their utmost to send him about his business. In the end he had to be brutal and point out just how imperative it was he hear their story in the privacy of their own home, rather than in open court, which was where it would surely end. They reluctantly let him in, but Verity was frozen out. They requested that she leave and she had no choice but to comply, informing her husband she would wait his arrival at the Pump-rooms.

Mrs Wolstencroft wasted no time on pleasantries, "Let me tell you, sir, that I greatly resent this intrusion upon my privacy."

"I'm sure you do, madam, but that is no concern of mine. I have been asked to investigate the untimely death of Mrs Dunstable, and I fully intend to do so." It was most uncommon for Underwood to be so blunt, but something in the woman's attitude made his hackles rise, besides which, he was getting tired and discouraged, not only with the murder, but with his private life too. Just as he had found some common ground with Verity, something like this would occur to drive a wedge between them, and he was finding the situation wearing.

The reply he received was a disgusted, "Well!" but he had no further difficulty in getting answers to his questions – whether they were truthful or accurate answers was an entirely different matter.

"I might as well tell you, without preamble, that I am aware of the true nature of your relationship to Miss Beresford, so pray do not waste my time in denying it."

"Dear God! How did you discover…?"

"Mrs Dunstable left a notebook – but I assure you as I have assured others, the moment this is over, I shall burn the evidence."

Mrs Wolstencroft had difficulty in bringing herself to thank him for this kindness, but Miss Beresford said, in heartfelt tones, "We are grateful, Mr Underwood."

He inclined his head in acknowledgement of her comment, then began his interview, "When did you remove your daughter from Mrs Dunstable's care and begin to call her your niece?"

"About three years ago. My husband and parents had passed away, so anyone who knew I had no niece was not there to betray me."

"Had you maintained your contact with Mrs Dunstable through all your daughter's childhood?"

"I could only manage to see her once a year. My husband had a detestation of spa towns, so I was able to convince him to let me come here for one week every year for my health. Mrs Dunstable would bring Adeline here to me for that one precious week."

"Did she blackmail you?"

Mrs Wolstencroft paled slightly, licked her lips nervously and glanced towards her daughter, "Not exactly, but I paid for the holiday for us all, and Mrs Dunstable liked to stay in the best hotels, and would suffer nothing which was not of the highest quality. I also paid considerably more for Adeline's keep than it would have cost me to send a boy to the finest schools in the land, but I felt Mrs Dunstable's discretion was worth the money."

The exchange of looks was not lost on Underwood, and he instantly knew there was something the ladies were not telling him. He hazarded a guess and was stunned by the reaction, "What made you lose confidence in Mrs Dunstable?"

Adeline leapt to her feet and began to pace the room in agitation, "Tell him the whole truth, Mother, for God's sake!"

Tears glistened in Mrs Wolstencroft's eyes, "Do not upset yourself, my love. It has nothing to do with the case, and there is no reason why you should parade your shame before this man."

The girl turned on her, aggression contorting her face, "It is not I who should be ashamed, but the men who…" her voice faded into a sob and she flung herself on to the settee in a passion of weeping.

Underwood raised a brow at her mother. She drew in a deep breath and admitted quietly, "There was one year, when Adeline was twelve, I could not raise the money to pay Mrs Dunstable. She forced my daughter to earn her keep by … as…" her voice sank so low Underwood could barely hear her, "a prostitute."

Underwood was appalled, "At the age of twelve?" he asked in a stunned under voice, "Dear God! What kind of a man wishes to use a child in that way? And what manner of woman was she to allow it?"

She shook her head wearily. She had tortured herself for years asking the same question, and many others of a similar sort, whilst watching her child suffer mental agonies because of her horrific experiences. Her disbelief at the perversions of which some of the male population were capable matched his own. Her compassionate gaze rested on her daughter's prone form, the anguish at her own helplessness writ clearly upon her haggard features, "I swore then that I would move heaven and earth to get Adeline away from her, but I could not afford to offend her. She knew too much and could do us both too much damage."

"And yet you have been giving every indication of friendship with the woman."

"It was necessary. It seemed we would never be free of her. A young man of good family has proposed to Adeline. She accepted and against my will, his family sent an announcement to the newspapers. It did not take Mrs Dunstable long to contact me and to invite us both here to see her, for 'old times' sake' she said. I knew what that meant. We were going to have to pay again for her silence."

Underwood looked thoughtfully at her, "I feel it only fair to warn you that what you have just told me makes you a suspect in the murder of Mrs Dunstable."

"I understand that, but I am sick of living with lies. If I had hidden this from you and it had been discovered later, it would have looked worse for me. I cannot win it seems. Well, I did not murder Josie Dunstable, but I am not going to pretend I am sorry she is dead. In fact I am exceedingly glad. Make of that what you will, Mr Underwood, but I beg you, do not punish my child any more. She has been through enough."

Underwood took his leave, feeling even more morose than he had previously. The notion that the world was a far better place for having lost Mrs Josephine Dunstable was beginning to take hold of his imagination, and he had to remind himself that it was not her capacity for good or evil which was at the centre of the investigation.

He found Verity waiting for him, as arranged, but for once her eyes were not turned eagerly towards the door awaiting his arrival, but instead covertly observing Gil, who was sitting with Mrs Pennington and her son.

Underwood saw his brother with a woman, but he didn't believe it, "Who is Gil's companion?"

"He has not confided her name to me, but when he walked in he went straight to her side, without even noticing my presence."

Underwood gave a snort of unkind laughter, "Well, let us hope it is not too long before we are thrusting a wife upon him."

"Thrusting? Is that how you feel about marriage?" she asked diffidently.

He was tired, disheartened and discouraged by what he had learned of Mrs Dunstable, therefore he did nothing to correct the error he had made, "For much of the time, yes," he said coolly, "Now, shall we continue on our way, or do you wish me to go alone?"

Her voice was equally if not more cold as she replied, "Not at all. By all means let us go. I have no wish to remain here and watch men and women make fools of themselves over each other."

They were obliged to hire a carriage to take them to the address provided by Oliver Dunstable, which proved to be a pretty little cottage in a small village some three or four miles outside Hanbury.

The young lady who answered the door was pretty in a doll-like way, and quite obviously as feather-brained as she was attractive. Verity unkindly thought of her as the female counterpart of the dense Oliver, a man for whom she had no liking, less respect and little sympathy. In this she and Underwood differed for he merely needed right to prevail; personalities mattered very little. But she could not help but feel that people who had been stupid and wicked enough to fall into difficulties caused by their own moral decline, would reap all the punishment they so richly deserved. Her clerical father's simple doctrine had been that goodness was its own reward.

As the conversation progressed it was borne in upon Underwood and Verity that if Dunstable had chosen to murder his wife, he had picked an unfortunate accomplice. She answered all their questions with a fullness and candour which irritated Verity and embarrassed Underwood.

She was so vague on days and dates that she was worse than useless as an alibi, but Underwood himself felt that might be no bad thing. His own hope was to keep Miss Frederica Marsh entirely out of the case, for Dunstable's life, in the event of a court appearance, might very well depend on convincing a jury of his devotion to his dead wife and his incapability of committing so foul a crime. Underwood hoped to prove Dunstable innocent of murder without recourse to his mistress.

The girl apparently found nothing wrong with her own morals or those of her lover, continually referring to the fact that they were 'so much in love' as though, thought Verity bitterly, that excused their behaviour and made everything they did together acceptable. She seemed to have no feelings of guilt or remorse towards the dead Josie, only loudly bewailing the fact that Oliver had been 'forced' from time to time to do his conjugal duty by his elderly spouse. Neither Verity nor Underwood had any desire to hear these details – on the contrary! – but Miss Marsh ploughed on regardless, entirely oblivious of the expressions of deep distaste on the faces of her guests.

It was only as they were preparing to leave that she gave a piece of information which stilled them both, all thought of flight immediately banished.

"One last question, Miss Marsh, if you please. Being aware, as you undoubtedly were, that Dunstable was already married, were there never any discussions between you relating to your own nuptials?"

"Not at first, but of course the subject arose when I told him I am going to have a baby."

Underwood's mouth actually dropped open, so dazed was he by this ingenuous remark, and Verity drew in her breath so sharply that the sound was clearly audible, "Did you say there is to be a child as a result of your association with Mr Dunstable?" she asked quietly, not entirely sure she had heard aright.

"Oh yes! Oliver was a little surprised at first too, but he assured me everything would be happily resolved and we would be married before the baby was born – and behold, we shall be. Oliver is so wonderful, is he not?"

"Wonderful," murmured Underwood with deep feeling and glanced at his wife. Verity's face was blank, she gave no indication of the varied emotions which assailed her, merely offering her hand to Miss Marsh and thanking her politely for her hospitality.

They climbed into the waiting carriage without exchanging a word, and it was not until the hamlet was fading into the distance that Underwood risked a comment,

"It would seem, my dear, you were right and I was wrong. There are more reasons to kill than merely money."

"I fear that may well be the case. Are you still confident that Oliver Dunstable did not murder his wife?"

"If you want me to be brutally honest, no. I can scarcely believe it, but Oliver could well be cleverer than either of us ever imagined."

"That is hard to believe," returned Verity sardonically. She really did not like Dunstable, but her feelings towards any man who betrayed his wife were growing daily more bitter.

Underwood gave a short laugh, "Poor Oliver, you really do detest him, don't you?"

"You have no idea how much."

CHAPTER ELEVEN

'Beneficium Accipere Libertatem Est Vendere' – To accept a favour is to sell one's freedom

Dusk was coming on apace and Underwood stared moodily out of the carriage window. Verity, pale and exhausted, had fallen asleep against the worn velvet squabbs of the hired hack and Underwood envied her the ability to slumber after the shock they had just sustained.

Where did Miss Marsh's admission leave them now? Oliver Dunstable not only had every reason to wish his wife dead, he also seemed to have promised that very thing. He had motive, opportunity, and means all within his grasp, so could Underwood be quite so certain he had judged his man correctly – and more importantly, what hope did he have of convincing a jury in the face of such damning evidence?

Underwood was thrown forward, suddenly and violently, as the carriage came to an unexpected halt and he heard the terrified whinnying of the startled horses, accompanied by the loud curses of the driver.

He let down the window with a clatter and thrust his head out, "What goes on?" he called quietly, so as not to wake his sleeping wife.

The vehicle moved jerkily backwards and forwards slightly as the elderly whipster tried to bring his frightened steeds under control, "There's a man lying in the road, sir," came the reply from the box, "He looks to be in a bad way."

"Good gad! We didn't run over him, did we?" exclaimed Underwood in concern, struggling to undo the door, which proved at first, unyielding.

"No, no, sir. I think he must have been set upon by footpads."

Underwood burst through the door as it suddenly swung open and found himself almost falling out onto the dusty highroad. He righted himself and squinted into the gathering twilight, barely able to discern the figure of the man who had staggered in front of their vehicle, before collapsing in a heap on the road, almost under the dangerously stamping hooves of the panicked horses.

Of one accord the driver and Underwood ran to the front of the carriage, the former to grasp the nosebands of his animals, the latter to see what aid could be given to the obviously injured man.

As he rolled the man onto his back, Underwood suffered a slight jolt, for the victim was black-skinned, something rarely seen in such a remote area of England at this time. Black people were quite widespread in London and other large cities, for slavery had been rife in the previous century, and Underwood had taught several African Princes at his university, but he had not been expecting to come across anyone here of Negro descent. It caused him no more than a momentary hesitation, however, for the man was severely beaten and was covered in blood and bruises. Underwood hoisted him into a semi-recumbent position and spoke gently to him,

"If I help you, do you think you could make it into the carriage? I'm sorry not to be able to merely lift you and save you the effort, but I doubt my ability." He spoke nothing less than the truth, for now he was nearer, he could see the man was of huge proportions, taller than Underwood's six feet by a good four or five inches, and immeasurably broader than his rescuer's slim physique.

At that moment a sleepy Verity joined them and called anxiously into the twilight, "What is wrong, Underwood? Why have we stopped?"

The sound of a woman's voice seemed to jerk the man back into consciousness, for he sat upright and muttered between swollen and bloody lips, "For God's sake get the girl away from here. They may still be lurking about."

"Come then," said Underwood decisively, "let us be on our way."

The man staggered to his feet, upheld by Underwood and they managed, with difficulty, to get to the carriage door, whereupon the man more fell than climbed into the vehicle. With a supreme effort Underwood hoisted inside the legs which still stuck out into the road, handed the bemused Verity over their sprawling guest, leapt in after her and called to the driver with an exceedingly coarse expression gleaned from his sporting students, "Spring 'em!" The driver needed no second bidding and with a bellow to the horses, and an expert, and exceptionally loud crack of the whip, they were speedily carried the remaining couple of miles to Hanbury.

Once back in the warm, candle-lit homeliness of the vicarage, the injured man soon found himself stripped of his torn, muddy and bloodstained coat. Verity's gentle but competent hands were washing

87

his cuts and Dr Herbert was diagnosing cracked ribs and binding them for him, Gil was making tea in his own ineffable way and Underwood was questioning him about his mishap.

His story was a strange one, and tragic in its way, though Tobias Hambleton, for that was his name, proved to be amazingly philosophical and had not a bitter bone in his body, though his listeners thought he had reason enough.

He had been taken from Africa – what part he had no idea – as a babe in his mother's arms, as so many hundreds of others had been, and subsequently sold into slavery, as a body servant to a titled lady in London. Through his babyhood and small childhood she had kept him by her, much as one might keep a pet dog. He slept in a little cot at the foot of her bed, and followed her throughout the day, fetching and carrying for her. There had never been a formal education, but a governess of the family's children had secretly taught him to read and write. All too soon he had out grown the sweet and cuddly stage and a tall gangling youth had no place in a lady's household. He had first been sent to help in the stables, where he had been given the hardest and most unpleasant tasks, but where he had developed the muscles which were later to be his salvation.

Soon the other servants had baulked at working and eating with him, for in their ignorance they had no idea how to treat this alien presence, who spoke, because his formative years, like a gentleman, and really had no idea how to perform the duties he was assigned. At around the same time the idea of slavery had become an anachronism, and Toby had progressed from lap dog to embarrassment. He found himself free, but cast out into the streets to earn his living as best he could. An outcast because of the colour of his skin, he did the only thing he knew and became a pugilist, for fights had been all too common in the stable yard. His fists became his saviour, but they placed him in his own particular hell. A gentle man, reared to serve a lady of quality, he found it increasingly difficult to batter his opponents senseless and bloody with his great strength.

This day had seen the moment when he had finally refused to do it any longer, and several disgruntled sportsmen had taken out their frustration on him. One man at a time, and they would have stood no chance, for in all his years of fighting he had sustained remarkably few injuries, but this was different. There were at least ten of them, and he had found himself firmly pinioned by half of them whilst the rest used fist and boot indiscriminately. He had regained his senses to find himself dumped in a ditch, only inches from the bottom and fortunate not to have drowned in the cold, muddy water. He had no idea how long he had lain there, only that on hearing hoof beats he had dragged himself out and staggered towards the sound, fearing that a night in the open in his state would probably have meant the end of him.

His audience was appalled by the story, and there was no hesitation in any of their voices when they all begged him to make free of their hospitality for as long as he felt the need. He grinned, ignoring split lips and showing beautiful white teeth which were miraculously unscathed by his ordeal, "You are all very kind."

"Not at all, Mr Hambleton," said Gil warmly, "We are only sorry that our fellow-countrymen have shown you less Christianity than they ought."

"Call me Toby, please – and as a Christian myself, I haven't exactly spent a life of saintliness. Ask anyone who has ever been in a mill with me."

They all smiled at this sally, though none thought he had been given very much choice in the matter.

"But to have thrown you out on the streets," protested Verity, "That really was unforgivable!"

"Not as unforgivable as the alternative, Miss," asserted Toby with emphasis, "Most men in my position would have been resold and shipped out to the plantations in the West Indies. There slavery still exists, and it's a death sentence for most. I'm just grateful my mistress could not bring herself to do that to me."

The silence which greeted this was broken by Oliver Dunstable strolling into the room, looking more relaxed than any man with a noose hanging over him had any right to, "Good evening all. What goes on here?"

Introductions were performed, then Mr Underwood looked grimly at him, "I'd like to speak to you, Mr Dunstable – now! You have some explaining to do."

*

Once again the vicar's study became the venue for a few choice words, "Mr Dunstable, you seem determined to bring about your demise by a hangman's rope, despite my best endeavours."

Oliver sank into a comfortable chair with a resigned and martyred air of a student about to be carpeted for an unfinished essay, "What ever the problem is, I dare swear you can solve it, Underwood," he said casually.

"Not being a miracle worker nor a midwife, I fear this little complication is quite beyond my powers, Mr Dunstable," answered the older man testily, "Why did you not confide your secret to me?"

"I didn't think it concerned anyone but Miss Marsh and myself. What has it to do with Josie's death?" muttered Oliver, a trifle sulkily.

"Didn't concern …!" Underwood roared, then trailed off, completely bereft, momentarily, of the power of reasonable communication. He took a deep breath, refreshed himself with a large pinch of snuff, and tired again, "Young man, the condition of your lady friend – I use the term advisedly! – bestows on you the perfect motive for having murdered your wife. If you now hasten into marriage with her, you will compound that supposition. All I need now to end the perfect day is for you to admit you attempted to terminate the pregnancy with tansy oil and we may as well start weaving the hemp ourselves."

Dunstable flushed to the roots of his hair, and then the blood drained as swiftly from his face as the full import of Underwood's words sank in, "I believe Frederica did try something of the sort…" he murmured reluctantly, "Didn't work though," he added somewhat bitterly.

Underwood stared at him for several incredulous seconds, "Do you mean to tell me you have had tansy in your possession in the recent past?"

"I suppose I have – but I swear to God I didn't know it was a poison."

"Then how do you suppose it manages to kill an unborn child, you blithering idiot?" roared Underwood, now completely out of patience and not much caring what he said, nor who heard him.

If it was possible, Dunstable grew even whiter, "I... I didn't think of it like that…"

"Your trouble, Mr Dunstable, is that you never think at all. If you did not commit this murder, you have played beautifully into the hands of those who did. I fear it is beyond even my ingenuity to salvage the situation."

"God! Don't say that. You can't believe I did it. You can't leave me to hang."

"Mr Dunstable," explained Underwood with admirable control, "if any court in the land hears that you had the means, the opportunity and the motive to kill your wife, then nothing short of Christ himself appearing to the jury to vouch for your innocence is going to save your neck – and even then they will ask to see the crucifixion wounds. God give me strength! Don't you see what you have done?"

Dunstable was almost snivelling with fright, "Please Underwood! You are my only friend, don't desert me now."

"Give me one good reason why I should not?"

"If not for myself, then for Frederica and the child! They are the real victims in all this!"

Underwood sank into a chair, holding his brow with one hand, "Good God, man, you have set me quite a task, haven't you?"

"Does that mean you'll help me?"

"It would appear so, but pray do not rely on the outcome being in your favour! I am going to need a miracle of epic proportions to save your worthless hide! You had better tell me where you purchased the tansy!"

"What?" He was still reeling from the explicit warning Underwood had issued and seemed confused and disorientated. Underwood repeated the question, and Dunstable stuttered a reply, scarcely aware of what he said. Underwood took note to the herbalist named by his companion, then left the young man alone with his thoughts.

*

Later in their bedroom, Verity, already tucked up in bed after her exhausting day, peeped at him over the edge of the covers as he performed his ablutions, "What did Mr Dunstable have to say for himself?"

Underwood lips were pursed in an expression of contempt and exasperation mixed, and he threw his coat violently towards a chair, "The man is a fool! God alone knows how I am going to get him out of this mess."

"Are you even going to try?"

"I have to. He did not kill his wife."

"You seem very sure, Cadmus. You were not so positive when you left Miss Marsh."

"Having spoken to him, I am now sure, beyond any doubt. Quite apart from anything else, he has not the intelligence to have planned any of this crime. My first assessment of him was correct. He could not organize a prayer meeting in a convent."

Verity giggled appreciatively, "Poor Cadmus. For a man who does not suffer fools gladly, you are having to spend a great deal of time with the biggest one of all."

"Quite!" he retorted, and climbed into bed beside her, "This has been planned meticulously, Verity, and infuriatingly, I am being manipulated into just the moves the real culprit had intended."

"What do you mean?"

"Always I am driven back to the same thing. Instead of being allowed to find out who killed Josie, I keep having to prove that Dunstable did not. It merely clouds the issue, as whoever plotted it knew it would. He or she is gambling on the fact that people always jump to the most obvious solution – in this case that Oliver killed his elderly wife, because he wanted her money, had grown tired of her, or wanted to marry his mistress – any reason would do. But even if there was someone on hand, such as myself, who would question these assumptions, then carefully laid traps along the way continually bring the issue back to proving Dunstable's innocence and *not* another's guilt."

"Then you think Miss Marsh's pregnancy was known to the real murderer?"

"Oh yes. I imagine the hapless Dunstable has been followed and observed for months, and has played quite happily into the hands of a ruthless killer. This moment has been chosen carefully, because all the pieces were in place. Dunstable has practically hanged himself. I should not be at all surprised to find he had taken the kindly advice of some well-wisher who told him where to buy tansy oil and what uses to put it to. The man walks around with his head in the clouds. He married Josie without a moment's thought as to what his future might be, tied to an old and sick woman, he began his affair in the same casual manner, not thinking how he could cope should she become pregnant, and he did not even have the sense to keep his private life, private."

"What are we to do about it?"

"I'm going to break out of this cycle, if it is the last thing I do. I'm tired of dancing to another's tune. Gratten is not helping matters, suspecting Dunstable and forcing me to keep bailing the boy out. I am going to see him tomorrow, then I am going to speak to Mrs Gedney – and the devil fly away with her husband if he tries to stop me."

"Cadmus, I worry about your motives."

He frowned at her, "What the hell is that supposed to mean?"

She almost quailed beneath the aggression in his voice, but bravely continued, "You seem so very sure Dunstable is innocent, but I wonder if your determination to clear his name stems not from your conviction of his innocence, but the conviction that you, having made known your opinion, cannot possibly admit to being wrong. You fly in the face of all the evidence with no more to back you than your own intuition…" Now her voice did trail away, for the scowl had grown black as night and she knew he was furiously angry with her.

"Thank you for that touching speech of support, dear wife."

Her voice trembled, but she refused to be cowed, "I will be supportive, Cadmus, when I think you are right, but I cannot quash my own opinions just because they do not tally with yours. If you wanted a compliant wife, you should have chosen one without a mind of her own."

The frown lifted as swiftly as it had descended, "Damn your principles, Verity. I don't think I will ever grow accustomed to having someone around me who is prepared to disagree. The position of tutor to a gaggle of boys was much more suited to my overbearing personality. Very well, I shall prove to you, too, that though Dunstable is an idiot, he is not a murderer."

"I'm not saying I think him guilty, I just don't have your confidence in his innocence."

"I accept your challenge, my dear. Dunstable shall be left without a stain on his character."

"He could never be that, Cadmus, after all he has done," she countered reasonably, "But I shall look forward to his being delivered from the gallows by your hand."

CHAPTER TWELVE

'Ab Asino Lanam' – Literally 'Wool from an ass' – Anyone who attempts the impossible is doomed to failure

It was quiet and cool in the church and with a feeling of relief and consolation; Gilbert sank to his knees at the altar rail and gave himself up to contemplation and peace. The vicarage was daily filling with more and more people and the vicar was finding it increasingly difficult to get time alone for the renewal of his inner spirit. The church was his last refuge and one where he knew his brother would not follow. Underwood avoided religion assiduously, unless forced.

Gil had intended to pray but he found his mind wandering. The colours which were cast upon the stone floor by the sun-filled stain-glass windows swam before his unfocused gaze. Never, in the past, had he felt that God was not with him when he entered a church, but he experienced nothing but emptiness and abandonment today. The knuckles of his intertwined fingers grew white and he unconsciously clenched his muscles. His face lost its customary calmness, and deep furrows marred his brow as he sank his head into his hands, "Oh God!" he groaned aloud, the words wrenched from him in anguish.

By the time he rose his knees ached with long contact with the cold floor and there was a determined set to his mouth which belied the misery in his eyes. He had struggled with his feelings for over an hour and had left his church decided upon a course of action.

The object of his deliberations was seated upon the stone bench set within the thick walls of the porch and she smiled tremulously when she saw him. There was no answering smile on his lips, but a slight tremble in his hand as he pulled the great oak door closed behind him, "Mrs Pennington, I did not expect to see you here."

"Do I intrude upon your time?" she asked softly.

He quickly realized he sounded unfriendly and forced himself to be more solicitous, "Oh course not. Would you care to look around the church?"

"Some other time perhaps."

"Very well. Where is Alistair?"

"Some of the elderly ladies at the Pump-rooms insisted that I leave him in their charge and get a little air. They suggested I looked a little tired and..."

The way she trailed off without finishing the sentence made him glance sharply at her and he saw that she did indeed look in need of a respite from her nursing duties. She was terribly pale and looked even more unhappy than when he had first beheld her.

"Can I offer you some tea? It is only a step to the vicarage."

"I should like that very much, but do you think you could sit here with me for a moment first? I have something I would like to say to you."

"Certainly," his words held no hint of the reluctance he felt. Suddenly he wanted nothing less than to sit beside her, in his church porch, listening to whatever she had to say. He had the uncomfortable notion he was not going to enjoy the conversation.

He sat, but left as wide a gap between them as it was possible to do. She watched him, her eyes widening slightly when she noticed his distance and his discomfiture.

"Reverend Underwood, I must ask, have I offended you in some way?"

His startled glance flew to her face, then dropped immediately away, "Great Heavens! Of course not. What on earth gave you any such idea?"

"I... I noticed you seemed to be avoiding me. When you first made yourself known to Alistair and myself, I thought you wanted to offer the hand of friendship, but since then you have barely spoken to us, and when you do, you seem cold and distant – oh dear! I sound very forward and strange, but I was so alone and I felt instinctively you were a kind man..." she stopped abruptly, and turning her face away from him she tried again to explain, stumbling over her words, "Oh, what a fool I am making of myself. Pray excuse me, I was wrong to do this ... I shall leave you alone..." she rose to leave but he reached out and caught her hand.

"Please don't go, Mrs Pennington. This whole sorry mess is my fault and you do deserve an explanation."

Her shoulders shook, "I cannot stay here now. Let me compose myself. I can't bear for you to see me cry."

Impetuously he stood and grasped her shoulders, twisting her so that she was forced to face him, "I have merited the pain of witnessing your tears, my dear, since I am the cause of them. Can you forgive me?"

She began to sob in the heart-broken, unstoppable way children have and he pulled her into his arms, cradling her head against his shoulder, until he felt the warmth of her body seeping through his coat and he knew he was lost forever.

Little use now to tell himself a love affair with her was impossible; pointless indeed to hope that the first feelings he had for her would shrivel and die without nourishment. Gil had found the one woman in the world he could love and nothing was ever going to sway him. The brotherly fondness he had for Verity was nothing when compared to the passion which swept through his veins now. Holding his sister-in-law in his arms had filled him with nothing but sympathy for her plight; this holding of Catherine told him what he had been missing all his life.

He waited, his heart and his arms full for the first time in his existence, for her weeping to subside, then he released her and drew her back down onto the seat, retaining his hold on one small hand, "Now it is my turn to risk making a fool of myself," he told her gently, "You are quite correct in assuming I have been avoiding you. I have. The reason is simple; you are a Catholic."

"Oh!" She looked into his eyes, a spark of anger in her own, "I had not thought to hear such bigotry from you, sir! Does my religion really bar a friendship between us?"

"Not friendship, no. But I had not known you above five minutes when I realized I could never feel mere friendship for you. Catherine, you are the woman I want to marry – but I cannot!"

She gasped in shock, her eyes searching his face as though for confirmation that he really had spoken these words, "I had not thought anything of the kind – I cannot believe it – you scarcely know me."

He smiled wryly, aware that he had spoken too soon and too candidly, but not really caring very much, "I know you must think me odd, if not worse! But I have nothing to lose by not being perfectly honest. Those being my feelings, you can hardly blame me for attempting to cut the connection between us. I hoped to spare myself further misery, and scarcely dared hope that you too might suffer some unhappiness at our parting. In short, I thought if I did not see you, I would swiftly forget you, but it was a vain hope."

"I don't know what to say to you," she whispered hoarsely.

"There is nothing to say. Even supposing you came to feel as I do, there can be no future for us together. A vicar of the Church of England can no more have a Catholic wife than can the King."

She looked down at her hands, lying so small and serene in his. How strange that they should be so still, when inside she was a swirling mass of confused thoughts and emotions. She tried to crystallize at least one of those thoughts into a question, "Do you want Alistair and I to leave Hanbury?"

"Certainly not! Why should you be inconvenienced merely because the vicar of Hanbury is a romantic fool?"

"Then what? I have no desire to make things difficult for you."

"You will not. I will forget this conversation ever took place and you must do the same. Let me be of assistance to you and your son for as long as your visit lasts, then let us part as friends. Any consequences must be borne by me."

Tears welled into her eyes again; "I can't allow you to do that…"

"You can and you must. I had no right to burden you with this unasked for confession and the only way I can atone is to help you with Alistair."

"I don't know," she said doubtfully, "May I think about it?"

"Of course. Now, will you take tea with me?"

"No… I… Not today. I want to go home."

He kissed her hand then watched her as she walked away between the gravestones, her footsteps light and swift, barely restraining herself from breaking into a run. It was painful to Gil to imagine she could not wait to be out of his society, and he rose wearily and stepped out into the sunlight, blinking a little after the dark shadowiness of the porch. Only God knew what was going to happen next, but he, at least, had ceased to struggle against his fate.

*

Verity and Underwood were fortunate enough to find Mrs Gedney at home, and without the company of her husband. That she was not pleased to see them was painfully evident, though she had no choice but to entertain them since the housemaid showed them straight in to her instead of first enquiring if she were at home to visitors.

Her answers to Underwood's questions gave every appearance of having been meticulously rehearsed, but he persevered hoping to betray her into an indiscretion.

97

"I understand your husband and your mother were not exactly boon companions?"

"Not many men do have close relationships with their mother-in-law. It is not a connection which engenders affection, is it? And I must say I deeply resent your intrusion into my affairs. My family is no concern of yours," was the tart reply.

"That would usually be the case – and under normal circumstances nothing would prevail upon me to plumb the murky depths of your relationships…"

"*Murky depths?* How dare you! Leave my house at once. I will not sit here and be insulted."

Verity intercepted hastily, throwing a warning glance in her spouse's direction, for he was showing his animosity a little too plainly, "We beg your pardon, Mrs Gedney. My husband spoke thoughtlessly. You must take his eagerness to solve your mother's murder as his excuse."

"Your husband's rudeness is only part of my complaint, Mrs Underwood. Why are you wasting everyone's time, asking pointless questions, annoying and badgering people, when it is obvious to everyone else in Hanbury that my mother's worthless husband is the culprit?"

"That may very well be the truth," said Verity, with sweet reason, and completely ignoring Underwood's sharp intake of breath – the only indication he gave that he was extremely unhappy with the way the conversation was progressing, "But surely you owe it to your mother to be sure. The last thing you must desire is for Dunstable to be taken to court, then released on the strength of a vital piece of evidence which had been carelessly overlooked. Don't forget, there is only one chance to convict him. If he is found not guilty, he cannot be tried twice for the same crime. You and Mr Gedney seem to be of the opinion that we are trying to prove your stepfather innocent – nothing could be further from the truth. We are trying to make sure that when he is arrested for your mother's murder, there will be no possibility of any error being made."

Underwood wisely kept his thoughts to himself.

Mrs Gedney visibly relaxed, she even forced a small smile to her lips, "My dear Mrs Underwood, I wish you had been more clear in your intentions from the beginning. None of this ill-feeling need ever have occurred. Naturally, under those circumstances, my husband and I will endeavour to give you every assistance."

Having smoothed the path for him, Verity now stepped aside and allowed Underwood to resume his questioning, which he did with rather less vitriol than he had previously displayed, "Could you tell me, Mrs Gedney, how you knew it was tansy which had killed your mother?"

"I smelled it in the glass she had been drinking from."

"You are familiar enough with the odour to recognize it?"

Her sallow skin reddened slightly, "Is it a crime to be familiar with such things? Surely we no longer live in an age when a knowledge of herbs proclaims witchcraft?"

He wondered why she was being so defensive. The question was innocuous enough.

"Not at all," he said soothingly, "I merely wondered. Do you possess such knowledge?"

She shifted uncomfortably in her chair; "I possess some slight expertise. In the first months of my daughter's life, when her problems became evident, I passed through the ridiculous stage of trying various remedies and treatments, hoping to cure her of her afflictions. I have now only to feel ashamed that I was so foolish. I should have listened to my husband and not wasted time, effort and money on those charlatans and tricksters!"

"Nothing which gives us hope is ever foolish or a waste of time, Mrs Gedney," intercepted Verity quietly, knowing that should her baby be born in any way afflicted, she would do exactly the same thing.

"Perhaps not, but as my husband often said, there were better things upon which we could have spent the money."

Gambling, drunkenness and womanising, presumably, thought Underwood cynically – and a trifle unfairly, for though he had heard many bad reports of Gedney, philandering had not actually been one of them.

As though the thought of him had conjured him from the depths of hell, Gedney chose that precise moment to walk into the room. He had evidently been told of their presence for he spoke with a false heartiness which did nothing to hide his fury, "Well, my dear, I see we have visitors. What nonsense have you been talking?"

She appeared very nervous, twisting her hands and glancing apprehensively towards him, "Mr and Mrs Underwood were just explaining about Oliver, Adolphus. It seems we have been misjudging them."

99

His eyes narrowed slightly, as though he suspected a plot, even if his wife did not, "How interesting. Perhaps you can explain more fully to me when they have gone."

There could not be a clearer dismissal, but Underwood was a past master at being obtuse when it suited him and ignored the hint, though he noticed Verity half rose in her seat, only to sink back when she saw he was not intending to move.

"Well met, Gedney!" He spoke with equal heartiness, which rang quite as false as his host's, "The very man to whom I wished to speak."

"I can't imagine why. There is nothing I can tell you."

"On the contrary, you hold much information, and your wife has assured us of your co-operation."

"Has she indeed?" his tone boded ill for his wife and she knew it, for she visibly quailed, "How very presumptuous of her!"

"Could you tell me exactly when you arrived in Hanbury, Gedney?" asked Underwood, disregarding this comment. Gedney, seeing no particular threat in this question, answered without hesitation that they had arrived only two days before the death of Mrs Dunstable.

"You had not previously been here?"

"Not since last year, no. We always spend a week here in June so that my wife can join her mother, and various friends, in taking the waters."

"And you did not enter your mother-in-law's house until that last evening before her death, when you joined her for dinner?"

"No!"

"From whom did the box of bon-bons come?"

"No one knows. They were delivered to the house that afternoon, I believe, with no card or letter attached. We assumed the card had simply been lost. All her friends knew of her weakness for sweets, and she was often sent little gifts like that."

"So, they could have come from anyone – and they could have contained poison?"

"Anyone who knew her well would have felt quite safe in risking poisoned sweets, knowing that she usually ate them all herself – but even if she had offered them around, one or two bon-bons would not have harmed the recipient. From what my wife has told me, tansy is only poisonous if taken in excess."

"So I understand. Thank you, Gedney. You have been most helpful. Could I presume to ask one more thing? From where did you acquire your herbal remedies, Mrs Gedney?"

"Most I have from Mr Sanderson of Welbourne Street, in Braxton, when I am in the district. Others I find in the wild, or even grow myself in my garden at home. I may not have been able to help Melissa, but I have helped many others with my receipts."

"Thank you. Good day to you both."

He waited until there were several hundred yards between them and the Gedney's door before he confided his thoughts to Verity, "I felt Gedney was a little *too* helpful, my dear. It was almost as though he were challenging us to prove Dunstable's innocence in the face of his obvious honesty. But I think we have our murderer, our method and our accomplice."

"Mr Gedney, in the bon-bons and Mrs Gedney?" guessed Verity.

"I would stake my life on it – though proving it is going to be the very devil. Gedney even told us why they had hit on tansy as their chosen poison."

"He did?"

"Yes, when he was at pains to point out that one or two bon-bons would not hurt if they should happen to fall into the wrong hands – you can be sure Mrs Gedney was not going to risk an accident to her child. They had to choose something which would only kill if overdosed upon, and they placed it in a food they knew Mrs Dunstable was greedy for, and could be expected to gorge herself upon."

"Of course. But how can we prove it?"

"Logic is altogether failing me on that point just now – but I trust something will trigger a solution."

Underwood was frustrated, but not at all surprised, to discover that Mr Gratten, though undeniably interested, was entirely unconvinced by any of these theories.

"Give me proof, Underwood, that's all I ask of you."

"You must give me more time for that, sir."

"Time is something we simply do not have. My superiors are beginning to put pressure on me to bring this case to a swift conclusion. To them it seems very straightforward. Dunstable killed his wife."

"But Gedney stands to gain far more from the old lady's death than Dunstable."

"The child Melissa does – and of what use is that to Gedney, if, as you claim, he is only interested in the money?"

"Sick children often die young, Mr Gratten."

Gratten, a fond father and a doting grandfather, was suitably horrified by this remark, "Dear God, no! The man could not sink so low."

"I fear he could, sir. I very much fear he could!"

CHAPTER THIRTEEN

*'Aut Viam Inveniam Aut Faciam' – Literally 'I'll either find a way
or make one' – Where there's a will there's a way*

True to his promise, Gil arranged a visit to the caves above
Hanbury for young Alistair, just as soon as the child was well enough
to make the journey.

Rather to his surprise his friends and family rallied around and it
was a large party that gathered in the early morning mist outside the
Bull Inn.

Toby, in spite of his still tightly strapped broken ribs, insisted that
none other than himself should have the privilege of pushing the
wheeled chair over the more difficult terrain and, in the meantime,
bore two stout poles which would eventually be threaded through the
arms of the chair and enable them to carry it over the rougher spots.
Underwood and Francis carried baskets containing their lunch, Ellen
and Verity bore smaller bags holding bottles of wine. Catherine held
waterproofs in case of rain and Gil found himself in charge of
Melissa, who had also been invited on the expedition, though her
parents had been excluded. The Gedneys had only allowed their child
to attend on the condition that Oliver Dunstable was not in the group,
but since he had already made arrangements to see Miss Marsh, this
caused no difficulty.

Catherine was inclined to be tearful at the kindness of the vicar
and his family, but he insisted upon making light of their sacrifice,
pointing out that they were all eager to witness the wonder of the
limestone caverns.

There was, in fact, to be only one drawback – to both Underwood
and Verity, rather a large one, though neither confided this to the
other. Verity had wanted Isobel Wynter to be invited, but could not do
so without including her sister. They were only awaiting the arrival of
the Wynter sisters and the two carriages which had been ordered to
take them as near to the caves as it was possible to drive.

As it happened both Isobel and Charlotte appeared just as the
vehicles came into view and with much bustle, laughter and confusion
their paraphernalia was stowed and they all scrambled aboard. The
road they took was a poor one to begin with, but it rapidly
deteriorated into little more than a track across the tussocky grass and

103

heather, causing the travellers to be tossed from side to side and provoking much hilarity. Alistair's face was alight with glee, for he was thoroughly enjoying watching the adults being subjected to such rough treatment, and in the face of such rare merriment from the sick child, no one considered their dignity a great loss, not even Underwood, who usually required to be perfectly groomed at all times.

When the carriages could go no further, the passengers alighted, and unstrapped Alistair's chair from the back of the first coach. The coachmen were left to tend to their animals and await their return for the well-deserved picnic.

Gil had overlooked no detail and there were two guides waiting for the party at the base of the final hill. Alistair's chair was lifted onto its poles by Gil, Toby, Underwood and Francis and they set forth.

It was no easy task man-handling the stricken boy over rocks and moss-covered boulders, but at last, breathless, but triumphant, they entered the caves.

A smooth, downward sloping path led to a low-roofed tunnel which forced the men to stoop, but allowed the ladies, except Charlotte who was particularly tall, to walk almost upright. Fortunately it was quite wide enough to take the wheeled chair, but poor Toby, who was by far the tallest of the party, had quite a struggle pushing it and walking in a crouched position at the same time. Their guides had given each of them a candle or a lantern so it was necessary to be wary of crowding too close to the person in front. Such was their preoccupation with this hazard and yet others caused by the uneven floor and low ceiling, that they were amazed when they at last emerged into the cathedral-proportioned cavern.

None had been prepared for the size and magnificence of the sight which met their eyes. Great pillars of glistening limestone seemed to support the dripping roof of the cave, though they were informed that this was not really the case, the columns were the result of stalactites and stalagmites respectively falling and rising to meet each other over thousands of years.

It was bitterly cold, but no one noticed the chill, so great was the awe they felt at the unexpected beauty of the sparkling stone. As they gazed about them, fantastic shapes leapt and receded in the flickering candlelight and it was several minutes before anyone was inclined to break the silence.

On and on into the blackness reached the caves, too vast to be imagined and naturally too dangerous to fully explore, though they were led a little further on to see the cold darkness of a subterranean lake.

Catherine smiled at Alistair's wide-eyed astonishment, and allowed him to reach forward and dip his fingers into the water, to feel for himself how icy it was.

It was with regret that they left the wonders of the caves behind them, but with profound relief that they emerged, squinting and half-blinded by the sunshine.

Their chosen picnic spot was charming, with a breath-taking view across the hills, a soft, bouncy sheep-cropped turf beneath them, convenient flat rocks off which they might dine, and a wind-breaking rocky outcrop to keep off the worst of the gusts. A small watercourse gurgled at their feet, wild flowers grew in profusion and the only nuisance was an occasional fly, which buzzed annoyingly about their heads as they ate.

With great good humour they invited their guides and drivers to join the feast and it was soon a very merry gathering, with Charlotte being gallantly, though respectfully, pursued by the guides, both personable young men, and Toby swapping pugilistic anecdotes with the two drivers.

The food was good and plentiful, Mrs Trent had surpassed herself, and the only untoward incident occurred when Underwood found a chicken leg he was about to bite into wrenched from his grasp by Melissa, who, due to her muteness was unable to request anything. This being the case, she had grown accustomed to helping herself whenever she wanted something. Underwood's surprise was comic to behold and everyone roared with laughter, even Melissa, though it was doubtful if she knew the real reason for their amusement.

When the food was finished, the adults relaxed and chatted. Francis and Ellen could only regret their son was too young to have enjoyed the treat, Catherine and Gil talked quietly, discovering each other, with perfect amity, whilst Melissa and Alistair played an hilarious game of catch, the boy proving himself quite capable of joining in, so long as the ball did not fall too far beyond the reach of his chair.

Verity took the opportunity to sketch not only the view, but her companions also, whilst they were unaware of being observed. Underwood watched her with undisguised admiration, for her talent was considerable. She seemed to be able to catch a perfect likeness with only a few deft strokes of her pencil, and he noticed, with amusement, that each picture was carefully dated and the place of execution noted.

"Why do you do that?" he asked, after watching her for some time.

"Draw?" she asked, puzzled, for he might just as well ask her why she breathed, and she thought he knew it.

"No; date, subject, place. It seems very organized behaviour for an artist. One always imagines talented people to be above such meticulous cataloguing."

She laughed, "Well, you are talented too, but you do not think yourself above order and structure in your work."

"True," he granted, oblivious of any lack of modesty of which he could be accused, "But I have not that extra creativity which sets the artist, the poet, the writer, apart from the common herd."

She laughed again, more heartily this time, "Now I know you are teasing me. You are a writer yourself – and in print."

"Ah, but only in Academia, that is quite different, and you haven't answered my question."

She blushed rosily; "You will think me terribly conceited if I tell you."

"Never! You are the least conceited woman I ever met – sometimes to your own detriment."

She could not meet his eyes as he said this, and refused to respond to the accusation, merely murmuring, "Of course it gives me pleasure to sketch, and serves as a reminder of my days, but I hope one day that my drawings will tell future generations how we lived, they are a sort of illustrated diary."

"I think that is a charming idea, and not in the least vain."

"Thank you."

"May I look?" With a nod she handed him the book. He noticed it was firmly bound, evidently rather an expensive purchase, for the paper was of good quality, and the pages could not be removed without tearing, so there was no margin for error. He realized as he flicked through that she had been busy whilst he had been taking his ease in Hanbury. Their visit was marked by at least one drawing, sometimes several, which she had done each day, sometimes in the early morning whilst waiting for him to ready himself for their daily sortie to the Pump-rooms, sometimes in the afternoons, in the quiet period just before tea. One in particular caught his attention, and with a carefully controlled edge of excitement to his voice he asked, "Do you remember drawing this, my dear?"

She glanced down without much interest, glanced away, then dragged her incredulous gaze back again, with a shock of recognition, "Good Heavens!" she breathed.

"Do you remember drawing it?"

"I do now that I have seen it again. I thought his face looked familiar, but I sketch so many people …"

Underwood held the book a little closer and scrutinised the figures at the bottom of the page – he needed spectacles sometimes, but was too vain to wear them,

"This date certainly doesn't agree with the information he gave us, Verity. According to this, he was in Hanbury at least three days before he had admitted to being there."

She lifted her eyes to his; "Does this mean we have him, Cadmus?"

"It could. We will have to question him again, and if he persists in the lie, then we certainly have something to present to Mr Gratten."

"Thank goodness for that."

Because they were in company with others, their conversation turned to other things, but their intense conversation had not been missed by several others in the party and not all were happy to see a lightening of the gloom, which had so recently surrounded them.

Charlotte flirted more outrageously than ever with her two country swains, but was infuriated to realize that Underwood was scarcely even aware of her presence, and far from being made jealous by her obvious popularity, was engrossed in his wife's conversation. Isobel watched everything with severe misgivings, knowing well that her sister was likely to reinforce her determined pursuit of Underwood, now that she had been thwarted.

Only Catherine and Gil seemed a world apart. True to his word, the vicar gave no sign, by word or action, that he considered the young widow to be anything other than a charming companion. She found it hard to believe he had ever spoken words of love to her, so calm was his demeanour, and she was acutely grateful that he had made it so easy for her to be in his company, for the truth was she very much enjoyed it. She had feared a feeling of embarrassment or even diffidence, but within seconds of being with her, he had set her at her ease. With this new relaxed atmosphere between them, Gil was at his best; content to be with her, without the weight of his unspoken

107

emotions casting a cloud over his personality, he was free to be the man only his family usually saw. Because of their differing religions, he was not required to be a minister – in fact was at some pains not to be so, and with this serious side to his nature removed, Catherine found a witty, humorous, kind and intelligent man.

As the sun began its slow descent towards the horizon, and the shadows grew long, they packed the remains of their feast into the baskets, hoisted them and themselves back into the carriages and set off for home, all content with what had been on the whole a very agreeable outing.

There were more treats in store, for Lady Hartley-Wells, much impressed by their Christian actions in caring for the two invalid children, had arranged a magnificent dinner party followed by a musical soiree.

Underwood was less than pleased when he was informed that he was to be part of the entertainment, but Verity's pleading glance could not be ignored, and he at last consented to performing a duet upon the pianoforte with his wife. He was a reticent man, but not entirely without vanity, so the enthusiastic applause was accepted with a wry smile and a kiss on his partner's hand.

One look at her sister's face caused Isobel even more discomfort. Charlotte was livid and made no attempt to hide it. She was sure now that Verity was deliberately showing off her talents in order to expose Charlotte's shortcomings. It seemed now that the whole day had been a procession of events which displayed all Verity's charms and accomplishments and Charlotte, who had at first been inclined to despise and discount the importance of her former governess, was now coming perilously close to hating her with a passion rarely experienced before.

Verity, blissfully unaware of all the malevolence, merely enjoyed the evening and was delighted to see that her husband and brother-in-law seemed to do likewise.

It was, perhaps, just as well that they had spent a pleasant day, for there was a shock awaiting them which was to seriously mar their memories of the occasion.

CHAPTER FOURTEEN

'Ad Utrumque Partatus' – Ready for either eventuality – good or bad

Underwood had no presentiment of disaster when he noticed a letter addressed to himself propped against the mantle clock. It was in Oliver Dunstable's rather untidy script, and if it looked to be even more of a scrawl than usual, Underwood merely put that down to being written in haste.

Written in haste indeed it was. As he scanned the few lines it contained, Underwood's face grew pale and Verity, always alert to her husband's moods asked, in sudden panic, "What has happened?"

Underwood sank into the nearest chair, crumpling the missive between his hands and dropping his head, as though physically crushed by the news it imparted,

"The witless idiot! The mindless, stupid, heedless young fool!"

"What is it?" demanded Verity, in a voice so compelling that he raised his head and looked at her, as though suddenly remembering her presence.

"I'm sorry, my dear, but if you only knew … Tell me, what could the boy do that would be more fatal than anything else?"

"He's run away?" suggested his wife tentatively.

"Worse! He's run away with Miss Marsh – and he fully intends to marry her."

"Good God!"

"'*Good*'! There is no goodness in the god that overlooks me. How am I to explain this to the Constable and the Magistrate? I persuaded them both to release Dunstable into my custody, assuring them of his continued presence in Hanbury. I'll be fortunate if I don't find myself behind bars, charged with aiding and abetting a murderer."

"It will not come to that, I'm sure. They know you acted with the best of intentions."

"You know what they say about the road to Hell and good intentions, Verity. Damn the boy! I could strangle him myself for this folly. What chance does he imagine he has now of avoiding the hangman's noose?"

"Perhaps he will leave the country."

"I suppose he may, but he must know he can never return if he does. His actions have confirmed him as his wife's murderer – and the real culprit will have evaded justice."

"If that is so, then there is nothing we can do about it, but I feel we ought to contact Mr Gratten immediately. The longer we delay, the worse it looks for us."

"Very true. I had better take myself off right away."

"Can you not send a message? You are so tired. It has been a long day…"

"It is going to be an even longer night. Don't wait up for me. I fear I may be late."

Verity looked into his eyes and she knew he feared he might not be coming home at all. He had spoken nothing less than the truth when he voiced a dread of gaol, though he had tried to make light of it not to frighten her. The constable was likely to take a very dim view of Underwood's loss of the major suspect in a murder investigation – especially when he had been so adamant in championing the one man everyone else thought guilty. Immediately she picked up her cape from where she had laid it on the sofa when they entered the house, and draped it about her shoulders,

"I'm coming with you."

"No."

"Please Cadmus. I will speak to Mr Gratten and explain how this was no fault of yours. He may be more inclined to listen to reason from a woman…"

"I said no, and I meant it. This is my error and I will take the consequences alone."

"But…"

He held up his hand for silence, "My dear, never since our wedding day have I asked you to honour the vow of obedience you made – I am asking you now."

"When we faced Gil at the altar, Cadmus, we also spoke of 'better and worse'," she reminded him gently. He smiled, the smile which reminded her why she loved him so desperately, because when it reached his grey eyes, it turned them smoky with desire, like embers which look dead, but which one knows one only has to stir to bring them back to a leaping flame.

"You must have known even then there was going to be far more 'worse' than 'better'."

"I wouldn't say that," she said throatily.

He reached out for her hand and kissed it, "Bless your heart for that, my dear, but still you stay here."

With a sigh she acceded to his order.

*

Mr Gratten greeted Underwood congenially, though he was evidently surprised at the tardiness of the visit, "'Evening Underwood, rather late for a social call, so I assume you have some news for me. Had a breakthrough, have you?"

"Not exactly. Shall we have a seat?"

Gratten obligingly led him into the drawing room and once they were both comfortably settled, Underwood wasted no time in breaking the bad news, "I'm sorry to have to tell you we have a problem, Mr Gratten – rather a serious one."

Poor Gratten, with no idea of the tidal wave that was about to engulf him, smiled cheerfully, "Whatever it is, I'm sure I can rely on you to solve it, dear fellow."

"Not this time, sir. Dunstable has taken it into his head to go travelling."

Underwood, rather callously, watched in complete fascination as the colour slowly drained from his companion's normally ruddy countenance; it was as though someone had turned off a tap and the blood had simply poured away. It was several tense seconds before the Constable was able to speak, then his voice was a croak of disbelief, "Travelling?" he repeated faintly, sounding winded, "Are you trying to tell me he has left Hanbury – after all the warnings he was given of the serious consequences of such an action?"

"He has."

"But of course you know his destination?" His tone was more hopeful than the question implied.

"No."

"And he intends to return when?"

"The letter he left for me indicates that he does indeed intend to return when … when he has settled the business which calls him away, but whether he will actually do so is a matter for conjecture, as is the duration of his absence."

"Oh my God!" exclaimed Gratten, suddenly recovering full use of his voice, "This is dreadful. Do you realize what this means?"

Underwood felt that the elderly gentleman did not really require any input from him at this juncture, so wisely held his tongue. Gratten continued without drawing breath, "It means he did it. He has duped us all, with that heartfelt weeping, and youthful air of innocence. We have let a murderer escape. By Jupiter, Sir Alfred Dorrington is going to love this snippet."

Mr Underwood felt it behoved him to intervene, "I beg you will be calm, sir. It means nothing of the sort. Dunstable is the kind of hot-headed young fool who bows to the prevailing wind, but he is not a killer. The truth of the matter is he has a young lady friend who is expecting his child – he wants – not unnaturally – to marry her before the child is born."

If Underwood hoped this news would soften the blow for Gratten, he was destined to be sadly disappointed, for that gentleman grew almost apoplectic,

"Marriage… pregnancy… Oh God! Oh God!"

Underwood glanced swiftly about the room and spotted a decanter on a side table and quickly crossed the room to fill a glass for his afflicted companion. Gratten tossed off the liquid in one mouthful, then choked alarmingly and managed to gasp, "Ratafia for the ladies! Are you trying to kill me?" Underwood could only sympathize, the sickly sweet almond flavoured liqueur was not to his taste either.

"I do beg your pardon."

Gratten managed to bring himself under control and finally turned his anger upon the one who had been momentarily expecting it.

"This is your doing, Underwood. Why in hell did I ever listen to you? I should have followed my first instinct and thrown the young puppy straight into gaol."

"Mr Gratten, believe me I entirely understand your anger, but even in spite of this occurrence, I still maintain Dunstable is innocent of murdering his wife. Admittedly he is guilty of almost every other folly and vice you care to name, but that doesn't make him an assassin."

The constable, however, was in no mood for rational thought, "Give me one good reason why I should believe anything you say, and why I should not now throw you in prison for aiding the escape of a suspected felon."

"I don't have one," said Underwood candidly.

Gratten looked on the point of a heart attack, but he managed to hiss viciously, "Get out of my sight, Underwood. And pray, pray hard, that Mr Dunstable decides to return to Hanbury in the next few days."

*

Verity was in bed, though not asleep, when Underwood crept up the stairs, so as not to disturb the slumbering household, all of whom had fallen into bed before he and Verity had even read Dunstable's fateful missive, and so knew nothing of the latest developments. She laid aside her book as he entered the bedroom, and one look at his face told her not to try and say anything cheering. He began to dispiritedly divest himself of his garments and she watched him silently as he threw aside his coat and began to loosen his cravat. The relief she felt at his safe return was reflected in her loving glance, but Underwood did not look at her.

When he sank wearily into a chair and attempted to pull off his boots, she cast aside the covers and sped to aid him. He made no protest, as he would normally be inclined to do, but lay back and let her tug at the offending articles.

"You should have changed into your shoes before going out again this evening," she said, rather breathlessly, "I think your feet are swollen from all the walking in the hills."

He sat upright; "I know it. I've been longing to remove these damn boots for the last two hours at least."

"I'll get you some water from the kitchen, you can soak your feet."

He began to laugh, "How very domesticated we sound. Tell me something, my dear. Do you want your own house very much?"

"Not if you do not," she answered, too swiftly for it to be true.

He reached out a hand and grasping her wrist, pulled her down onto his lap, "Don't do that, dear one."

"What?"

"Subject yourself to my will. God knows I'm a selfish creature – Gil was right about that. If you continue to please me at your own expense, I shall soon be intolerable."

She smiled knowingly, "Oh dear, was Mr Gratten very angry? He must have carpeted you very thoroughly indeed to have roused this mood of penitence."

"Horrid child!" he murmured, and kissed her.

She lay quietly in his arms for a few moments, her head nestled against his shoulder, "I do want my own house, Cadmus," she ventured presently.

He had almost fallen asleep, so cosy had been their position, but this brought him to full wakefulness, "I've been a knave, haven't I?"

"A little thoughtless, perhaps, but you are right, it is my fault. I should have told you, not expected you to read my mind – I ought to know by now that you are not in the least perceptive and the most insensitive…"

He stopped her mid-sentence, "Yes, yes, I see. There is no need to labour the point."

She giggled softly against his neck, "Poor Cadmus, is the whole world against you?"

"It certainly seems so," he agreed feelingly, "Now, since we finally have the truth from you, perhaps you would care to confide the rest of your plans – for I have no doubt you have them aplenty."

She sat up, suddenly full of energy, "Well, there is a lovely house, right here in Hanbury…"

"I thought there might be," he said, with an air of resignation, "At least that will be convenient for visiting me in the local gaol…"

All thought of domesticity fled from her mind and she looked at him with great concern, "Is it really that serious, or are you merely teasing?"

"A little of both, I'm afraid. Gratten is not pleased – in fact this incident has sent him into something of a panic, but I don't imagine I stand in immediate danger of being hauled off by the militia. Things may grow more desperate, however, if Dunstable decides to flee the country. Gratten may feel the need to present the local magistrate with a scapegoat, and if it is not to be Dunstable, it may well be me."

Verity threw her arms protectively about him, as though by doing so she could fend off the threat to his person, "Don't! Oh, pray don't! I can't bear the idea."

He patted her shoulder gently, rather surprised by the passionate display, for relations between them had been somewhat distant of late and he had been beginning to fear the adoration she had appeared to bestow on him in the first months of their marriage was fading, "Come now, there's no need for this. I'm not breaking rocks or picking oakum yet"

His only answer was a muffled sob and he cursed himself for having so distressed her, "Good Heavens, Verity, this isn't like you."

She knew it, but still she could not stem the tears, it was as though she had no control over her emotions. Imagining how it would feel to have him taken from her, bearing her baby alone, surviving every day without him, she lived every agonising moment of it in the space of those few seconds and it sent her into a sort of frenzy. Soon her weeping had grown so intense that sobs shook her whole body and Underwood was panicked into speaking harshly to her. Suddenly she had to get off his knee and rush to the washstand, where she began to retch painfully and very profitably, much to his concern and astonishment.

When the attack seemed to have abated, he lifted her off her feet and deposited her on the bed; "I'm going to wake Francis."

She lay back on the pillows, totally spent, her hair damp with perspiration, her face reddened and blotched with tears, "No, please don't. I'm better now."

"Verity, you've been unwell for weeks now."

She opened her lips to tell him the reason, but suddenly realized she could not. The knowledge that she was to have a child would lay an intolerable burden of worry upon him, should the threat of prison become a reality. It would be better to wait a few days, then tell him when all was calm again.

"No, really, I am better. It was foolish of me to get so upset. I'm just tired – over tired. And I have been fretting about our not having a house, but now you have promised, and I shall brighten up, I swear it."

He hesitated, torn by the desire to have her consult the doctor, but reluctant to distress her again by insisting upon it. She saw that she had him and pressed home her advantage, turning over onto her side and firmly closing her eyes, "I'm so weary, Cadmus, please just let us get some sleep."

He could not but agree with that, but there was the wash basin to empty and the rest of his clothes to shed. By the time he had climbed, exhausted, into the bed beside her, she gave every appearance of being fast asleep. Except for the occasional hiccupping breath, such as a child gives when it has fallen asleep on tears, she seemed quite peaceful, but Underwood stared at her for several minutes in the guttering candlelight, a slight frown creasing his brow, before he finally snuffed the candle and closed his eyes.

CHAPTER FIFTEEN

'Nemo Me Impune Lacessit' – No one provokes me with impunity

Dunstable's disappearance caused much consternation in the vicarage the following morning. Underwood's first instinct had been to keep the whole matter to himself and Verity, but with his brother's house bursting at the seams with guests, it rapidly became obvious no such secret could be kept.

Gil, much to Underwood's surprise, tended to view the elopement with approval – except, of course, for the difficulty it promoted for Underwood himself.

"Gil, what has happened to you, old fellow? I should have expected one of your calling to be threatening hell-fire and eternal damnation for the unfortunate couple."

Gil, who had certainly never been heard to say anything so unforgiving, merely smiled, "You will have your little joke, won't you, Chuffy?"

"I wasn't joking," asserted Mr Underwood, "Dunstable's behaviour has been thoroughly reprehensible from beginning to end – and was never worse than when he dropped me right in the mire and left me to flounder out of it as best I might."

"But he does seem to be attempting to put at least some of the coil to rights. His baby will now be born in wedlock."

Underwood was at his most sardonic when he responded, "You can have no notion how much better that makes *me* feel."

There was nothing else to do but continue their daily lives and wait for any further developments, so presently they made their usual pilgrimage to the Pump-rooms, where Underwood severely bade his wife sit and drink her water – every last drop.

He managed to catch Francis alone by the fountain and asked him in a concerned undertone what he thought ailed Verity. The doctor was distressed to have to lie to his friend, and silently resolved to speak firmly to Verity at the next available opportunity, but he had given his word, so nothing would prevail upon him to give her away, "What does she say is wrong?" he asked warily.

"That she has been fretting because we have no home of our own."

"Oh, well," said the doctor decidedly, "there you have it. Of course she feels odd living with your relations. She thinks she is being a burden. Imagine how you would feel under similar circumstances. Women get these strange humours from time to time. She'll be as right as ninepence when she has her own place."

With that Underwood had to be content.

Fortunately there were several events that helped to take his mind off his vague concerns for his wife, the most prominent being the arrival of a host of new visitors to Hanbury Spa. Gil, who knew everyone thanks to his infallible system of gossip gathering, was able to furnish them with names and brief biographies of some of the more diverting characters, and the morning was spent in amused contemplation of some amiable and elderly eccentrics.

The first of the new arrivals were Mrs Sophie Fancourt and her son Algernon. She was a sprightly little woman, barely four feet six, he a stooping six-footer. The Underwood party were astounded to be informed that Mrs Fancourt was not a day less than ninety, and her bachelor son almost seventy. Her only concession to age was to admit to a little deafness, and the carrying of a silver-handled can, which she clearly did not need. She had not a tooth in her head and her sight was not as quick as it had once been, so her son carried out an incessant commentary of everything which went on around them. Unfortunately her deafness meant that every remark of his was answered with an "Eh?" from her, which required him to repeat his every utterance more loudly. After so many years of this tedious interchange, no one observing them could ever understand why he did not simply speak more loudly in the first place, and so negate the necessity of the repetition, but he never did, so consequently she missed half the things he had been at pains to point out to her. Their conversations were hilarious, but infuriatingly frustrating to listen to – and naturally, since they were held at top volume, impossible to ignore.

"Look mother, Sir Barnaby has just walked by."

"Eh?"

"SIR BARNABY! Never mind, you've missed him now." She turned her head, and said loudly, "Isn't that the back of Sir Barnaby's head? Why did you not tell me, Algy?"

"I did. Is that a pigeon or a turtle dove?"

"Eh?"

"PIGEON OR DOVE? It's gone now."

She looked up; "I don't see anything."

"No, you missed it."

After watching this for some time, Underwood dug Gil in the ribs, "That will be you and mother if you don't find yourself a wife, brother."

Gil gave Underwood a stern glare, "Don't be so unkind. Mother isn't even slightly deaf."

"She will be by the time she's ninety!"

"Who says I won't be married anyway?" This rejoinder was only wrenched from Gil by the extreme irritation he felt at his brother's smug taunting, and he could have bitten his tongue the moment the words were out of his mouth, for naturally Underwood was not about to allow anything so provocative to pass unheeded.

"Have you someone in mind, Gilbert?"

"No."

"Mrs Pennington is an excessively charming woman, don't you think?" hazarded the irrepressible Underwood.

"Exceptionally charming," agreed Gil, with as much disinterest as he could muster.

He was saved from further annoyance by Toby, who had quickly become privy to all their lives, and who now leant forward and hissed warningly, "Beware, gentlemen! Mr Gedney is heading this way – and he seems mightily pleased with himself."

"Oh no," muttered Underwood feelingly, "That is all I need to make the day perfect."

Gedney was quite as obnoxious as everyone had expected him to be. From the odiously knowing smirk on his face, to the arrogant stance he took up in front of them, he proclaimed triumph, "I hear your house guest has taken to his heels. Ha! Quite a facer for you, Underwood. The wife and I are debating whether or not to sue you. If we can't get the murderer, why not the idiot who let him escape, eh? We'll inform you of our decision in due course."

"Very well," said Underwood calmly.

"Who is that person?" enquired Mrs Fancourt loudly, from her seat a few feet away from Underwood.

"Don't know him," returned her son, without interest.

"Eh?"

"DON'T KNOW!" roared Algy.

"Don't want to know, either," commented Mrs Fancourt, "What's he want to yell for? We're none of us deaf – nor interested in his business."

Gedney turned a dull red and threw a venomous look at the old lady, which she returned, stare for stare, even raising her ornate lorgnette to her faded blue eyes, a wealth of contempt in the gesture. His glance fell first, and he lowered his voice a little, "You've not heard the last of this, Underwood, believe me."

"That in itself would be a novel experience, Gedney," he responded coolly, his lips still twitching at the unconscious humour displayed by the Fancourts.

The man looked confused, "What the devil is that supposed to mean?"

"Believing you. I've never had cause to do any such thing, thus far into our acquaintance."

"Very amusing!"

"I do my poor best. Tell me, Gedney, whilst I have your attention, when did you say you had arrived in Hanbury?"

Gedney grinned, "Still trying it on, eh? Well, it won't do you a scrap of good, not now. I arrived on the twenty third, with my wife and family."

"And you swear you were not in town before that date?"

"I've not been in Hanbury since last year, when my mother-in-law last visited."

"Thank you."

Underwood then turned and addressed some remark to Toby, so Gedney could only feel himself summarily dismissed, he hesitated, apparently about to say more, then with a contemptuous, "Pah!" he went away.

"We have our answer, Verity," whispered Underwood. She nodded, much to the mystification of the rest of the group.

Fortunately there were more new arrivals in the Pump-rooms to distract attention from this exchange, so the couple never found themselves questioned by their companions as might have been the case under other circumstances.

The same Sir Barnaby Pepper, whom Mrs Fancourt had missed only minutes before, returned accompanied by a finely dressed young dandy, who swaggered in, raising his quizzing glass indolently to his eye and sweeping his gaze about the room, "Sink me, father, the place is a mausoleum!"

"Don't be impertinent, you young puppy," spluttered the severely embarrassed Sir Barnaby, only too aware of the furious glances being sent in their direction.

The son was entirely unmoved by his father's exasperation, or the tacit disapproval of the gathering, merely dropping his glass on its ribbon and adding, "You're right, Pa, I take it back, some of 'em are undoubtedly breathing."

Verity could not restrain a choke of laughter and this drew the exquisite's attention to her, "By Jupiter, not only a live one, but young and pretty enough to take a chap's interest. My dear girl, allow me to present myself, Vivian Pepper, at your service."

Verity, much amused, took the proffered hand and admired his perfect bow, "How do you do, Mr Pepper, my name is Underwood."

"Your name cannot simply be Underwood. Such a divine creature must have a prefix."

"I do – Mrs"

He smiled, "Ah! That complicates matters, rather. Might I have the honour of apologising to Mr Underwood?"

That particular gentleman had been watching this scene unfold in bemused silence, but at the mention of his own name, he rose to his feet, "Your servant, sir," he said wryly, but with a perfectly executed bow.

Mr Pepper glanced at him for the first time and his expression of faint boredom was altered at once into one of startled recognition, "By Jove! It cannot be Snuff Underwood. I thought the name had a familiar ring."

"Still playing the Bond Street Beau, I see, my dear Vivian."

The young gentleman allowed a pained expression to pass across his handsome features, "Snuff, please! You ought to know better. A Pink of the Ton, nothing less."

"Quite so," answered Underwood, with mock humility, "Tell me, did you ever pass your finals?"

"Good gad, no!" exclaimed Pepper, with deep loathing, "Don't have anything to do with the word 'final', altogether too serious a notion for the likes of me."

"I can imagine it would be."

"So, Snuff, can it be true that you are really leg-shackled to this lovely creature?" asked Pepper, turning his devastating smile back upon the astonished Verity.

"*Leg-shackled*?" retorted Underwood in a pained voice, "What an appalling turn of phrase you possess, you abominable boy. If you refer to marriage, then yes, this is indeed my wife, Verity."

"How the devil did you persuade her up the aisle, Snuff? Inherit a fortune?"

"Certainly not! There is more to a man than riches and fine clothes - speaking of which, where *did* you get that waistcoat?"

Mr Pepper drew aside his coat to further display the offending article of clothing, which was extremely loud, every inch of cloth being covered with embroidered flowers, birds and cherubs, "Oh, do you think it a mistake?" was his disappointed comment, "I own I wasn't quite sure about it myself, but I risked it, since we are in the Provinces."

"You'll frighten the horses with it!" asserted Underwood cordially, "What brings you into the wilds of Derbyshire?"

"Oh, visiting some old tabby – relation of m'father. He thinks we should do the pretty and get m'self a mention in the Will."

"Not Lady Hartley-Wells, by any chance?" guessed Underwood shrewdly.

"The very same. Do you know her?"

"I do – and if you'll take a piece of friendly advice, don't attempt to see her whilst wearing that waistcoat."

When Vivian had sauntered away in search of his father, or more probably, unmarried quarry, Verity's attention was drawn once again by a young man, but this time it was overpowering pity which was the cause and not mere amusement. The bright red of his tunic lent a gaiety to his demeanour, which was utterly destroyed when a glance revealed that his bath chair was a tragic necessity. His face was handsome, his upper body strongly muscled, but both his legs were gone.

"Oh, Gil," whispered Verity, "Who is that?"

Gil followed the direction of her eyes and his face split into a delighted grin, "So Major Jeremy James Thornycroft is back in Hanbury. Don't waste your pity on the man, Verity. You'll never meet a more wicked flirt, a more avid gambler or a more insane lunatic. He uses his pathetic state to capture girl's hearts, and to hold off the Magistrate when his folly leads him into court. Come and let me introduce you. You'll rarely spend a more amusing half hour."

*

Charlotte Wynter was furious. All her plans had gone awry and she could find no way to untangle the mess. The picnic in the hills had been the ideal opportunity to arrange matters so that she could have been close to Underwood, taking his attention away from his mousy little wife. She could have claimed his hand to help her over rocks, perhaps twisting her ankle and finding herself once more in his arms – it had worked before, when he had first fallen in love with her, but in the event she had not dared risk any such subterfuge, for she had been made only too aware that any accident would have ended with her being clasped to the excessively hairy chest of one of the guides, or worst still, the carriage drivers.

Isobel's pronounced amusement at her abject failure to secure Underwood was even more galling, for she had, very unkindly, made much of the affection shown by Underwood towards his wife. Charlotte could not believe any man could prefer the boring, bluestocking former governess to her own stunning beauty, and she felt sure Underwood was simply being gallant – not that she felt this did him any discredit. It was very laudable that he was an honourable man, but honour could not be allowed to stand in the way of a love such as theirs.

The time had come to use more obvious methods, and to make Underwood notice her again, she would employ almost any trick – and what was more, she would shake Verity out of that fool's paradise of hers. She must be made to understand whom it was Underwood truly loved.

Unwittingly, Isobel gave her the perfect chance to catch her prey alone.

"Lady Hartley-Wells has invited several of the ladies to play whist and take tea this afternoon, Lottie. Do you care to join us?"

"Which ladies?" inquired Charlotte, without much interest. She was finding life in the spa deadly dull, but she was determined to stay, so any diversion was welcome. But she was not such a fool as to commit herself to an afternoon of tedium. If the ladies named by Isobel were vaguely entertaining, she would join them, otherwise she would have a convenient headache.

"Ellen, Verity, Catherine Pennington and myself. There will doubtless be others too, but I misremember their names."

Charlotte had been about to accept since she liked Ellen, and knew her well, but a sudden flash of inspiration made her hastily retract, "Yes – oh no, wait! This afternoon, you said? I had forgotten until just now. Reverend Underwood asked me to help with the church flowers. He says I have a real talent for making pretty displays."

Isobel scrutinized her sister's face, but could see no trace of guile. Her first reaction was to offer to help too, but she was eager to join her friends, and Charlotte must be safe enough in Gil's company, he would hardly allow her to pursue his brother without protest.

"Very well. I shall see you later."

"Yes, later," answered her sister vaguely, already plotting the contents of the letter she would presently send to Mr Underwood.

Gil was very pleasantly surprised when Charlotte ran him to ground at the Pump-rooms and quietly offered to do the church flowers for him. He thought it immensely touching that she should forego an afternoon of pleasure in the company of her friends in order to beautify the church in readiness for Sunday's services. When lightly quizzed on the cause of this self-sacrifice, she explained that the patience and forbearance of young Alistair in the face of such long-standing illness, offered a salutary lesson in humility and gratitude to the Lord for her own rude health, and he found these sentiments struck a chord with him. With a warm smile he assured her of a hearty tea in the vicarage when her self-imposed task was done.

She had been alone in the church for no more than ten minutes when Underwood joined her. He walked down the aisle to where she stood in the Lady Chapel, her arms full of fragrant blooms, and wasted no time on niceties, "I'm very busy, Charlotte, and can spare you only a few minutes. What is so urgent that I must speak to you here and now?"

"You are unkind, Mr Underwood. Here am I, in the direst need of a friend's counsel and you cannot wait to be away."

"Have you no other friends?" asked the gallant and honourable gentleman tersely.

She gave a fair imitation of a broken-hearted sob and buried her face in the flowers.

"Oh, gad! Not more tears," muttered Underwood, who had seen enough of weeping women in the past few days, to last him a lifetime, but he had the grace to be sorry for his impatience, "Come now, Charlotte. Weeping never solved anything, as far as I am aware. What is this trouble you are in?"

"It is Edwin. He is bringing terrible pressure to bear upon me. He has written to say that if I do not agree to marry him, he will cast my sisters and I out of the house. He says he has no obligation to keep us all, now that our father and his wife are dead."

"I own I'm amazed you still wish to reside there. I would find it an imposition to have to share a roof with the man. If you really want my advice, I'd say it was an ideal opportunity for you to cut all connection with your unhappy past."

She raised tear-drenched eyes to his face, "But where shall we go? Isobel is far from well, and we have very little money of our own."

"Don't you have any other relations who would take you in?"

Anger, not tears, made her eyes glisten, "Would you have me live on the bounty of some reluctant relative? Never! I should rather die on the street than beg a bed for myself and my sisters."

"Very laudable – but hardly wise," admonished the strictly practical Underwood, "Well, I don't know why you have come to me with this tale of woe. I have no solution. I imagine Gil would be of more assistance. He must know of some genteel occupation suitable to you. Some old lady needing a companion perhaps…"

"A Wynter of Wynter Court working for a living?" she interrupted haughtily, "Have you completely taken leave of your senses – or are you merely the most insensitive creature alive?"

He laughed reminiscently, "Oh, I have it on the best authority that I am entirely insensitive."

She cast aside the flowers and approached him more closely, "I don't believe it," she breathed huskily, looking mistily up into his face. Before he knew what were her intentions, she had put her hands behind his head and drawn him inexorably towards her. Their lips met briefly, then he tried to pull away from her, but she was surprisingly strong and a further kiss was placed on his unwilling mouth before he gripped her wrists and wrenched himself out of her grasp, "Don't do that again, Charlotte!"

"Why not? You enjoyed it as much as I," she whispered.

"Do you want me to insult you?" he countered harshly.

She gasped and stepped back from him, for in asking the question he had done just that, "What have I done that you should hate me so?" she asked in genuine distress.

"I don't hate you – but I must say I don't like you very much either."

"I was prepared to … offer myself to you."

"That, I'm afraid, was painfully evident."

She raised her hand to strike him, but he wasn't about to submit to that indignity. He caught her wrist again, but this time his grip made her wince with pain.

"You, Miss, are a hussy! Selfish, unprincipled and thoroughly spoiled. I can only be grateful that fate intervened and prevented our marriage, for I realize now that my days would have been a living hell, with the misery of your infidelities grinding my pride and manhood into the mire."

"I wouldn't!" she cried in sudden anguish, "I would not have been unfaithful to you."

"You think not? I know differently. You are one of those people who only want what they cannot have. Now, I suggest you get down on your knees before the altar and beg pardon for having defiled the house of God with this unsavoury exhibition."

"You don't even believe in God," she snivelled miserably.

"I may not, but the faith of others is enough to sanctify this building in my eyes."

He turned to leave her and not even the sound of her weeping made him hesitate. The slamming of the oak door was the only indication he gave of the depth of his anger – anger which was, alas, aimed directly at her. She knew now the true meaning of desolation and half fearfully she looked about her, superstitiously aware that she did indeed believe in a vengeful God and that she had sinned grievously in His house.

CHAPTER SIXTEEN

***'Si Vis Pacem, Para Bellum'** – If you wish for peace, be ready for war*

Gilbert was in the vicarage garden and saw his brother storm out of the church, slamming the door behind him, an expression of fury contorting his features, and his pace far quicker than the vicar had witnessed for many a year, but as he attempted to follow, he was thwarted by the arrival on the scene of his housekeeper.

She looked so indignant that he imagined for a moment that she must also have caught sight of the irate Underwood, but her first words put flight to this notion,

"Reverend, there is a gentleman asking to see you – a gentleman of the cloth."

"Of the cloth?" he repeated absently, still staring after the long departed Underwood, "What? The Dean? The Bishop?"

She shook her head firmly and elucidated, "Not our cloth, sir! The other!"

"The other?" Now he was completely mystified, "What other? What are you talking about, Mrs Trent?"

"It's a priest."

"Priest?" Gil was still baffled, for he considered himself a priest, but even as she spoke, he became afflicted by a curious and oppressive premonition of disaster; he had the strangest sensation of trying to fight his way up through muddy water, always just a breath away from comprehension, from the air of life.

"He's a Roman Catholic Priest," hissed Mrs Trent, still too appalled by this unprecedented occurrence to speak aloud.

It was as though a light had pierced the darkness, but with understanding came panic. There could be only one reason for this unexpected visit – Catherine or her son. Gil promptly forgot his brother, "Where have you left him?"

"In your study, sir," she said, adding maliciously, "I was tempted to tell him to go about his business, but thought it would come better from you."

"Thank you," said Gil and took to his heels. Mrs Trent was left open-mouthed on the lawn, watching his receding figure, his black garments lifting and flapping behind him in the wind of his speed.

At last she recovered sufficiently to shake her head and mutter darkly, "I never thought I'd live to see the day when the True Church would run at the bidding of the Papists."

Meanwhile Gil burst into his study to be confronted by an elderly man, his black hat in his hands, and an expression of disapproval on his face.

"Reverend Mr Underwood, I presume?" he asked coldly. Gil, trying to gather his dignity, but failing miserably due to his extreme breathlessness, could only nod.

"My name is Fullick, Father John Fullick."

Gil was finally able to calm his breathing sufficiently to be able to reply, "Good day to you, sir," and hold out his hand. His visitor merely glanced at the proffered extremity as though it were something unclean, and declined to take it.

"This is not a social call, sir!"

"That much I had already guessed, but I see no reason for incivility. I assume you have some message for me?" Gil let his hand drop, sorry now that he had tried to offer it.

"Not a message, but a warning." Gil was by now thoroughly baffled, and his physiognomy showed it, for the priest gave a short, humourless laugh and added, "Pretence at injured innocence does not fool me, young man. I do not take kindly to poaching, Underwood, be it of livestock or souls."

"I beg your pardon?"

"So you should. Mrs Pennington has been a good and devout daughter of the Church all her life. She has received the sacraments of Baptism, Confession, Communion, Confirmation and Matrimony with a rare grace, when her son dies, she will take Holy Orders. She does not require the assistance or interference of Heathens!"

As this tirade progressed Gil found his temper rising and by the end of it he had never in his life been closer to smashing his fist into the face of another human being. He discovered that the sensation of rising fury was a curiously invigorating one. He smiled with grim humour, "Mrs Pennington must have been very attracted by my faith to have engendered such panic in you, sir! I wonder why that should be?"

The sarcasm was not lost on the priest, for he flushed darkly and spoke through gritted teeth, "I think it more likely it is your ingratiating manner than your faith, which has momentarily blinded this poor sheep to her religious duty."

"Poor sheep!" snapped Gil, with rare impatience, "She is a grown woman, with a mind of her own – and a remarkably intelligent one, at that. Now, I think we have nothing more to say to each other. Let me show you out."

"Don't bother, I shall leave, but not before I have repeated my warning. If I hear that you have been seen keeping company with Mrs Pennington again, I shall address my complaints to your Bishop. I suspect he will view your relationship with my parishioner in the same poor light that I do myself."

The vicar was very sure he was right, but he made no reply, merely crossing the room and holding the door open for the priest to pass through it. As he did so, the desire to plant his boot in the nether regions of his uninvited guest almost overpowered him. Fortunately for the pride and dignity of both parties, he managed to restrain himself.

When he was once more alone he threw himself into the chair at his desk, and stared unseeing at the neatly written sermon that lay before him. He thought over what the priest had said to him and was relieved to discover that it was not Catherine herself who had spoken of him to her confessor. The words, 'If I hear Mrs Pennington has been seen …' told him that the gossips had been busy again. If this gave him a crumb of comfort, it was only a crumb, for Catherine had made it clear she did not reciprocate his feelings, and in the face of such powerful opposition, it was highly unlikely she would choose to be defiant for his sake. Much as he hated to admit it, he had no hope that he would ever see Catherine Pennington or her son again.

*

Verity returned from Lady Hartley-Wells' card party unutterably weary, and went straight upstairs, intending to rest for an hour or so before dinner. Finding a piece of crumpled paper on the floor next to the bed, she bent to retrieve it and in doing so recognized the handwriting of her erstwhile pupil. She was puzzled for she knew she had never taken delivery of a letter from Charlotte Wynter. With a sudden qualm she realized that if the note had not been sent to her, then it could only be for Underwood.

She held it clenched in her fist, her knuckles shining white against the dark stuff of her skirt. It was not her habit to read the private correspondence of others, but she hesitated only seconds before she sank to her knees at the side of the bed and smoothed the thick sheet of parchment out upon the coverlet. At first the words jumped and blurred before her eyes, but she determinedly blinked away her foolish tears and read:

Dear Mr Underwood,
    I am engaged to do the flowers in the church this afternoon, and I beg you will meet me there. I am in the direst trouble and only you can help me.
    You must know what I mean, and you could not be so cruel as to ignore the plea of one who has much call upon you.
Yours as ever,
C.W.

Verity fought an overwhelming nausea. Certain phrases leapt off the page at her and seemed to hit her like physical blows. "…in the direst trouble … one who has much call upon you …"

When an unmarried girl spoke of "direst trouble", she could only mean one thing, couldn't she?

Verity tried to bring herself under control, but the words spun in her mind, allowing no sensible thought to penetrate, "…direst trouble … only you can help… much call upon you… yours as ever …"

She continued to kneel on the floor for some considerable time, until the ache in her joints and a sudden savage pain in the pit of her stomach brought her to her senses. She must be calm. She had nothing left but the child she carried, so she must not harm it with stupid, rash behaviour.

She rose slowly, went to the washstand and splashed her face with cold water. When she felt a little steadier, she went slowly down the stairs, to see Gil in his study.

She was too distraught to notice he himself was far from calm, merely asking,

"Tell me, Gil, did Cadmus go into the church whilst Charlotte was there?"

"He did – but he did not stay above five minutes, and came rushing out as though the hounds of hell were on his tail!"

He had thought her pale when she entered the room, but as these words she grew ashen. He rushed to her side and was just in time to catch her as she fainted.

His shout of dismay brought half the household running to his aid, and Verity returned to consciousness, laid out on a chaise longue, to find a crowd about her, all talking at once, recommending various remedies from burnt feathers to hartshorn to brandy and hot, sweet tea.

Francis was the last to arrive and he immediately took charge, shooing all from the room, whilst taking Verity's wrist between firm, cool fingers.

"What brought this on?" he asked, as soon as they were alone. She told him, in a dull, lifeless voice, which did nothing to convince him she was not distressed beyond bearing.

"You foolish girl!" he said briskly, when the recital was at an end, "Are you trying to ensure that this child is born with a hare-lip or a club-foot?"

She sat swiftly up and clawed wildly at his arm in a panic, "Oh, no! That is not a possibility, is it?" she cried in horror.

He pushed her gently back into a reclining position, "Not at the moment, but you are certainly not doing yourself or your baby any good at all."

Two tears trickled pathetically down her pale cheeks, "But what am I to do?"

"Be sensible, Verity, for Heaven's sake! Do you really believe Underwood is carrying on an intrigue with Charlotte? Do you think he has given her a child? It seems to me you have a very poor opinion of your husband's morals – and with very little reason."

"You think I am wrong?"

"I *know* you are."

"Then how do you explain the letter?"

"I fully admit, I cannot, without knowing the full story, but I would guess Miss Wynter is bored, and is planning all kinds of mischief simply to pass the time. She has never cared to find herself thwarted, and Underwood recovered from the heart-break of their parting far too quickly for her liking."

"Do you really think so?"

"Yes, I really do. Have you told him yet of your condition? He might be a little more solicitous toward you if he knew."

"No."

"You ought to be ashamed of yourself, Verity. Do you not think Underwood has the right to know of his impending fatherhood?"

"I suppose so."

"Then do something about it, for my sake, if not your own. It is damnable having to lie to him. "

"I will. I promise, I will."

"Where is he, anyway? He wasn't amongst the gaggle I sent out of here just now."

"No one seems to know."

*

It was late when Underwood returned to the vicarage, to be greeted by his brother and told of Verity's swoon. He showed great concern and was about to run up the stairs when Gil caught his arm, "Where have you been?"

"The Bull," answered Underwood tersely.

"The *Bull*!" repeated the vicar in amazement, "*You* have been in a Public house all evening?"

"I have," replied his brother, with great dignity, "I met up with Major Thornycroft and we drank a great deal of brandy."

"Oh," said Gil, abashed. There did not seem to be anything else to say, so Gil merely added, "Well, I trust you are not going to make a habit of it. Don't wake Verity if she is asleep. Francis has seen her and assures me there is nothing to worry about."

"Francis has been doing a great deal of assuring – and I have done a considerable amount of worrying," responded Underwood testily, and left his brother alone in the dimly lit hall.

Gil was about to mount the stairs himself, for the rest of the household was abed, when he heard an urgent tapping on the front door. He was not particularly perturbed, for it was no uncommon thing for a clergyman to be required at all sorts of odd hours. He opened the door and was confronted by a black-shrouded female figure, a hooded cloak pulled far over her head and successfully disguising her identity. Even as he opened his mouth to speak, the woman raised her face to look at him and it was caught in the light of the candle he held. Gil

136

thrust out his hand and dragged her roughly inside, retaining his clasp on her hand until they were closeted in his study, whereupon he dropped it as though it burned his flesh.

"It was madness for you to come here at this time of night!"

"I don't care. I had to see you. You have had a visitor. What did he say to you?" Her words tumbled over each other in her haste to get them out, and he smiled slightly at the panic in her voice.

He saw that it was his clear duty to make this easy for her, so he said, "I have no wish to sound churlish, but that really is none of your affair."

With a gesture he bade her sit on the chaise longue whilst he took his accustomed place at the desk. She obeyed, the hood falling back to reveal the fact that she had been in some agitation when she had come to him, for her hair had escaped its pins and the lace cap she habitually wore, as befitted her widowed status, and it cascaded over her shoulders, causing Gil to draw in his breath sharply before he managed to control his astonishment. She had lovely hair and the look of wildness it lent to her was curiously compelling. He couldn't recall ever having seen a woman without her hair neatly and demurely secured, and he was astounded by the emotions it roused in him.

"How can you say that? Of course it is my affair," she looked and sounded panic-stricken and he held up his hand as though to fend off an attack.

"Hush! I beg of you to calm yourself. You will wake everyone, then we will have no chance of keeping this between ourselves."

She lowered her voice, but her words were heavy with threat, "Your reputation obviously means a great deal to you, Reverend Underwood, so I warn you now, if you do not tell me what passed between you and the priest, I will scream at the top of my voice – explain that away, if you can!"

He blanched, "Pray do not do anything so foolish. I promise you it is your reputation I cherish, not my own."

"Then do not risk either. Tell me!"

"Very well. Father Fullick requested that I cease to encourage you into keeping company with my circle of friends, that is all."

"Liar," she said softly, "I know what he is like. He threatened you, didn't he?"

"Only with a complaint to my Bishop – nothing very unpleasant or frightening, I assure you."

She looked at him, holding his gaze in her own, "Are you going to give way to his threats?"

"The decision is not mine, Mrs Pennington. It is yours. I had no intention of mentioning his visit to you, though evidently you have your own methods of discovering these things."

"It is not my decision," she cried, ignoring the latter part of this speech, "How can I risk your livelihood and your vocation?"

He could not bear to look at her any longer, so he rose and strolled to the window, staring out into the darkness, "I think you need not worry on that score. The Bishop does not take the same dim view of friendship between those of differing religions, as is evident in your own church. I happen to know he dines regularly with a Jewish friend of his."

"Not just a liar, but an accomplished liar!" she murmured admiringly.

He turned swiftly, ready to hotly deny her accusation, but when he met her eyes, so guileless and bright in the candlelight, he found himself grinning ruefully, "Evidently not accomplished enough. I promise you he does have an acquaintance of the Jewish faith, but perhaps he is not yet quite broadminded enough to dine under his roof."

"I'd lay a wager he is not."

He crossed the room to a table that held a salver, decanter and glasses, and poured them each a sherry, "Why have you come here?" he asked, as he handed her the drink.

"To tell you… that he was not speaking on my behalf. I was furious when I found he had been to see you."

"I would be less than honest if I did not admit that for one moment I feared he might be doing just that – but it was only for a moment."

"Thank you."

"Is it true you intend to enter a convent?" he asked suddenly, probably the sherry had gone to his head, for he had tossed it off in one swallow.

She sipped a little of her own drink before replying, "I think I might have chosen to flee from the world and hide, yes. I imagined I would never fall in love again."

She thought he had not heard her, for he gave no reaction, simply returning to his chair and placing his empty glass on the desk before him, "If you took the veil, they would cut off all your hair," he said quietly looking down at his folded hands, then he raised his eyes to her face and added, "I think that would be a great pity."

Their eyes held for a few fraught seconds, then she took a deep breath and asked, "Have I been mistaken in coming here?"

"It was not prudent."

"Must I go away and never come back?"

"That would also be a great pity."

"Is that all you have to say?"

"It is all I am at liberty to say."

She stood up, drained her glass, shuddered slightly as the alcohol hit the back of her throat, then set it down on a small table. She pulled her hood over her head and said quietly, "I see I was in error. I should have realized convention would be too strong for you."

She strode towards the door, eager to be away from the scene of her humiliation, but as she reached for the handle, he overtook her and covered her hand with his own, effectively preventing her egress. Turning around she found herself very close against him. He gently prised her fingers from the knob, but continued to hold her hand behind her back, "Don't go," he whispered, so that she hardly heard him.

"I must. I should not have come here. I should not have accused you of being afraid to defy convention. It was cruel, I know…"

"It would be more cruel to leave me now."

His eyes were deep brown, almost black in the candlelight, and she felt herself relaxing against him, almost drowning in their darkness, like the subterranean lake he had shown her, but this was not icy cold drowning, but a sinking into warmth, into bone-melting heat, so that she lost all will power and could do nothing to fight against it. She spoke in a hoarse whisper, the words tumbling from her trembling lips, her body shaking as though from fear or bitter cold, "If I stay any longer, I shall want you to kiss me, I will not have the strength of mind to get up and go. I shall be here all night in your arms, and in the morning my reputation will be lost forever, and I shan't care…"

"Catherine," he said, "Marry me."

Her head fell against his shoulder and dragging the hood roughly from her, he did what he had been longing to do all evening, and buried his face in her hair.

CHAPTER SEVENTEEN

'Quis Separabit?' – Who shall divide us?

Dawn had just driven away the last remnants of night when Underwood staggered down the stairs, heading for the kitchen and tea, his head aching abominably, his mouth furred and dry. It took him several seconds to realize that it was rather unusual to meet Gil, looking as though he had been up all night, just creeping in through the front door. He winced as even the soft closing of the door scraped along a nerve, "Where the devil have you been?" he muttered hoarsely.

Gil recovered from the surprise of the meeting swiftly, and looking his sibling up and down said kindly, "You look as though you need a cup of tea as much as I do. Come along – and I must say, you are being well served for your misdemeanours!"

"Never mind my misdemeanours! What about yours?" growled Underwood, in no mood for a lecture, and certainly not one from his younger sibling.

Gil led the way down the dark passageway to the kitchen and once there insisted on stirring up the fire and placing the kettle on the reddened embers before answering his brother, then Underwood almost wished he had not asked. There were certain advantages which one took for granted when possessing a clergyman for a brother, and not having to listen to admissions of midnight assignations with attractive young ladies usually numbered amongst them.

"Good God, Gil! Are you telling me she stayed all night?"

"I have just returned from walking her home. We watched the dawn come up over the church."

"My dear fellow, when you decide to break out of your shackles, you certainly don't indulge in any half measures, do you?"

With a cup of Gil's tea inside him, Underwood could even raise a small laugh, but Gil looked both guilt-stricken and horrified that he should have been so misunderstood, "My dear Chuffy! What do you take me for? Nothing happened, I swear it – well, nothing of an untoward nature anyway."

"She was here, alone with you, unchaperoned, all night! If that is not untoward enough for you, I don't know what is."

"Well, yes, I realize it looks very bad, but what I am trying to tell you is that we only talked – and, well, kissed. But we did not anticipate our marriage vows," explained Gil hastily, self-condemnation written in every line of his worried frown.

Underwood unkindly roared with laughter, "I never supposed for a moment you did. It might have done you a lot of good if you had."

"Do you mind? You are speaking of the woman I intend to make my wife."

"I should hope you do. You could do nothing else and retain your honour. Don't you understand, you have compromised her beyond repair?"

Gil knew Underwood was at his sardonic best. He had no thought ever to bow to convention himself, but even so, his words hit home, "No one knew she was here," he murmured defensively.

"It is to be hoped you are right. Dammit Gil, are you trying to get yourself unfrocked?"

"I think it will come to that, anyway. I don't see how I can marry a Catholic and remain in the Ministry."

Underwood was only too aware how much this eventuality would hurt his brother, and he instantly ceased to tease, "Will she not convert?" he asked seriously.

"She says yes, but it is a great deal for me to ask of her."

"I don't agree. If the God you both believe in is the loving and forgiving being you constantly assure me He is, then she can be true to her faith in her heart, and still retain her place in Heaven."

142

Gil was strangely uncomforted by this, "Chuffy, you are incorrigible! It is very easy for you to be so dismissive, but there are those of us who think there is slightly more to it than that."

"More fool you," said Underwood firmly, "Pour me another cup of tea. I'm going back to bed. I feel like the very devil!"

"Sometimes you talk like him," admonished Gil feelingly, but he fetched the tea.

*

It was much later that same morning that Verity and her husband strolled into the Pump-rooms and everyone was astounded to see that as well as making Verity swallow her dose, Underwood also took a glass of the waters.

This was unprecedented, for though Underwood was a hypochondriac of the first order, he had so far into their visit been vociferous in his condemnation of Spa's over-inflated claims in general and Hanbury in particular. He felt that all who paid good money simply to drink water were being foolish in the extreme. However, Francis had wickedly confided that Hanbury's waters were a sovereign cure for hangovers, and Underwood was feeling just bad enough to try anything. Naturally no one else in the room was privy to this information, so his actions remained a talking point for over a week, especially when it was not repeated. Underwood, to his chagrin, discovered that Hanbury Water had no more effect on his headache than had hartshorn, *sal volatile,* or bathing his brow with lavender water.

Charlotte glanced disdainfully in his direction when she saw him enter, then began to sparkle and flirt to such an extent that she very soon had a crowd of admirers about her. A second glance told her that his pale countenance and lethargic mien were sure signs of jealousy and she was deeply gratified. Underwood, however, had not even noticed she was in the

143

room. Verity, amused and sympathetic by turns, was the only other person in the room who knew of his plight and was very gentle with him, for which he was prodigiously grateful.

He was less than pleased, however, when Vivian Pepper left his father, Lady Hartley-Wells and Mrs Wolstencroft to their cups of water and whisked Adeline across the room to join the Underwoods and Major Thornycroft.

Having met Charlotte Wynter and taken her in immediate dislike, due no doubt to her overweening vanity, he had decided to snub her by making Verity the object of his attentions. Underwood scathingly reported that the mutual detestation between Charlotte and the dandy had arisen because neither could bear to associate with persons who outshone themselves in terms of attractiveness and self-interest.

Verity did not care to know the reason, she merely enjoyed the rare sensation of putting Charlotte's pretty nose out of joint, for put out she was! She was horrified that plain little Verity should hold the attention of the two most worldly and handsome men Hanbury presently contained - she did not count Major Thornycroft in this assessment, for to her, he was simply an object of pity and revulsion, and she felt it unutterably tasteless of Verity to flirt with him. It really wasn't fair, she thought stormily, maliciously observing the group of her laughing elders. Verity hadn't half her beauty, though she had to grudgingly admit that recently Mrs Underwood had greatly improved in looks, for there was something about her which had quite altered her face and figure – a contentment perhaps? Charlotte did not wish to pursue this line of thought and sulkily turned away.

Presently, however, she had recovered and had become her usual ebullient self. She was too young not to enjoy life to the full, even when she believed her heart to be broken. Someone mentioned the idea of a riding expedition to the nearby ruins of a castle, and Isobel, aware that Verity had been a keen equestrienne, hastily included her friend in the invitation.

Verity was tempted. She had not ridden for months and it would be a treat. She looked at her husband and he gallantly told her that though nothing would prevail upon him to sit upon an *eqqus caballus*, he had no objection to her proposed jaunt. When Vivian Pepper added his pleas for her company, archly declaring he was desperate to be alone with her, away from the unfriendly presence of her husband, she was swayed still further. It only took one look at the furious expression on Charlotte's face to make the decision final.

Major Thornycroft appealed to the obviously uninterested Adeline Beresford that she take pity upon him, and stay and bear him company when these callous youngsters went on their outing. She gave him a sad smile, "Certainly, I'm afraid of horses…"

"Such beauty should be afraid of nothing," he declared passionately, taking her hand and placing a fervent kiss upon it. Adeline gently withdrew her hand, but her smile grew a little warmer.

She happened to catch his eye and saw a glimpse of his agony when he listened to the others discussing the horses they intended to hire or borrow. Surprised at her own temerity she asked softly, "It matters very much to you, doesn't it, Major?"

"Hurts like the very devil, sweetheart," he assured her with a grin, "But I'll be damned before I let them know it. Can you imagine anything worse than the whole world tip-toeing around you, trying not to mention anything which might injure your sensibilities?"

She shook her head, but her eyes were thoughtful.

Consequently there was a gathering of young people, suitably attired and mounted, outside the vicarage at three o'clock that afternoon. Charlotte had recognized an opportunity to shine in Underwood's eyes, for he knew she admired her ability to ride well, therefore she had ensured Verity's animal was quite as wild-eyed and skittish as her own, never imagining that demure little Verity was more than equal to the challenge.

She was also miffed to notice that Verity's riding habit was quite as spectacular as her own – though a good deal tighter than it had been at the time of purchase. Mrs Underwood the elder had left nothing undone in equipping her new daughter-in-law for life in a fashionable Spa town.

Underwood obligingly helped his wife to mount and was watching with interest as she gathered up the reins and brought her dancing horse under instant control. His look of admiration was not lost on Charlotte, who was just wondering what she could do about it, when Gil came out of the house and with a touching concern for his sister-in-law, but no thought, said swiftly, "Verity, are you sure you should be riding in your condition?"

As soon as the words were out of his mouth, Gil could have bitten his tongue, but there was no recalling them. Verity looked aghast at having been thus exposed, and her eyes flew guiltily to Underwood's face, but it seemed for a moment that her husband had either not heard his brother's words, or had not understood the import of them. As she looked down at him, Verity saw by the change on his face that the words had finally sunk in and waited with bated breath for the inevitable storm to break.

He raised his eyes to hers, his face set and white, "Get down, Verity. I have something to say to you."

Blood rushed into her face, but a diamond-hard determination shone in her eyes. No man was going to speak to her in that tone and have her meekly obey.

"It must wait until later. I am delaying everyone, as it is."

"Everyone else is leaving. *You* are staying here." With that he grasped her bridle and cast an icy glance about him. The young people needed no second bidding, all being only too horribly familiar with the tone of parental disapproval that his voice held. Only Vivian hesitated, for he had grown exceptionally fond of the gentle Verity, but even he was quelled by the delicacy of the situation. Even one of his self-consequence could not but realize that this was something which must stay private between husband and wife.

Charlotte looked so stunned that Isobel was forced to lean forward and take her horse's reins in her own hands. Of one accord, the party clicked their mounts into action and within minutes the hoof beats died in the distance, but not before they had heard Charlotte's anguished question drift back on the wind, "Does this mean she is going to have his baby?"

"Oh hush, Charlotte, for pity's sake!" replied Vivian, an unmistakable sneer in his voice. In his opinion only an imbecile could have misunderstood what had just occurred.

Tears of mortification gathered in Verity's eyes, but she refused to let them fall, "How dare you make a fool of me like this? If you do not release my bridle, I'll never forgive you."

The look he gave her was coldly contemptuous, "And I'll never forgive you if you damage my child," he said and walked into the house.

Verity threw an imploring look at Gil, but he shook his head briefly, "Don't risk it, Verity. Go in to him. I'll look after the horse."

"I can't ... I can't face him," she whispered in anguish.

"Better now than later, my dear."

He was waiting for her in the study, as she knew he would be, but he had been kinder than she had thought, for he was not seated behind the desk, like an angry school master, but had taken a stance in front of the empty grate, his elbow resting on the mantle, one finger pressed to his lips, and a faraway look in his eyes.

"You had better sit."

Her first reaction was to argue that she did not need a seat, that if he could stand, so could she, but she suddenly found her legs shaking so beneath her that she doubted her ability to stay upright for very much longer. He waited for her to cross to the old chaise longue then continued, "I presume my understanding is not at fault, and you are indeed pregnant?"

The fact that he used so stark a word, so rarely heard amongst the middle classes, who had a range of quaint euphemisms, always delicately whispered, struck a chill into her heart. He was not pleased, she could see that now. He was furious with her. He had not wanted children.

She nodded miserably.

"And my brother knew of it?"

Another nod.

"Anyone else?"

"Francis and Ellen," she whispered, suddenly aware how very hurtful this sounded to him.

"May I be allowed to ask why I was not informed, when half our acquaintance was privy to the secret?"

"I was…" Her voice died in her throat, she swallowed deeply and tried again, "I was afraid to tell you."

He accepted this in such profound silence that she could not help but shoot a look towards him. His face was a mask of indifference; she would never see the pain that answer had inflicted upon him. It was as though they were strangers, for this was not the Underwood she loved. He could never have looked at her with such icy disdain, such loathing.

"Really? When did I turn into such an ogre that I could not be told something so fundamental?"

She almost started out of her seat to fly to him, to throw herself into his arms and beg his forgiveness, but the expression of abhorrence on his face forced her back more brutally than a blow would have done, "I never said … anything so cruel. I … I thought you did not care …for … for children. I didn't know how to tell you … then there was … Charlotte."

He lifted his hand, "Don't, pray, mention that young woman's name to me!" She was startled at the vehemence with which he said this, but there were too many other things on her mind just then to examine it more closely.

"I cannot help it if you have given me reason to think you would be displeased…" she said, more strongly now.

148

"I fail to see how I have done such a thing. As far as I am aware, the subject of offspring has never been broached."

"It was – once. I asked if you liked children and you answered that you thought them a confounded nuisance…" her voice broke on a sob, but he was too furious to consider her feelings.

"You have an extremely disconcerting – not to say provoking - inclination to view everything I say as carven in stone. I meant other people's children, naturally. My own … ours…" he stopped too overcome by a mixture of confusing emotions to continue.

Verity knew she had hurt him, probably more deeply than he would ever admit, and the only thing she could say to him was pathetic and inadequate, "I'm so sorry, Cadmus."

He ignored her, as she knew she deserved.

"Perhaps you would like to confide when I was to be allowed to know of this momentous event," he continued, as though she had not spoken, "A month from the birth, perhaps – a week?"

"I know it will not sound true, now, but it was to have been this evening, I promise…"

"Do you have any notion – or even care – of the anguish you have inflicted upon me? I have been frantic for weeks, thinking you seriously ill and hiding it from me – and now I find…" He trailed off, unable to put into words the depth of anger, relief and confusion which swept over him.

They were silent for a moment; she weeping quietly; he trying to master the words, which he wanted to fling at her, but knew he could not, the hurt he wanted to repay. At last he was sufficiently calm to ask, "Do I have to beg to be told what date you expect your confinement?"

"I don't know precisely – I think it will be December," she murmured, desperately wiping away her tears with shaking fingers, thoroughly demoralised.

"Thank you," he said coldly.

He went out and left her to reflect upon this misery of her existence. It was to grow more miserable still; for when she finally dragged her weary bones up the stairs, she found he had taken all his things from their room and placed them in another.

She threw herself on the bed she had shared with him and sobbed in good earnest.

CHAPTER EIGHTEEN

'Quot Homines, Tot Sententiae' – So many men, so many opinions

Gratten paced the floor, observed with cool interest by his visitor.

"This is very confusing, sir, I don't mind admitting it. But you did right to come to me – oh, yes, indeed you did."

"Well, you must see the difficulty faced by myself and my colleague. We needed a judgement on the matter and you seemed to be the proper person."

"Quite right, quite right, but I think we will wait for Underwood's arrival before we make any decisions. He has… er… has been helping me with my enquiries."

It never occurred to Gratten that a note from him to Underwood might instil serious misgivings. In the excitement of new revelations, he had quite forgotten their previous encounter and he wondered vaguely why Underwood should have a curious air of diffidence about him when he was shown into the magistrate's library.

"My dear fellow, allow me to introduce Mr Wilkins," Underwood accepted the introduction and the change of manner with equanimity. It would appear Mr Wilkins was in some way responsible for this dramatic alteration of manner towards him from Mr Gratten, and he would undoubtedly be informed of the reason presently. He did not have long to wait.

"I beg you, sir, that you tell Mr Underwood exactly what you have told me."

"Certainly, Mr Gratten, I should be delighted."

Wilkins, it seemed, worked for an Assurance Company, a concept which had grown increasingly popular since the Peninsular Wars, when the loss of the breadwinner could have a devastating effect upon a soldier's family. His friend Johnson did likewise. In the course of the previous week, both

151

gentlemen had received a claim on the life of Mrs Josephine Dunstable, and both had seen the curious newspaper report, which had stated that the death of Mrs Dunstable was being treated as suspicious. In the usual way of things, it would be far from both their thoughts to discuss the private business of their respective offices, but this coincidence had been too great to ignore, so Wilkins had volunteered to travel North and present the facts to the gentleman in charge of the case.

Underwood was very interested indeed, "Are you at liberty to disclose the name or names of those who benefit from these policies?"

"I am, sir. My employer and that of Mr Johnson were most concerned that the lady might possibly have been murdered for the sake of the insurance money, which in both cases amounted to a not inconsiderable sum."

"The names, then, if you please," prompted Underwood, who never had any patience with pomposity and verbosity, unless it was his own.

"The policy with my company is made out to Mr A. Gedney – I might add that his wife and daughter are also insured with us, he being the sole beneficiary."

Gratten and Underwood passed a speaking glance, "Is his life insured for the benefit of his family?"

"Strangely enough, no."

"How odd that he should be so very certain of his surviving all his family members," commented Underwood cynically, "Is Mr Johnson's policy the same?"

"No, sir. Mr Johnson is to pay a Miss Adeline Beresford."

Now that was unexpected, and Underwood raised an eyebrow, "But I was under the impression that only close kin could insure a life? Miss Beresford is not related to Mrs Dunstable, is she?"

"She certainly is – legally adopted daughter. Beresford was the name of Mrs Dunstable's first husband."

"Is that so? How odd that Mrs Wolstencroft and Miss Beresford did not furnish me with that information, Mr Wilkins."

"Well, if they killed the old lady, it is hardly surprising, is it?"

"Under those circumstances, not at all. Tell me, do you know of any policies which benefit Oliver Dunstable?"

"No, but now you mention the name, Mr Gedney has a policy on his life too. His father-in-law, I understand?"

"He is, but logically, Gedney would be most unlikely to collect on a man so many years his junior."

Mr Wilkins was evidently baffled by this pronouncement; "Do you mean that the father-in-law is a much younger man than his son-in-law?"

"Much younger," asserted Underwood firmly.

"How very odd," said Wilkins, but with a shrug of his shoulders. He was a man who was quite accustomed to the many vagaries of his fellow man, and generally took even the most peculiar events in his stride, "Well, I need not scruple to tell you that we will not be paying either of these policies until we are quite sure no blame attaches to the beneficiaries."

"Very wise, sir. And I would like to thank you for your help. This information could be of vital importance, quite vital."

Mr Gratten was not a subtle man and he now made it more than evident he would like Mr Wilkins to leave so that he could discuss these new developments with Underwood. Mr Wilkins could take a hint. He shook hands with both men and obligingly took himself off, telling Gratten he would be staying at the Bull for the next few days, should he be required again.

"What do you make of all that, Underwood?" asked Gratten, as soon as the door closed.

"I think it is time to speak to Rachael Collinson, Mrs Wolstencroft and Miss Beresford again. These ladies have been withholding information, and I want to know the reason why."

Gratten was suddenly aware that Underwood had come at his call without any recriminations for past behaviour, and he had to admit now that, though Oliver Dunstable was undoubtedly a half-wit, it was looking more and more likely Underwood had been right all along and he was not a murderer. He felt compelled to mention this to his companion, though apologies never came easily to one of his ilk.

"This is very decent of you, Underwood, very decent, especially as I was a little …er … shall we say, hard on you the last time we met?"

Underwood smiled grimly, "Pray think no more about it, Mr Gratten. I have had experiences over the past twenty-four hours which have quite cast our little *contretemps* into the shade."

"Oh? Anything I can help you with?"

"Not unless you know about women."

"Ah! Which of us does, my friend, which of us does?"

"Quite!" said Mr Underwood bitterly, "Certainly not I."

*

He had the grace, however, to feel a qualm of guilt when he set forth, alone, to visit the ladies. He knew Verity had been as eager to solve the mystery of Mrs Dunstable's death as he was himself, and she would be devastated to know he was now acting without her, but his pain and anger were still too deep and raw to permit her re-entry into his good books just yet.

Consequently his expression had never been more forbidding or his manner less amiable, especially with Collinson, for whom he had never cared anyway. He thought her callous, calculating and thoroughly unpleasant, and he showed no mercy when he spoke to her. For the first time since he had met her, she lost her air of self-assurance. He actually managed to frighten her into thinking about the consequences

154

of her bad behaviour, and it was a very chastened young lady who answered his brusque questions.

"Miss Collinson, I am exceedingly tired of being trifled with over this matter, and I fully intend to discover the truth, or see someone suffer the full force of the law."

"I don't know what you mean. I haven't done nothing. Why are you always picking on me?"

"Your employer was probably murdered, yet you have given information reluctantly, have been rude and unhelpful. If you wish my suspicions to be directed towards a person who had constant contact with the victim, who handled her food, her drink, and her medicines…"

She paled visibly, "Are you trying to push the blame onto me...?" she stuttered incredulously.

"Someone is going to hang for this crime, Miss – and if you want that person to be you, just continue the way you are." His eyes held such a depth of contempt for her that she had no choice but to believe he was capable of laying evidence against her and letting her hang.

"But I didn't do it … Please, sir, you've got to believe me. I swear to God, all I've ever done is do as I'm told to do."

"Then she was murdered?"

She nodded.

"Who told you what to do?"

She swallowed convulsively, "Mrs Dunstable was my employer."

"And who else paid you, Miss Collinson?"

Her eyes slid slyly away from his intense gaze; "I don't know what you mean."

"Oh, I think you do. There are one or two things I need to have clarified, are you going to co-operate?"

"Yes," she said sourly.

Even at this admission of defeat, he did not allow his severity to relax, "Mr Gedney asserts he did not arrive in Hanbury until he came with his wife on the twenty-third of

June, but I have evidence to prove he was here some days before that, and he then entered the Dunstable house. Did you act as go-between, telling him when it was safe for him to enter the house without being observed or disturbed?"

"Yes."

"What did he do?"

"I don't know. I just let him in, then I left him. I had to find out when the house would have fewest servants present, then leave a message for him at the Bluebell Inn out Northcross way. I then let him in."

"And you really have no idea what he did?"

"No."

Damaging, but not enough. Gedney could have wanted to enter the house for a dozen reasons, and if he were glib enough, he could convince any jury that he was not a murderer, but was there for quite different purposes. He might, for example, have been eager to see the old lady's will, to know for sure what he might expect to gain on her demise. He could very well be aware of her blackmailing activities, and, being short of money himself, might have been attempting to remove the little black book and earn himself a commission.

"You stated the box of bon-bons was a gift from Mrs Gedney. Are you sure of that?"

"Not really. Everyone who knew her sent her bon-bons. She had several boxes delivered that week. I couldn't be sure which box she opened that night."

"Why did you not say that when I first asked you?"

"I don't like Mrs Gedney."

Underwood, who thought he was beyond being shocked by anything, was appalled. It seemed the girl would have been quite happy to see her employer's daughter in the dock, accused of murder. This was going much further than he imagined even she would dare. He had a sudden flash of inspiration. He scrutinized her face; "Do you have any followers, Miss Collinson?" She blushed deeply and this, coupled with her vehement, indeed violent, denial, told Underwood that she had something to hide. He left the line of questioning for the moment and noticed that she seemed immensely relieved that he had done so.

"We listed everything Mrs Dunstable had eaten and drunk that day, but I omitted to ask if she consumed anything when she retired. Did she?"

Collinson thought carefully, then, appearing to remember, she nodded vigorously, "Yes, I had forgotten, but Mrs Gedney came to her room with a pot of herbal tea. They chatted as she drank it – seemed quite friendly with each other for a change."

Underwood declined to show any interest in this snippet and continued smoothly, "Who, exactly, sent Mrs Dunstable bon-bons that week?"

"Lady Hartley-Wells, Miss Beresford, Mrs Arbuthnot…"

"Anyone else?"

"I can't remember."

"Very well, that will do for now. If you remember anything else, you are to let me know at once."

"I will – oh, Mr Dunstable gave her two boxes as well."

"Good gad! She did have a sweet tooth, didn't she?"

For the first time a ghost of a smile passed over her features, "She did. It's a wonder she was so thin, by rights, she should have rivalled the *'Victory'* for bulk."

"So it would seem."

*

When he was shown into her drawing room, he found Miss Beresford there alone, and though he made no comment upon it, he thought she looked extremely unwell. She offered him refreshment, which he declined.

"I understand congratulations are in order, Mr Underwood. I'm afraid your news is all over Hanbury by now. It is, perhaps, not common for such an event to be made a subject of gossip, but Charlotte Wynter has taken it upon herself to broadcast the scene played out yesterday afternoon at the vicarage."

He controlled his fury with admirable strength of mind; "Miss Wynter takes too much upon herself!" The comment was stoic enough, considering his own opinion of Verity's behaviour and Charlotte's malice.

"Pray don't scold her, sir. I, for one, am only too delighted to hear some happy news for a change. My own affairs have descended into chaos and I can only be grateful that the whole world is not plunged into a similar misery."

The bitterness in her tone did nothing to encourage him to continue, but he knew he must do so, "I'm sorry to hear that. Might I enquire as to the cause of your distress?"

"Why, the murder of Mrs Dunstable, what else? Josie threatened to end my engagement by exposing my shame to my betrothed, but that has happened anyway. By dying in such tawdry circumstances, she has scotched my romance. The first hint of scandal and he has run for cover like a rabbit!"

"He has broken your betrothal for so tenuous a connection with Mrs Dunstable's death?"

"He – or at least his parents – have certainly done so. But let us speak of something else. I admit I do not want to dwell on my troubles. Tell me to what do I owe the honour of this visit?"

"I hesitate to lay greater burdens upon you Miss Beresford, but there are one or two questions I must ask."

"Pray continue."

"Is it true Mrs Dunstable legally adopted you?"

Her teeth sank into her lower lip and her fingers twisted themselves into knots, but she gave no other indication the question was not welcome, "Yes."

"Might I ask why you did not think to mention it sooner?"

"It is not something of which I am particularly proud, and I did not think it relevant."

"Then why hold a life policy on the woman?"

She drew in a shocked breath, "How did you know about that?"

"I hate to sound pedantic, but I am here to ask questions, not to answer them. Suffice it to say, I do know about it."

She recovered herself swiftly, "I presume there is no law against holding such a policy?"

"No, but there are laws against benefiting from such a policy by means of murder, Miss Beresford."

"May I ask if that is the only reason you hold me in suspicion of committing murder?"

"I would not go so far as to say I do hold you in suspicion, but I must explore every possibility. It now seems you would benefit financially from your adopted mother's death, you have admitted wishing her ill, for reasons of revenge, you were one of the persons who sent her sweets which might have contained poison..."

She lifted her chin proudly, "Very well," she said with great dignity, "You need not say any more. I admit I did it. I murdered my hated legal mother. I sent her bon-bons filled with poison. Now take me away and hang me! What do I care?"

Her trembling lower lip told Underwood she cared more than she desired him to know. He wanted to smile at her childish response to pain, but it was altogether too serious a matter to be ignored or trivialised, "Miss Beresford, please do not treat this lightly. If you repeat that confession, I shall be obliged to act upon it."

"Act upon it with my blessing. I've lost the only man I shall ever love. Why not let the hangman save me the tedium of killing myself! I repeat, I killed Josie Dunstable with poisoned bon-bons. If you do not take me into custody now, I shall go to Mr Gratten and reiterate before witnesses..." her voice grew increasingly loud and hysterical, and Underwood thought it best to humour her.

"Very well. Would you like to pack a small valise?"

"Aren't you afraid I will try to run away?"

159

"No, I trust you."

"You should not – I am a murderess!"

"Even murderesses have some honour," he responded calmly.

"But I do not. My body has been bought and sold, doesn't that take away any claim to honour I might have had?"

"Anything bad which happens to a child rebounds upon its guardians, Miss Beresford. I would place the blame for the past squarely upon the shoulders of Mrs Dunstable, then forget it forever."

She looked thoughtfully at him, "Tell me, Mr Underwood, if you loved a woman, would you let such considerations keep you from her?"

"Not for a second."

"Do you think the man I was to marry was justified in breaking our engagement?"

"I think him a knave and a fool, Miss Beresford, and though I hesitate to suggest it to you, I think you are well rid of him. And, I might add, he is certainly not worth dying for!"

"No," she said, as though pondering upon the wisdom of his words.

"Do you now wish to revoke your statement regarding the death of Mrs Dunstable?"

"No."

CHAPTER NINETEEN

'Falsus In Uno, Falsus In Omnibus' – False in one thing,
false in all things

Twenty days after she died in Underwood's arms, Josephine
Dunstable was finally laid to rest in the peat soil of Gil's
churchyard. Her funeral was well attended, but it was mostly
due to the morbid curiosity of the populace. There were
probably only two mourners who felt any genuine affection for
the dead woman; her old friend, Lady Hartley-Wells, and the
man who thought of himself as her son, Geoffrey Beresford –
and, of course, only he, Gedney and Underwood were actually
present at the burial, for women did not traditionally attend
funerals, though they might join the wake afterwards.

Mrs Arbuthnot could barely contain her joy and pride at the
presence of Mr Beresford and Underwood wondered anew how
she could have warned him against disclosing her secret, then
be so openly adoring herself and not expect people to guess.
However, it seemed they did not. No one appeared to be very
much surprised that a woman could hold her Godson in such
reverence, evidently attributing this eccentricity to her own
childless state.

Mr Gedney was stoic until the moment the coffin was
lowered, then lost no time in castigating Underwood for his
tardiness in bringing to justice the foul murderess, Adeline
Beresford, to justice. Calling her a viper in his mother-in-law's
bosom was one of the least offensive things he said. He was
silenced by one of Underwood's most contemptuous looks,
something in the eyes warning him he was treading a very thin
line. Wisely he left whatever else he had to say for another
time.

Verity, still horribly humiliated by the public knowledge of
her condition, had wanted to stay away from the consuming of
the funereal meats, but Gil persuaded her otherwise. He

sensibly pointed out that she was going to have to face people sooner or later, and perhaps the best moment would be when they would have something far more scandalous to feast upon. The astounding news of Miss Beresford's confession was still the *cause celebre* in Hanbury, and nothing Underwood said or did could stem the gossip. He knew she was not the culprit, but whilst she maintained her stubborn refusal to retract, Gratten was only too delighted to take her word. This arrest removed a very tricky burden from his shoulders, and the fact that it transferred that burden to the unfortunate Underwood, bothered him not one whit.

The after funeral gathering took place in one of the private salons of the White Hart and it was here that Geoffrey Beresford approached Underwood and begged the favour of a few minutes private speech. The vicar's brother desired nothing less, but manners forced him to accede. They retired to a quiet corner and for the first time Geoffrey allowed his concern for his adopted sister to show. Throughout the service and the burial he had preserved his dignity, even when Gedney had begun his diatribe, merely casting the man a disdainful glance. Now he displayed his feelings before Underwood, much to that gentleman's discomfort.

"My Godmother has told me of your involvement in all this, Mr Underwood, so I beg you will tell me if Adeline is really guilty of doing this terrible thing."

"Since I do not possess the power of clairvoyance, sir, I cannot be positive that Miss Beresford is lying when she admits to the crime, but I strongly suspect she has allowed herself to reach such a depth of misery that she has confessed in order to escape from a life she no longer feels holds any happiness for her, either now, or in the future."

Geoffrey looked astounded, and more than somewhat distressed, "Do you mean to tell me she is prepared to go as far as allowing herself to be tried and hanged for this murder, even though she is innocent?"

"Unless someone can persuade her otherwise, I'm very much afraid that may well happen. No jury will ignore a confession, even if it be patently false – and hers is not. She did have the motive and opportunity. The real perpetrators are exceedingly unlikely to save her neck and risk their own with a last minute confession. And I have to say I am not having an easy time finding the proof that condemns them and saves her. Not unnaturally the authorities think they have a culprit and are uninterested in pursuing the matter further."

"I know my sister is incapable of committing this crime, Mr Underwood."

"I could not agree more."

"You will not, then, give up on her?"

"Certainly not, but she has set me no easy task."

"I understand that. Perhaps if I went to see her?"

"I think that would be an excellent idea. She's little more than a child, Mr Beresford, and most children find it very difficult to imagine a brighter future when they are in despair. Experience teaches us all that things *do* change, but she has not that experience yet. If you could convince her that life should never end for anyone at eighteen."

"I will do my poor best, Mr Underwood, and I shall look forward to a satisfactory culmination to your deliberations."

Shortly after this conversation, Underwood, Verity, Gil and their house guests returned to the vicarage, most of them having taken part in the funerary feast in an extremely desultory manner, especially Underwood, though this was not entirely due to his preoccupation with the Beresford brother and sister. It was a very subdued gathering which met in the parlour after the ladies had removed their capes and bonnets.

Gil handed round sherry, which no one particularly wanted, but which they all obediently took anyway. The atmosphere was heavy with unspoken emotions, for everyone knew of Verity and Underwood's difficulties. They had scarcely exchanged a word in days, and the vicar at least, knew of the separate bedrooms. Francis and Ellen were to leave the following day for their own home, and this added to Verity's unhappiness. She was dreading being left alone with the brothers once more, knowing that Gil, being Gil, must say something to his sibling, and she feared it would be entirely the wrong thing, and make a bad situation disastrous! She fervently wished tomorrow would never come.

*

The stench of horse sweat, old leather and closely crammed humanity made the bile rise in Verity's throat, but she forced a smile to her lips. She could not let Ellen climb into the waiting stage, then travel all the way home, fretting for her friend, for who knew when they would meet again?

It had taken every ounce of self-control she possessed to keep the secret of her melancholy from the Herberts, and not for anything would Ellen have told her that she had spectacularly failed to do any such thing. In turn, nothing would have prevailed upon Verity to burden her friends with her troubles, knowing, as she did, there was no help they could offer, and they must therefore spend the entire journey, and probably some considerable time after that, worrying about her.

Ellen embraced her closely, guessing more than Verity knew. She had thought from the beginning that it was foolish in the extreme to keep Underwood in ignorance and Ellen's soft heart ached for them both, but especially for Verity, for whom she had a very deep and real affection. The only gift she could give her friend now was her silence. Nothing would be more fatal to her composure than any mention of her problems.

So, Ellen, Francis and young Francis were carried away from Hanbury by the stage and Verity watched the vehicle until it disappeared from view, feeling more desolate than she had for many years.

Gil and Toby had come with her to bid farewell to the departing guests, but Underwood was preoccupied with his investigations and had said his goodbyes at breakfast.

As they strolled back to the vicarage, Toby remarked thoughtfully, "I think it is also time for me to be moving on. My ribs are more or less healed now, and I cannot impose on you good people forever."

Verity raised troubled eyes to his, "But where will you go – and what will you do?"

Toby grinned down at her, the affection in his voice removing any sting from his words, "Mrs Underwood, don't you have troubles enough of your own, without taking on everyone else's?"

She felt compelled to give him an answering smile, "Is that your way of telling me to mind my own affairs?"

"Could be."

"Mr Underwood will be sorry to see you leave."

"Mr Underwood has better things than that to be sorry about," he responded tersely, a reaction which was most uncommon in the affable giant. Verity lapsed into blushing silence.

*

The Bluebell Inn, on the Northcross road, was not much frequented, being, as it was, situated very near to a major tollgate, and therefore tending to attract a passing trade which was all too eager to pass and get the toll out of the way. Couple this with a surly landlord, a bad cook and two unattractive barmaids, it frankly did not have much to recommend it. Unless, of course, one required discretion or even secrecy. It was the sort of place, thought Underwood, ducking his head to avoid cracking his skull on a low doorframe, which footpads and highwaymen would use as a meeting place or hideout. Ideal, in fact, for the use to which Gedney had apparently put it.

The landlord possessed a remarkably poor memory of the patrons he entertained, until Underwood reached his price, then he became voluble. Armed with two of Verity's swift, but true to life sketches, Underwood asked his questions. The landlord's answers were much as he expected in all but one respect.

Yes, he had taken messages from a girl who resembled the picture of Collinson, and he had given them to a man akin to Gedney's, and vice-versa. What was more, the two had met frequently and hired a room in the Bluebell – no, not the coffee room, an upstairs room, and it took no imagination whatever to guess for what purpose they had wanted to use it.

Underwood paid lavishly for ale he had not drunk, then returned as quickly as he could to Hanbury.

Miss Collinson was found in the boarding house where she had been residing since the death of her mistress and consequently the loss of her work and home. She greeted Underwood with a world-weary sigh, "Oh, not you again! I thought I had seen the last of you. For God's sake, can't you leave me alone?"

"I can – if you welcome death," answered her tormentor mildly.

She shot a scared look in his direction, "What are you talking about?"

"Miss Collinson, you know too much. You are running a terrible risk. Gedney will stop at nothing to bring this matter to a successful conclusion. You have outlived your usefulness. He has killed once, do you really think he cares how many more have to die?"

"Adolphus wouldn't hurt me," she countered furiously.

"He'll hurt anyone who stands in his way."

"I don't stand in his way…" she trailed off, suddenly aware she had said too much.

"It is errors such as that which will sign your death warrant, Miss Collinson. He has been given a breathing space by this foolishness of Miss Beresford, but he knows I am not about to surrender. You have been his lover, you have been made privy to his plans, you have helped him to execute them – do you really believe he is not going to try and close your mouth – forever?"

"You are just trying to frighten me, trying to make me give him away," she was almost sobbing with fear, but she would not listen to his counsel, "I won't do it. Get out of here! Go away and don't come near me again. He'll kill you, if you don't leave it!"

"I will not leave it, Miss. And Gedney won't even try to kill me, because he is a coward at heart. I fail to see what attraction he holds for you or any other woman, but evidently there is something. But have it your own way. Trust Gedney instead of me, and see how long you survive."

"I will!"

*

"Could I ask you to do something for me, Toby?" asked Underwood, after a great deal of thought, when he met the big man in the hallway of the vicarage some time later.

"Depends what it is," responded Toby with more honesty than willingness.

Underwood did not seem to notice the distinct lack of enthusiasm and quickly outlined what he had learned on his trip to the Bluebell Inn. "I need you to follow Rachael Collinson – discreetly – and make sure no harm comes to her."

Toby was a good deal more interested after he heard this, "Do you think something is going to happen to her?"

"I know it, Toby. Unless we save her, she is a dead woman."

"You are sure of that?"

"Oh yes, undoubtedly. Knowledge is a dangerous thing."

"Then surely you are in more danger than her."

"Gedney knows I need proof to hang him – and I don't have it, but she does."

"Will the landlord of the Bluebell admit he has spoken to you? Would it not be safer for him to deny you ever approached him?"

"Of course it would – but Gedney is a thoroughly unpopular character, and people seem to delight in betraying him. One could almost feel sorry for him. I can imagine the pleasure mine host will take in puncturing the man's obnoxious arrogance. Besides, if he doesn't tell Gedney I am closing in, Collinson will. She will now run to her lover as fast as her legs will carry her, telling him the game is up and begging him to flee with her. He'll help her swiftly away – but not in the way she hopes."

"I don't have much choice but to delay my departure for a few more days then, do I?"

Underwood lifted an enquiring brow, "Why? Were you thinking of leaving?"

"Yes."

"Do you have any plans?"

"No."

"Then why go? I thought my brother had made it abundantly clear you were welcome to stay at the vicarage *ad infinitum*."

"He did, but I no longer care for the prevailing atmosphere."

Underwood's characteristic little frown briefly creased his brow and Toby wondered how he was going to react to this obvious piece of criticism. He was almost foolishly relieved when his companion answered candidly, "I can't say I blame you, my friend, I'm not too happy about it myself."

Aware that he had scored a direct hit, Toby grinned, reached out a huge hand and gripped Underwood's shoulder, "Then do something to remedy it, Mr Underwood!"

"Easier said than done, Toby. She has destroyed all the trust I held in her, keeping this from me."

"That was never her intention."

"I know it – but to tell me she is afraid of me! Good God, what have I ever done to deserve that?"

"Only your wife can answer that, sir. Talk to her."

But Underwood shook his head; "I can't Toby. I could not, just at the moment, dredge up enough self-control to confront her. I'm not only hurt, I am also incredibly angry." He hesitated, then managed to laugh, "I don't know why I'm burdening you with my confidences – I can assure you it is not my habit to discuss my feelings with anyone. Get yourself off on your guard duty – and don't let Collinson out of your sight for a moment!"

CHAPTER TWENTY

'Curae Leves Loquuntur Ingentes Stupent' – *Slight griefs talk, great ones are speechless*

Verity and Underwood continued to meet as strangers. He enquired politely after her health each day, and escorted her to the Pump-rooms, to concerts and assemblies, but every moment in his presence was torture to Verity, who lashed herself into an orgy of self-pity and self-blame. He would never, ever forgive her, they would never recapture the easy friendship they had shared – and she did not blame him! She had behaved abominably. She was worse than a faithless wife to have kept such a secret from him.

Gil tried to talk to them both, at various times, but failed miserably. Underwood was still far from forgiving him for knowing of Verity's pregnancy and failing to inform his brother – or advising Verity to do so. Verity merely sobbed and cried in exasperation, "For Heaven's sake, Gil, do not try to mend it. You will only say something dreadful and then where shall I be?" Much offended, the vicar did as he was bid and left them to their own devices. He had troubles enough of his own. Alistair Pennington had begun to fail fast and Gil had to bear the anguish of both watching the beloved boy slowly dying and his mother grow daily more distraught. He felt – and was – entirely helpless and hopeless, and under those circumstances, it seemed both Underwood and Verity were behaving in a pettishly puerile way, which shamed them when compared to the bravery or little Alistair.

Naturally this did little to cheer Verity, who was more than aware of her failings as a wife, a mother and a friend. The only brightness in her life came in the rather surprising form of Vivian Pepper, who had fallen dramatically in love with her when he had discovered, or so he imagined, that she was trapped in a loveless marriage with a much older man. Her condition merely added to the tragic aspect of the case and he felt at his most romantic when he fantasized them running away together and his raising of the undeserving Underwood's blond and angelic son.

Verity, naively thinking him a nice, kind-hearted boy who was being polite to an elderly matron, unwisely allowed him to squire her about town. Her husband, well acquainted with calf-love, recognized the symptoms immediately and was infuriated that she should be encouraging Pepper's presumptuous and obvious advances. He refused to be drawn by her foolish attempts to make him jealous and concentrated even more avidly on solving the mysterious death of Mrs Dunstable.

He travelled to Manchester to question the herbalist whom, it seemed, had supplied Dunstable, his wife, her daughter and Gedney himself.

Mr Flynn was understandably shocked and distressed to learn that Mrs Dunstable, an old and valued customer, had died of an overdose of tansy, and he was only too willing to impart any information which might be of use.

With the aid of Verity's drawings, and his own exceptional memory, Mr Flynn identified all the major players in the drama and Underwood could not help but reflect upon how much Verity could have assisted him in the questioning of the elderly man, and how invaluable her sketches had been. He was missing her badly, not just her company, but her wisdom, her insight and her support. Without her by his side, this was a dreary business, grinding its weary way to a depressing conclusion. No longer did he feel the thrill of the chase, the excitement of pitting his wits against those of an opponent worth of his steel. The whole affair had degenerated into a sordid little murder of a cruel, avaricious woman by a greedy, callous and unscrupulous man.

Gone was Underwood's passion for justice; in its place, mere duty. He had set himself the task and now he was honour bound to finish it.

His lethargy was briefly banished, however, when Mr Flynn produced a fact that had a profound effect on the case, "I can confirm that Mr Dunstable and Mrs Gedney purchased tansy oil, amongst other things, from me. Mr Gedney, however, has never, to my knowledge, bought any such thing. He asked for advice on identifying tansy growing in its wild state, but he never bought any oil."

"Really? But surely that has no bearing on the case, for he would have used the oil purchased by his wife."

"Not to have killed his mother-in-law. Mrs Gedney bought the smallest bottle I sell. It might have a detrimental effect on one's digestive system, but it wouldn't kill anyone."

"Are you sure?" Mr Flynn nodded emphatically.

"Then he must have planned all along to take it from the wild and extract the oil himself."

"I doubt it. It is no easy task, extracting essential oils from plants, sir. It is a long, drawn out process of boiling and distilling."

"Could he have poisoned her with the plant itself?"

"I suppose so, but I imagine it would be no easy task to persuade her to take it. Would you?"

Mr Underwood laughed mirthlessly; "I wouldn't take the time of day from Gedney, let alone eat anything he offered me. So what is the solution?"

"He could have infused dried leaves in boiling water and made what could be loosely described as 'tea'."

"Tea? Herbal tea? Who mentioned herbal tea?" Mr Flynn, baffled by this musing aloud on the part of his visitor, could offer no help, so he merely shrugged.

"Good God! It wasn't just the wine or the bon-bons. The *coup de grace* was delivered in the bedtime herbal tea."

"Dear, dear," murmured Mr Flynn faintly. He had been hoping that these accusations would be dropped and the whole episode proved to be some ghastly and unfortunate error. He had never before been involved in nefarious goings on – however distantly, and he would have preferred it to remain that way.

Underwood, his attention taken by the elderly gentleman's obvious distress, kindly changed the direction of the conversation, all the while thinking how useful Verity's calming presence would have been at this juncture, "Correct me if I am wrong, but I believe I have read recently, in pursuing this case, that touching tansy plants can cause a nasty rash, somewhat similar, I imagine, to nettle stings?"

"No, it isn't quite the same, for not everyone is susceptible to tansy as they are to *urticaria*, but it can irritate the skin of those sensitive to it."

"Thank you, Mr Flynn, you have been most helpful."

*

Though he had known he would not be met at the stage by any of his family, for the simple reason that they had not been informed of his time of arrival, Underwood was still curiously down-hearted to be set down once more outside the Royal Hotel in Hanbury. He suddenly fully understood Verity's desire for her own home. It would be pleasant now, after a long journey, to be heading for one's own hearth, knowing a loving family was waiting eagerly for the wanderer's return. Instead he was destined for a chilly vicarage and an even chillier reception.

As he walked back he happened to pass the home of Mrs Pennington and chanced to meet Gil just coming out of the front door, looking sadly weary and pale. Underwood noticed his demeanour, but made no comment upon it, only hailing him, for the vicar seemed unaware of his approach. Gil summoned a

173

welcoming smile when he saw his brother, "It's good to see you home, Chuffy. A comfortable journey, I trust?"

"You trust in vain," replied Underwood tersely, thinking longingly of the day when someone should invent a way of smoothing the roads, or stop the interminable swaying of horse-drawn vehicles, "How does Verity do?"

"She's very well. The sickness seems to have ceased, I'm delighted to report. I left her not half an hour ago, just preparing to put up her feet and consume a box of bon-bons some kind soul has sent her."

The colour drained from Underwood's face "Bon-bons? Oh, my God!" Without saying another word, or waiting for his brother to speak again, he set off at a run, leaving Gil to stare after him, a startled expression on his face.

Underwood was not a man much given to physical exercise, but he ran as though the hounds of hell were on his heels, the blood pounding in his head, his breath dragged out of his lungs in laboured gasps. It was not just the unaccustomed exertion which caused these exaggerated reactions, but the very real fear that Verity was, at that very moment, eating sweetmeats which might be laced with a toxin designed to kill her unborn child, if not herself. He was sent headlong into a panic the like of which he had never before experienced, lashing himself into a frenzy, blaming himself for his stupidity and pride. Why the devil had he not warned her about accepting gifts of food and drink, which came from an unknown source?

He thrust open the front door with such violence that it bounced against the wall and sprang back, almost hitting him, but he cared not. He hurtled down the hall and burst into the parlour, grasping the door handle for support, his chest heaving with the strain of drawing in enough breath to enable him to gasp, "Verity! For God's sake, don't eat the bon-bons!"

At least eight pairs of shocked eyes were turned upon him, and one or two tiny screams came from startled mouths. It would be hard to say who was more flustered by this

174

unexpected entrance. It had never occurred to Underwood that his wife might have visitors, and they in turn had never seen a madman force his way into the serenity of a vicarage tea party.

Verity turned a furious face upon him, her own heart pounding with shock, and rising to her feet she swiftly ushered him back out into the hall, closing the door behind her and castigating him in a vicious whisper, "What in Heaven's name do you think you are doing? Lady Hartley-Wells nearly had a seizure! And I know you are jealous of Vivian Pepper, but to forbid me to eat his bon-bons is the outside of enough. How dare you?"

Underwood listened to these words without immediate comprehension, and he stared foolishly at her for a few seconds before the most vital thing she had said filtered through to his stunned brain, "Those damned bon-bons were from *Vivian Pepper*?" he demanded hoarsely.

"Yes. Did you not know?"

"No," he muttered grimly, "I did not!"

"Then what was that all about?" She gestured towards the closed door of the parlour.

"Gil intimated you had received them anonymously."

It was her turn to look baffled, but only for a short time, then her puzzled expression was replaced by one of even greater fury than before, "So, you think I am too witless to know not to accept unsolicited gifts? Well, thank you for your confidence in my intelligence. You must think me a complete fool!" She thrust him impatiently aside, not waiting to hear his protests, and went back into her guests, closing the door firmly in his face. Underwood sank wearily into a convenient chair and raised his hand to his brow to wipe away the beads of sweat clustered there. The feeling of deflation was complete. Never had a knight galloped so gallantly to rescue his lady from peril only to fall flat on his face at her feet.

He was going to kill his brother when he saw him again!

*

Geoffrey Beresford met them the following morning at the Pump-rooms to take his leave of them before quitting Hanbury. He was morose, having failed to convince his adopted sister to retract her confession, and, what was worse, he had to work hard at persuading her mother not to make the same gesture and admit to the murder in order to save her only child.

"Adeline is adamant, Underwood. Only the Fates know what can be done now. I think she has some silly notion that her trouble will bring Robertson hot-foot to Hanbury, to rescue her – and if he doesn't, then she imagines he will spend the rest of his life regretting his part in her death."

"Presumably Robertson is the erstwhile betrothed?"

"Yes."

"Do you know the man?"

"Oh, yes. I met him at the engagement party."

"Is he likely to come here as she hopes?"

"My first action, on hearing about all this, was to write to him and beg him to come here with me to see her."

"His answer?"

"Completely hopeless. It was a resounding no. He is utterly spineless! I have no idea what she ever saw in the man to recommend him. He has acted from the first as though he was doing her untold honour in marrying her, for she is practically penniless. In his eyes she has forsaken any chance of a reconciliation. He would let her hang and not lift a finger."

Major Thornycroft had been listening to this conversation with interest, though ostensibly he had been flirting with Verity. When Beresford had shaken their hands and taken his leave, he addressed himself to Underwood, "Do you think Miss Beresford would see me?"

Underwood scanned the face of his companion, trying to fathom the depth of feeling which lay behind this request. Thornycroft rarely gave the impression of being anything other than a wild romancer. He even had several differing versions of how he lost his legs, though all included descriptions of his gallant action in battle. If one story was to be believed, it was Napoleon's own sabre which had sliced the limbs from under the courageous Major.

"What makes you think you would be any more successful than her brother?"

"There is much common ground between us."

On the surface this was a ridiculous statement, for there could be little comparison between a girl so young she had barely left the school-room, and a soldier in his thirties, who by his own admission was a hardened drinker and rake, but Underwood sensed the pain they both had to endure. Both were battle-scarred, maimed by life and felt unloved.

"Very well," he agreed, "I'll speak to Gratten. It had better be soon though. She is about to be transferred from Hanbury's own 'lock up' to the gaol at Derby, to await trial."

"The sooner the better."

*

It was a pale-faced young woman who greeted them, her hair scraped back from her face in a severe style which did little to relieve the harrowed expression in her eyes.

For once Underwood took no part in the conversation, beyond asking how she did. Her reply of, "I'm well enough, thank you," could safely be discounted.

The Major allowed Underwood to wheel him across the room, so that he was beside her chair, then with a jerk of his head, he dismissed his porter. Underwood grinned ruefully and retreated to a seat at the far side of the room, leaving the floor to Thornycroft, whilst hoping he had done the right thing in trusting him with the tender heart of the young girl.

"Robertson is not going to come here, Adeline," began Major Thornycroft, with no preamble.

"I did not think he would."

"Yes, you did. You've been hoping against hope that he loved you enough to save you – but it's an empty gesture, because he doesn't give a damn!"

Tears glistened in her eyes, "Are you pleased to turn the knife in my breast, Major? Believe me, you need not bother. No one could twist it more painfully than I do myself."

"I'm not trying to hurt you, sweetheart, but only make you see what a fool you are being. Do you think that pompous ass is going to torture himself for the rest of his life because you are dead? He won't. He'll have forgotten you in a sennight."

She gave a grim smile, "Thank you, sir, for reminding me how utterly worthless I am, how ugly, how forgettable. Of course no man could love me!"

"You are wrong about that. I'm more than half in love with you myself – but do you think I could ever have told you if none of this had happened? You speak of worthless, ugly, forgettable – and you sum me up in those three words. Add pitiful cripple and you have it all. But I'll be damned before I would let any of those cold-hearted little witches know how they wound me with every sympathetic stare, with every glance of contempt and disgust. The fault lies with Robertson, not with you. When I tell you he doesn't give a damn, I'm criticising him, not you."

Tears slid slowly down her cheeks; "You don't know me. You could never say you loved me if you knew…"

"I'm half a man, Adeline, what right do you think I have to see flaws in you? If you told me now you had killed your mother, it would not change my feelings."

She laughed through her tears, "But I didn't…"

He pulled her into his arms and quickly kissed her cheek, "I know that. And I don't care whatever else it is you think you have done."

"You would care, if you knew."

"It could not be any worse than all my follies, my dear. Now, are you going to stop this nonsense and let Underwood get you out of here?"

"I suppose so," she hesitated then looked into his eyes, "Did you mean any of that, or were you just being kind?"

"It's not my nature to be kind."

"I think it is. Are you really in love with me?"

She could see he regretted having said it, he grinned, but it did nothing to hide the pain in his eyes, "Lord, what have I been saying? Bless you child! I'm in love with every woman I meet, knowing I'm safe from their wiles."

"Don't you want to be married?"

"God, no! What sort of a man would I be, shackling some woman to a cripple? I've nothing to offer on the marriage mart, sweetheart. A small pension, a huge mound of gambling debts – even with legs, I wouldn't be much of a catch."

"I think you are perfect," she whispered.

He hugged her, roaring with laughter, "For god's sake, get us out of here, Underwood. The woman belongs in Bedlam, not gaol!"

CHAPTER TWENTY-ONE

***'Proprium Humani Ingenii Est Odisse Quem Laeseris' – It is
human nature to hate a person whom you have injured***

Toby had spent an incredibly boring few days. Following
Rachael Collinson was wearisome. Out of work and barred
from leaving Hanbury to find new employment, she did very
little but wander from kitchen to kitchen, drinking tea and
gossiping with her cronies, but he had promised Underwood
and he always kept his word. Privately he thought the vicar's
brother was over-reacting to the possible danger Collinson was
courting. Toby had seen no evidence of any peril; on the
contrary, she led a life of mundane safety, which he had not in
the least enjoyed sharing, even for a few hours a day. He was
sick of snatched meals, and hanging around street corners
waiting for her to do something interesting.

On the evening after Underwood's return, he was loitering
outside her boarding house, waiting for the light in her bedroom
to dim, knowing that was the signal for him to hasten back to
the vicarage and hopefully a hot meal. Even as he gazed up the
candle was extinguished, but for once his instincts told him to
wait a little before leaving and to his astonishment his patience
was rewarded.

The caped and hooded figure of Collinson stole out of the
door and down the steps. There was no hesitation in her pace;
she knew exactly where she was going – and she had no idea
she was under observation.

Toby dogged her steps until they reached the less salubrious
end of town, where she slipped into a common alehouse. Toby
went across and peered in through a window, considering it too
dangerous to enter the place, for though it was dimly lit and
smoky, he was a rather conspicuous man. He saw her sit in a
high-sided booth, and he recognized the man who presently
joined her, though unfortunately he was never to be privy to the

conversation, but he felt that judging by their gestures, and her wild expression, the content was neither friendly nor satisfactory to either party.

Presently they rose to leave, and Toby shrank back into the shadow of the wall, watching the man walk away, followed some minutes later by the girl.

By now much more interested in his task, Toby fell into step some yards behind her, not near enough for her to be aware of him, but with every sense alert. Something told him that if Underwood was right, this was the moment of Collinson's greatest danger.

The streets were unlighted and it was almost as if some part of his unease communicated itself to the girl, for her footsteps quickened and panic sounded in every click of her heels.

With a speed which shocked Toby a dark figure suddenly appeared from the pitch blackness of an alleyway and with a gurgling, hastily stifled scream, Collinson was dragged backwards into the dark.

Toby ran, his weight causing the pounding of his feet to echo and crack between the closely crowded buildings. Into the alley he sped, then hesitated, trying to accustom his eyes to the lightless murk. It seemed an eternity before he could make out the crouched figure huddled over the prone female form. A roar of fury burst from him, which he afterwards regretted, for it occurred to him the man was so intent on his task it might have been possible for Toby to approach him and grapple him to the ground. As it was, he looked up, saw the furious bulk of Toby bearing down on him and wisely took to his heels, leaving Collinson insensible and possibly dead.

Toby was beside her in a moment, feeling frantically for a heartbeat, a pulse which would show her assailant had failed in his task, but his panic grew as it became more and more unlikely that she had survived the attack. It was only as his fingers quested in the darkness that he realized the cord which had been thrown over her head and tightened about her throat was still biting cruelly into the soft skin. He dragged it away with a force which ripped off two of his fingernails, but the pain of which he did not feel until hours later.

There was still no response, and with sweat gathering on his brow and dripping down his face, he hoisted the inert form into his arms, and set off at an unsteady run to the vicarage.

Fortunately Toby knew the vicar never locked the door until the family retired to bed, so he burst into the hall, thence into the parlour, calling at the top of his voice for aid as he did so.

The family came running and in a few, breathless words, Toby explained what had happened, whilst laying his burden on the sofa. Underwood was swiftly on his knees, tearing at Collinson's clothing in his hurry to loosen the cord which held her cape in place, and then attempting to find a pulse in her neck.

"I don't think she's breathing," he said in despair, "If she is, it is just barely!"

Verity pushed him firmly to one side, aware, as he was not, of the intricacies of female attire, "Help me turn her over, we must cut the strings of her stays."

Within seconds a knife had been produced, and Collinson's best muslin was reduced to rags and the laces of her stays slashed through. The violence with which she was thrown over again onto her back seemed to force the air from her lungs and with a gurgling groan, she breathed.

"Thank God!" murmured Gil fervently.

"No, thank Toby!" said Underwood heartily, taking his handkerchief from his pocket and wiping his sweat-streaked face, "That was a truly horrible five minutes. I thought we had lost her."

He picked up the knotted rope which still hung, though loosely now, about her throat, "A clumsy garrotte, the knots are not even positioned correctly, too far apart. This was not used by a professional footpad. He would know that the knots have to fall either side of the windpipe to ensure no sound issues from the victim. These would have been almost under her ears, no wonder it did not kill her straight away."

"Perhaps death was not the intention. Mayhap the man meant only to rob or rape her whilst she was unconscious," suggested Gil, always willing to give the benefit of the doubt, even if it was to the committing of a slightly lesser crime than murder.

Toby shook his head, "He wanted her dead, I would stake my life on it. He was still twisting the rope when I came upon him and she was obviously unconscious then. Why not take her purse, or her virtue then run?"

"Quite," agreed Underwood brusquely, "Could it have been our friend, Toby?"

"I can't be sure of that. All I know is he left before her, and he probably knew her route, but in the darkness, I could not swear it was him.

"That's a pity, but the girl may have recognized him. If she ever wakes, we may find out."

Gil gazed down at the insensible Collinson with great concern; "Do you really think she may not regain her senses, Chuffy?"

"It is always possible. She has been brutally attacked, and was barely breathing for several minutes. She seems to have been lucky, but it may not yet prove to be the case."

"We had better get her into a warm bed and call the doctor to her," said Verity, with great common sense.

Toby lifted his burden once more and she followed him out of the room. Underwood gazed thoughtfully after them, "I knew he was unscrupulous, Gil, but I swear I never wanted him to kill again. Snuffing the life from an old woman is evil enough, but there is something undeniably chilling about strangling a girl at the very beginning of her life."

"Yet you set Toby to guard her."

"Thank God I did – but it was a precaution only. The girl was his mistress, I honestly thought he must have some regard for her that would protect her."

"Are you so sure it was Gedney?"

"Well, for once, our friend Dunstable had done the right thing in being out of town when the attack happened. If he should happen to turn up tomorrow, with no alibi for this evening, even I will have to begin doubting his innocence," replied Underwood with a laugh.

*

The doctor shook his head over Collinson in a thoroughly depressing manner, "I might as well be frank with you, Mrs Underwood, she is a very sick girl. If she lasts the night, you might have a chance of pulling her through."

Verity wished he would do less assuming disaster and more doctoring, but she could understand his pessimism. The girl looked even more ghastly now dressed in a white night gown, which was all too reminiscent of a shroud, laid out flat and motionless on the bed. She was so impossibly still and pale that she might be dead already but for the slight rise and fall of her breast and the livid bruises on her neck, which seemed to grow more angry and purple even as she watched.

"Is there anything we can do to make her more comfortable?" she asked diffidently, trying to jerk him into action without offending him.

"She looks perfectly comfortable to me," he answered, with indifference   "You can moisten her lips with a wet feather if you want to."

Verity could not keep a horrified expression passing across her face at his callousness, but he smiled understandingly, "You've done as much as you can, my dear, the rest is in God's hands. The girl will live or die, as He wills. I cannot help her. Bathe her bruises with witch hazel and keep her quiet, that's all

184

I can advise. She may wake as though nothing has happened, but I doubt it. More likely she will find her larynx had been so severely crushed that she cannot speak, either temporarily or permanently, I know not which. She may have been deprived of air for so long that her organs have been damaged, including her brain. You may end this with a gibbering wreck on your hands – time will tell. I'll call back in the morning. Of course, if she doesn't wake quite soon, she will die from lack of water and food, unless we force feed her – even then her throat may be too damaged to allow her to swallow."

When he had gone, Gil quietly came in to see how things were going and found his sister-in-law sitting by the bed, gazing at the recumbent Collinson. Without looking up she said, "When my time comes, Gil, for pity's sake, don't let that Job's comforter within a mile of me."

Gil laughed quietly, "I'm so sorry, my dear. Dr Burford was out on a case, so we had to settle for Haining. I've just taken it upon myself to dismiss him from Alistair's case, and the boy seems brighter for his loss."

She turned swiftly, "I'm so sorry, Gil, with my troubles, I have been too selfish to ask how Alistair is doing."

"I understand," he assured her, "And as it happens, I think he may recover. Haining is one of those dreadful men who think we should bow to the Lord's will and let the sick die peacefully, without the distress of a fight for life – as though he were in direct contact with the Almighty, and knows which should live and which should die! I sent him about his business and sat by Alistair for an hour coaxing him into eating a cup of custard. The poor little man had been fretfully turning his food away, and Haining told Catherine not to force him."

"Oh, Gil! He said he would come back in the morning – is there any way you can turn him away?"

"Leave it to me."

He fetched a chair from by the wall and sat beside her, "Let me help you, Verity. I can't stand much more of this madness! I know you think I will make things worse, but tell me honestly, how much worse could they be?"

Tears trickled slowly down her face; "They could not, of course. But I know you would be wasting your time. Underwood is never going to forgive me for this."

"My dear, you speak as though you had committed some cardinal error, and Underwood is some fearsome tyrant. I cannot believe things have come to such a pass between you."

"Neither can I – and the only conclusion I can reach is that if he loved me as I love him, none of this would have happened. I would not have felt the need to keep the secret from him, and if I had, he would not have hated me for doing so."

"Verity, he does not hate you…"

"Yes, he does!" Sobs broke from her, stifled so that she should not disturb the sleeper, for even in her distress her first thoughts were of others, "He does. And I cannot bear it." She stood and her chair fell over backwards with a crash, much to her horror, but the noise did not penetrate the coma of the unfortunate Collinson, "I cannot bear it for one more day, to see him looking through me as though I do not exist for him. It is breaking my heart."

She brushed past him, trying to reach the door, but he caught her hand, "Verity, you must not think these things. I know he has been angry, but I promise you he will calm down. It is not the end of the world."

She dragged her fingers from his grasp; "It is for me. I don't think he has ever known how I adore him. He is my reason for living, Gil, stupid fool that I am, to fall in love with a man who wanted someone else – and so deeply too. What was I about, letting him have my heart? I should have held something back, but I did not. I have destroyed myself!"

This remark engendered real panic in Gil for he took her words literally and was assailed by the sickening fear that she might attempt to do herself some harm. She seemed distraught enough even for that. His dread showed in his face when he cried, "Verity, for God's sake…"

"Oh don't concern yourself, Gil. I won't kill myself. I have a baby to think about, but I must do something, or go mad."

"Please don't do anything until I have spoken to Chuffy…"

"I forbid you to do anything of the sort. He has humiliated me enough. I'll not hand him the rest of my pride on a platter, so that he can throw it back in my face."

"But if he knew how upset you are, how ill all this is making you…"

"If he cannot see that with his own eyes, then he does not deserve to be told!"

Gil felt as though he was parrying the thrusts of an expert swordsman armed only with a fish knife. With the pride of Verity on one hand and that of his brother on the other, he was very much between the devil and the deep blue sea. He had only two choices; either keep out of the argument, or speak to Underwood without telling Verity he had done so. He was reluctant to take the latter course, being a man of honour, but the consequences of either action could be equally disastrous, and he could only conclude that had he at least tried to set things right, then he could at least live with himself.

He said no more, but let Verity leave him. He heard her cross the landing and go into her own room. He stayed by the patient until he was relieved by the housekeeper about an hour later, then he went to seek his brother.

It was much later than he had thought, for Underwood was alone in the parlour, the fire sunk to mere embers. Toby had evidently retired and judging from his sleepy expression, Underwood did not intend to linger very long either, though he did summon the energy to ask, "How is the patient?"

Gil did not bother to restrain the curt reply which sprang to his lips, "Asleep still," he snapped, "I wish the same could be said for your wife."

187

That brought Underwood sitting upright, his voice betraying a concern his face tried to hide, "Has Verity complained of insomnia?"

"Verity never complains. Not even when she is being treated appallingly by the man who swore to love and cherish her not eight months ago."

He had the grace to look slightly shame-faced, but there was an edge to his voice which showed Gil that the wound was still raw, "I believe she made similar vows – along with honour and obey."

Gil softened his tone a little and spoke in a conciliatory way which did nothing to appease his brother, "Verity is well aware she has behaved badly, Chuffy, but surely the punishment is now vastly outweighing the crime. What did she do, after all, but keep something from you, which you felt you ought to have known. Many women do the same, wanting the first few dangerous months to be over before confiding the news."

"If that was the case, perhaps you would like to explain why a mere brother-in-law was privy to the secret?"

Gil was a man who rarely blushed, but that stinging comment brought the blood rushing into his cheeks for he had the distinct impression there was more behind the question than was at first apparent, "I have been about in the world more than you, Chuffy. Verity did not tell me – I guessed – in fact, I believe it was I who told her what ailed her."

"How very gallant! Now the question that haunts me is why did you not then tell me? I have been reticent, Gil, because, apart from being my brother, you are a man for whom I have a great regard, but I must tell you now that some weeks ago, I awoke to find Verity gone and when I went in search of her, I happened across the two of you, in the kitchen, embracing. Being a trusting sort of man, I attributed this to the affection I know you share, but by God! When I find you knew of my wife's pregnancy when I did not, I find that trust slipping from my grasp like water between my fingers."

His voice grew louder as he spoke and Gil went white as the implication of his words hit home like physical blows, "What … what are you saying, Chuffy?"

"Don't use that stupid name, Gilbert. We are not boys any longer!"

Gil was slashed to the heart by the vicious edge to his brother's tone. Never in his life had Underwood spoken to him with such malice. It took several seconds for him to recover sufficiently to frame a reply, "Are you suggesting that you think I am having a love affair with your wife?" his voice was barely above a whisper and Underwood's face was ashen when he listened to his brother put his confused thoughts into words. If he admitted the truth, he did not know what he believed. He had never been more hurt or angry, and he was utterly confounded by a situation of which he had no experience and over which he had no control. The stark blankness of his brother's expression was enough to make him regret the words he had used, but the doubt was there and he could not now deny it.

He breathed deeply and answered as evenly as he was able, "You asked Verity to marry you before I did, you wrote to her – not to me! – to request this visit; you knew about her baby – a baby which she fully admits she was too frightened to tell me about. And in the early hours of the morning I found her – in her night attire, mark you! – in your arms. You tell me, Gil, what should I be thinking? What would you say if the situation were reversed?"

"I don't know, Cadmus. I have no answer for you. I can only tell you that Verity and I both love you."

"Your affection for me is not the issue. It is your feelings for each other which concerns me."

Gil threw him a look of profound contempt, "You do not deserve the devotion Verity has lavished upon you. You are a selfish, thoughtless fool!"

With that he was gone. Underwood stared sightlessly at the door, his thoughts unfathomable behind the impassive set of his features.

CHAPTER TWENTY-TWO

'Medice, Cura Te Ipsum' – *Physician, heal thyself*

An early morning visit to Mr Gratten was just what Underwood needed to complete his dose of the megrims, but he went anyway.

The Gratten family were still at breakfast when he arrived, so he was left to kick his heels in a small room off the hall for a quarter of an hour until the Constable sent for him.

Fifteen minutes of solitary cogitation did nothing to improve his mood and Gratten was immediately aware of things being vastly wrong when he faced his visitor across his impressive desk, "More bad news, I see, Underwood?" he said tersely.

"It's that obvious, is it? Well, I suppose it rather depends upon your point of view," was the bitter reply, "Miss Collinson has been attacked and only escaped with her life because I had set Toby on her trail. He witnessed the incident and stopped it."

"Good gad! This is terrible – but you say she survived?"

"Only just – and may not yet. She is still unconscious."

"Poor girl," he said automatically, "But you hinted that this might not be entirely bad news – why so? In what way, pray, could it be construed as anything other than tragic?"

"You are right, of course. It is tragic and I had no right to intimate otherwise. I was merely considering that one man at least can be relieved that the assault happened when he was out of town. Dunstable cannot possibly be held responsible for this, thank God."

Mr Gratten's face became severe. "Don't thank Him too soon, Underwood. Apparently He had another trick to play on you and your friend. Dunstable and his bride arrived back in Hanbury yesterday afternoon. He came immediately to me to apologise for absconding, explaining the delicate condition of the woman who is now his wife, and telling me that he had returned in order to fulfil your own instructions. I took pity on him, feeling he was no threat, and allowed him to return to his wife on the understanding that he would come to me today and give a full account of himself."

Underwood stared at him, utterly incredulous, "Please tell me you are playing some not-very-amusing hoax on me, Gratten!"

"'Afraid not, my dear fellow. Dunstable is back. If Collinson knows anything, then the man who killed Mrs Dunstable would want the girl dead too. Dunstable has chosen exactly the wrong moment to come back – if he is innocent!"

"Or someone else has chosen exactly the right moment to attack Collinson. Damn, I am not fated to have a moment's luck with this case. No doubt his only alibi for last night will be that witless wife of his."

"No doubt," Gratten hesitated, looking thoughtfully at his companion before adding quietly, "You know, Underwood, the time may have come for you to admit defeat. Dunstable really is the only sensible suspect in this case. He was the only one to benefit from the old woman's death; he had motive, means and opportunity. Collinson was our only witness and she has now been half-killed, just as Dunstable arrives back in town. Don't you think that's rather overwhelming evidence?"

"Yes, I'm afraid I do."

"Are you going to admit defeat and let me arrest Oliver Dunstable?"

"Will you allow me one last favour, before I do?"

Gratten, who was an irascible man, but not impervious to the charm of the vicar's brother, who had risen in his estimation during their association, was only too willing to oblige – but only within the confines of his duty.

"I'll do my best – what is it?"

"Let the world think Collinson is dead – just for a few days, at least."

The Constable shook his head dubiously; "I don't see how it can be done, my friend. If she had died there would have to be a

192

Coroner's Inquest. How do I explain the lack of an inquest to the public, or the lack of a body to the Coroner?"

"Yes, I hadn't thought of that. I see the difficulty. Very well, you'll have to arrest Dunstable, but I want it to be assumed Collinson is much worse than she presently seems. As far as everyone is concerned, she is despaired of, and we are only waiting on her demise in order to charge Dunstable with her murder also."

Gratten eyed his companion warily, "This sounds like complete submission, Underwood, and yet I have the distinct impression that it is not."

"Nonsense, Mr Gratten. I cede utterly. Dunstable is the murderer of his wife and the assailant of Rachael Collinson."

*

Since the church was the only place Gil could be sure of not being overheard, it was there he asked Verity to join him to discuss their predicament.

She came readily enough, hardly prepared for the thunderbolt which was about to strike her. Gil, uncharacteristically furious with his stubborn, unreasonable sibling, made no attempt to lighten the blow, "I spoke to Underwood last night, and he, in so many words, accuses us of having an affair."

Verity was already pale, she had daily grown more colourless for weeks, almost as though the child within her was leeching the very life from her, but this drove the last vestiges of blood from her cheeks and Gil thought she was about to faint yet again. He thrust out a steadying hand to catch her should she fall, but she cringed from his touch as though it were the hand of a leper extended to her.

"He said that?" she whispered, her eyes huge, dark and full of pain. Gil instantly regretted his hastiness and lack of diplomacy, but could not now unsay the words.

"It … it was what he intimated," he adjusted weakly, aware that any retraction was too late, then added with slightly more spirit, "I admit I was never nearer to striking him."

"Why did you not?" she spat, suddenly vicious, "Why don't you try and knock some sense into his stupid head!"

Gil forced a smile, albeit a wry one, "I'm afraid that is not really my way of dealing with things, my dear."

"I wish it were. I wish you had hit him hard. He deserves it for even thinking such disgusting things."

The vicar was rather taken aback to be referred to as 'disgusting', but he knew what she meant and tried not to take her vehemence personally, "He does, but I fear you will have to find some other gallant to beat him for you. I really could not bring myself to do it."

Verity looked thoughtful, "I wonder if Vivian would…" she murmured, then shook her head, "No, he would be too afraid of ruining his clothes with blood."

"Verity!" admonished Gil, really shocked that she could even consider violence. He spoke so seriously that she found herself laughing a little.

"Oh Gil, I did not mean it. I can't imagine Underwood engaging in fisticuffs – and certainly not with you or Vivian Pepper. But what am I to do? If he can really believe such a thing of us, there is no hope."

"Balderdash! There is always hope. You must now sit him down and talk sensibly to him. This not-speaking nonsense has gone quite far enough."

"No, the time for talking is gone. I know what I must do. I'm so sorry Gil. You can't begin to understand how mortified I am to have come between you and your brother, but I promise, it will soon be in the past."

"What are you going to do, Verity?" he asked, greatly concerned by her suddenly determined tone and the martial lift to her chin. She was a woman preparing for battle and he knew it.

194

"Never mind me. You have your own life to live. Isn't it time you went to see how Alistair does?"

Gil consulted the watch in his waistcoat pocket, "By Jupiter, you are right. I should have been with Catherine ten minutes ago. You'll forgive me, Verity, if I go. Good luck with my witless brother."

*

An atmosphere of harmony and relaxation hovered about the lovers. The new Mrs Dunstable was reclining on a chaise longue; a tasselled silk shawl spread over her feet, legs and her now all too obviously expanded middle. Underwood, who had never much associated with women, still less pregnant ones, was astounded that so short a length of time could make such a difference to her bulk, though he naturally made no comment upon his observations. The doting husband and expectant father was feeding her pieces of fruit from a china dish. He merely glanced over his shoulder at their entrance, grinned amiably and said, "Well met, Underwood. Allow me to present Mrs Dunstable," for all the world as though he had done something exceptionally clever in marrying his already pregnant mistress, with the threat of a murder charge hanging over his head. Gratten summed up Underwood's own feeling admirably with a contemptuous snort.

"We have met once before," said the vicar's brother stoically, "though under happier circumstances. Dunstable, I'm sorry to have to tell you that I can no longer prevent Mr Gratten from performing his duty as Constable of Hanbury. He has come to arrest you for the murder of Josephine Dunstable and the attempted murder of Rachael Collinson."

Oliver leapt to his feet, the dish of fruit flying from his hand and landing with a clatter, but miraculously unbroken, on the polished wooden floor, "What the devil!"

195

Underwood crossed the room to retrieve the abused porcelain, and absent-mindedly handed it to the young woman, who was so stunned that she simply took it from him and sat cradling it to her breast, as though it were her child.

"Dear God! You know I did not do this, Underwood. You cannot mean to desert me now."

"I'm sorry, Oliver, but I have no choice. In the absence of any shred of evidence to prove your innocence, Mr Gratten feels he has wasted enough time."

Dunstable's face twisted into ugly fury, "God damn your hide, Underwood! I only came back because you swore you would help me. Frederica and I were all set for France, but the little woman believed in you and persuaded me back to clear my name. Now you tell me that I'll hang for a crime I didn't commit!"

"Have you any proof of that assertion, Mr Dunstable?" asked Gratten quietly.

"You know damn well I have not!"

"Then I must ask you to come with me."

These quietly spoken words caused all hell to break loose.

*

Underwood returned to the vicarage in the late afternoon, his mood as grey as the lowering skies, which presaged rain before the day was out.

Dunstable, hardly surprisingly, had taken the physical act of arrest very badly, having convinced himself and his bride that Underwood had arranged everything for their safety, and he could not bring himself to believe the nightmare had actually happened. The object of this misplaced confidence was physically, mentally and emotionally drained by the raw passions which his and Gratten's arrival had provoked. He was not a particularly demonstrative man himself and he had found the display of grief, fury, fear and a dozen more minor feelings,

196

not only wearing, but also intensely embarrassing. He could only wish Dunstable and his spouse had possessed more self-control – preferably from the very beginning of their association.

He found he had entered the house only a few seconds after his brother, who was standing in the hall, reading a letter, which he had apparently found on the hall table.

Aware that he had behaved unforgivably the night before, Underwood now desired nothing more than to slip past the vicar unnoticed and gain the comparative peace of his room, but it was not to be. As the door had opened Gil raised his eyes from the missive and looked grimly at his sibling, "I think you had better read this, brother."

"Not now, if you don't mind, Gil. I'm exhausted. It has been a very trying day…"

"The day is not yet over," interrupted Gil harshly, "I think you will find your wife has left you."

Underwood's head jerked up, *"What?"*

Gil thrust the piece of paper into his hands, "Read for yourself. She says she can't bear any more. She has gone from here, and she has left no indication of her destination."

The shocked husband quickly recovered himself, determined to show his brother a level of dignity not displayed by the Dunstables, "Of course, she has gone to Mother. Where else does she have?"

The vicar wore an expression of contempt, which was almost alien to one of his kindly and forgiving nature, "I hope to God you are right. For a woman to be alone in the world in her condition is not a position I would envy."

Underwood raised his eyes from the note written in Verity's hand, but shaky and tear-splashed in a way which pierced his heart not only with sorrow, but guilt, and he stared at his brother, "Thank you Gil, that was just what I needed to hear at this moment."

197

Such was Underwood's pride, he was determined not to deviate one iota from his usual routine. Having convinced himself during the course of a long, and largely sleepless night, that Verity's only possible haven was with his mother, and she would indeed relish the idea he was frantically searching for her, he forced himself to make his usual trip to the Pump-rooms. His relief at seeing the friendly countenance of Major Thornycroft was no less deep for not being shown.

"Good day to you, Jeremy. Is it my imagination, or are we rather thin of company here today?"

The Major gave him a knowing glance; "You seem rather thin of company yourself. No Verity or Gil? All is well, I trust?"

Underwood threw him a look of mild loathing, "Damn you, Major! Am I to gather from that sly comment you are fully acquainted with the trouble in the Underwood household?"

The Major grinned, "I have my sources of information," he admitted smugly.

"Since you have the confidence of every woman in Hanbury, you no doubt know how abominably I have treated my poor wife, and where she is now residing? Which one of the tabbies is sheltering her, Jeremy?"

"To the former question, the answer is yes, but if it comforts you any, I can fully appreciate your annoyance. I would have been a little put out myself."

"Thank you," muttered Underwood sardonically.

"Well, it makes a man look a rare fool when he is the last to know of his own impending paternity."

"Is that remark designed to make me feel better or worse, Thornycroft?"

The Major grinned again, but with the slightest edge of unkindness, "Better, of course, my friend."

"Good, then make me feel better still, and tell me where my wife is hiding herself."

"Now, that I don't know, sorry."

"You wouldn't tell me if you did know, would you?" His only reply was a shake of the head, but Underwood could not be sure if it denoted denial, or merely weariness at the folly of his fellow man.

"I shall not press you. No doubt she will come running back when she comes to her senses."

"I would not rely on that, if I were you, my friend. Women can be damnable awkward creatures when they get an idea into their heads."

"Not Verity!" asserted Underwood firmly, "She does not have an awkward bone in her body. A sweeter, more biddable girl you are never likely to meet."

Thornycroft roared with laughter, "Good God, man, you really don't know the first thing about your wife, do you?"

Underwood chose to ignore this remark. What, after all, could the Major know about Verity? He could not have known her more than a few weeks.

"Where is everybody? I have never known the Pump-rooms so empty."

"Most of the tabbies are staying away because there was a rumour flying about that Dunstable was coming here this morning with his new wife. None of them want to be contaminated by her presence."

"Great Heavens! You are quite right, Major, women are strange creatures. What do they think the poor girl can do to them?"

"Give their daughters naughty ideas, I imagine. The wages of sin are supposed to be death, but she comes trotting back with a wedding ring on her finger. Not the sort of example which will make rebellious young ladies listen to Mama's strictures."

"Very true. Well, no doubt it will delight those same mamas to know that the Dunstable's sins, at least, have found them out. Mr Gratten arrested Oliver yesterday for the murder of his first wife. The second Mrs Dunstable stands in immediate danger of the same fate for aiding him."

The Major looked suitably serious, "I can't say I'm sorry, for that means Adeline Beresford need no longer fear the gallows, but I must admit to feeling somewhat confused. I thought you were maintaining Dunstable's innocence."

"I was."

"Had a change of heart?"

"Not exactly."

"So what next?" pursued the Major, reflecting that getting Underwood to show his feelings was like extracting a sentence from a foot soldier which did not include a volley of curses.

"I have no idea."

The Major scanned his companion's face, but still gained no insight into the thoughts hidden behind his impassive features, "I realize I have not known you for long, Underwood, but I must say you never struck me as a man who gives up so easily."

"Really?"

"Yes, really."

"Ah, well," he said comfortingly, "we are all of us wrong sometimes, Major, pray don't let it weigh too heavily upon you."

*

It was with a joyous smile that Catherine greeted Gil, running down the stairs into the hall of her house, "He is much better this morning, oh, my dear, I really think he is going to get better."

He took both her hands in his own, an answering smile on his lips, "That is good news indeed, my love."

Even in the midst of her own overwhelming emotions, her loving eyes could not miss the troubled look in his eyes, "Something is wrong, Gil. What is it?"

"Nothing that need concern you," he responded swiftly, knowing it was useless to deny the existence of a worry. Already she possessed an intuition about him that rather stunned him, "Pray think no more about it."

Her hand cupped his cheek as though he too were her sick child, "Anything which causes you distress is my concern." With that she seated herself determinedly on the third step and pulled him down beside her, "We neither of us will move from this spot until I am told the whole story."

He laughed, "I bow to a will stronger than my own. Verity has left town."

"By that I presume you mean to intimate she has left her husband?"

Gil, only too aware how shocking such an enterprise by any wife would be, had been extremely reluctant to place that explanation on Verity's actions, however his uncomfortable silence answered the question more eloquently than words ever could.

The breathy, "Oh dear!" hardly expressed her true feelings, but she felt lost for a wise or comforting comment, at least for the present. Once married, a woman almost literally belonged to her husband. There had even been instances of unsatisfactory wives being sold at auction by disgruntled spouses, though admittedly it was rare and generally amongst the poorer classes. Even so, the child Verity carried was the property of her husband and he could pursue her to reclaim his own, or force her to return to him, no matter how unwilling she might be. Men had the right to beat their wives; they automatically became the owners of all money and property after the wedding, unless her father had made provision in the form of a trust. Even a wife's personal earnings belonged to her husband and he could sue any employer who paid his wife without recourse to him. Naturally Underwood was no such ogre, but Verity had chosen a difficult path, and at worst could be laying herself open to persecution, the loss of her child, destitution…

Catherine's worried glance met Gil's, "Oh, my dear! Does your mother know? She will be so distressed."

"Underwood seems to think Verity will go home to mother, but I did not share his confidence, so I sent an express letter. If she returns her answer by the same method, we should know in a day or two if Verity is with her."

"And if she is not?"

"Then God alone knows what has become of her, for as far as we know, she has no living relatives at all."

CHAPTER TWENTY-THREE

'Suppressio Veri' – Deliberate suppression of the truth

The triumphant Gedney was never going to waste any time in seeking out Underwood and gloating noisily. Naturally he chose the Pump-rooms to stage his performance. Maximum audience to ensure the deepest humiliation for his victim.

"Well, Underwood, it looks as though Gratten has more intelligence than you ever suspected! He has finally arrested the murderous Dunstable, I hear."

"Your hearing is evidently acute, Gedney, and does not deceive you!" acknowledged the vicar's brother evenly.

Gedney leant forward so that his reddened face was within inches of Underwood's, causing him to turn his face slightly so that the foul, drink-sour breath was deflected to his cheek, "God rot you! You would have liked to see me swing, wouldn't you? You sanctimonious bastard!"

"There are ladies present, you ill-bred oaf, so I suggest you curb your language, or I will be forced to teach you some manners!"

Gedney staggered backwards, roaring with laughter, "Do you really think you could? Pray challenge me, my friend, for I'd like nothing more than to smash my fist into that smug face of yours!"

"The feeling is entirely mutual, believe me, however, I have never yet so far forgotten myself as to strike a drunken man, so I suggest you try and stay sober long enough to grant us both the satisfaction we so crave!"

"Drunk or sober, I can take you on!" growled Gedney, infuriated by the slur, but unfortunately quite unable to refute it.

"No doubt you think so, but I have no intention of finding out. The way my luck is running, the first blow I struck would spin you off your feet and you'd break your neck as you hit the floor! If I die by anything other than natural causes, I intend it to be with better reason than for ridding the world of your worthless hide!"

Gedney gathered what was left of his shredded dignity; "I'll be back, Underwood. Look to your safety!"

"Don't worry yourself on that score, Mr Gedney," he returned sweetly, "I fully intend to stay well away from dark passageways."

The drunken man glared suspiciously at him, his bloodshot eyes focusing with difficulty, "What the devil is that supposed to mean?"

"Did you not know? There is a maniac with a knotted rope on the loose in town. Rachael Collinson barely escaped with her life."

"I knew that, of course. That black ape of yours saved her – if it was not him who jumped on her in the first place. His tale of a gallant rescue is probably pure fantasy!"

Underwood was on his feet in a second, "By God, Gedney! You go too far. You are vastly offensive sober, unfathomably obnoxious drunk, but when you insult a friend of mine in that way, you are unspeakable!"

Both men were by now so involved in their dispute that they had quite forgotten their surroundings. So oblivious were they, that they were only brought to their senses by the round of applause which greeted Underwood's words, and the several shouted vilifications directed at the universally unpopular Gedney. His skin flushed almost purple and he turned on the gathering with an almost bestial snarl, "Be damned to you all! Keep out of it. This is a private conversation!"

"Then keep it that way!" snapped the Major with rapidly rising fury, "And get out of here before I shoot the legs from under you and cut you down to my size!"

"All right, Major, I can handle this situation," murmured Underwood, trying to placate without stripping the man's masculinity from him, but equally unable to let him offer to fight the odious Gedney.

"Oh, I know that, my friend, but I really should not allow you to soil your hands with such scum!"

Gedney threw him a look of intense loathing, "Why don't you shut your mouth and go back to the protection of the ladies' skirts, you pathetic little cripple!"

This was more than the residents of Hanbury were going to allow. Gedney found himself literally submerged beneath a barrage of complaints and outraged protests. Several ladies loudly demanded the immediate calling of the Constable and the Major was roaring for his seconds and his pistols.

With a wheel-chair bound man offering him a duel, Gedney did not have much choice but to leave, but he was evidently still fighting mad and Underwood decided he might just be wise to avoid his society for a few days.

Underwood was not a coward, he never backed down from a quarrel, and he would never refuse to pick up a gauntlet, once thrown down, but he was a peaceable man and the very thought of physical violence was deeply abhorrent to him. He would happily claim craven cowardice in order to diffuse a volatile situation, but it was very far from the truth. In fact he showed greater courage in facing such situations than many a man who flung himself into a fight without thinking of the consequences. It was far easier to be brave when animal instinct took over than when those instincts had been successfully controlled and one was coldly and fully aware of the damage about to be inflicted.

Major Thornycroft took one look at his companion's drained face and said, "Come, my friend, you need a stiff drink. Push me to the nearest hostelry."

"I don't need drink to give me Dutch courage!" was the slightly bitter response, but the Major laughed.

"Don't be a fool. One brandy is not going to turn you into another Gedney! And for myself, I desperately need a large whisky!"

Underwood, who had not thought himself quite so transparent, grinned wryly, "I suppose not."

They chose the White Boar, knowing it not to be one of Gedney's haunts, and Thornycroft insisted on paying his corner, despite Underwood's protests, "Put your money away. The King allows me a large enough pension to buy a few drinks, besides which, I intend to be unbearably impertinent, and that's always easier when your drinking partner stands in your debt."

Underwood accepted a large brandy and found himself a seat in a secluded corner with enough space beside him for the Major to draw in his wheeled chair,

"What form is this impertinence to take?" he asked, after a swallow of the reviving liquid.

"I want to know what the hell has gone wrong between you and Verity. The woman adores you, as any fool can plainly see, even a confirmed old cynic like myself. What the devil has happened to drive her away?"

The fact that he was able to hear this without anger or resentment surprised even Underwood, who would normally be furious to hear his private affairs discussed in a common ale house – or indeed anywhere else, but there was a sincerity about Thornycroft which took the sting from his comments. He cared – and for a man with troubles enough of his own, that showed a generosity of spirit which even the supposedly insensitive Underwood could appreciate. He took another gulp at his brandy and opened his heart, "I found I couldn't talk to her, Jeremy. It was not just the fact she had kept me in the dark, it was the idea of there being a child at all! I was not expecting it to happen. It never crossed my mind for a single second. And when I realized it was true, I simply could not cope with the knowledge. She thinks it is because I don't want children – God, if she knew I'm terrified of the prospect!"

Thornycroft was kind enough not to laugh out loud, but his lips twitched in appreciation of a private thought, "My dear fellow, how long were you confined to the monastic atmosphere of Cambridge? How could you possibly overlook that aspect of marriage? Your brother must have told you the purpose of marriage is procreation."

"Well, of course he had no need to! He tried, but I can't say I enjoyed our pre-nuptial lectures. He's my younger brother, for God's sake! I wasn't going to discuss those things with him," was the disgusted rejoinder.

"Then how could you not know that making love to your wife was probably going to result in a child."

"I'm over forty. I thought it was too late – and God knows it probably is! What kind of a father am I going to make at my time of life?"

"The best kind, you fool! Indulgent, doting and ever aware of the little miracle you have created, instead of taking your offspring for granted, as many a younger man has done! I don't mind telling you, I envy you. The chances of my planting my seed in fertile soil is fairly remote now." He slapped bitterly at what was left of his thighs.

"Nonsense," interjected Underwood, only too glad to divert the conversation from himself, "Adeline Beresford would marry you tomorrow. She's utterly infatuated, and you know it."

"She may be – but I wouldn't marry her. She's barely out of the schoolroom and has her whole life before her. She deserves more than a cripple for a husband!"

"You are arrogant, my friend!"

The Major looked suitably aghast at this stinging rebuke, "Good God! How came you to that conclusion? I thought I sounded rather noble and forbearing!"

"Exactly. Hiding behind your injuries, refusing to take the risk of being rejected. Not allowing the young woman to make her own choices so that the world will think you noble and self-sacrificing. Balderdash! You are headed for martyrdom, Major."

"I thought we came here to discuss you."

"I thought we came here for a drink."

"So we did." Major Thornycroft hailed the landlord, "Two more over here, my good man – and keep 'em coming!"

When their glasses were set before them, refilled, the Major continued, "What are you going to do about your wife?"

"None of your damned business," was the cheerful reply.

"In other words, you don't know what to do."

"In other words, I don't need to do a thing. She has flown back to my mother, and will presently be persuaded back under the old lady's protection. I will be given a severe dressing down, will immediately apologise sweetly and all will be forgotten."

His companion shook his head in disbelief, "No one as smug as you should be allowed such a lovely little wife"

"I'll make it up to her."

"I sincerely hope you do!"

"Are you going to propose to sweet Adeline?"

"None of your damned business – to borrow your own very evocative mode of expression."

Underwood, suddenly brandy-serious, gripped his friend firmly by the shoulder, "Don't be a fool, Jeremy! Don't let stupid pride stand in the way of happiness. Believe me, she carries scars as deep as yours. They are just not visible."

Thornycroft raised his eyes and looked into Underwood's, "You've hinted so before. Are you going to tell me what ails her?"

"No, that must lie with the lady, but if she ever trusts you enough to tell you, treat her kindly."

"You have my word on it."

"Good."

*

Completely unaware that he was destined to shortly suffer a double blow, Underwood pursued his enquiries with stoicism which astounded all whom knew of his wife's desertion.

Especially concerned was Lady Hartley-Wells, who sent him one of her more strongly worded invitations. Underwood grinned as he read it, debating whether to risk giving the old lady an apoplexy by refusing to attend. On reflection, however, he decided to go, as she sounded mildly frantic and he had little else to occupy him.

He was surprised to be greeted by a woman who was evidently struggling to control a rising panic, so unlike the usual forbidding demeanour of the redoubtable widow. They wasted no time in exchanging pleasantries, "Is it true Verity has gone?"

"Merely on a visit to my mother," he replied evenly, trying not to be irritated by this blunt style of questioning, and the unmannerly interest in his affairs.

She sank into a chair as though relief had knocked the legs from under her, and briefly rested her hand on her formidable breast, "Thank God!" Doubt seemed to assail her for she looked at him through narrowed lids and demanded, "You are quite sure of that, are you?"

He frowned, "Why do you ask?"

"Because that idiot of a nephew of mine left town the same day, and we haven't heard from him since"

It was Underwood's turn to slump into a convenient seat; "Vivian Pepper has left Hanbury?" he managed to murmur, still not quite able to assimilate the information fully.

She was frantic with worry and this made her more than usually irascible,

"Of course Vivian! How many idiot nephews do you think I possess?"

"I really have no idea."

"Don't be impertinent. And for pity's sake, open your ears. Do you walk around completely blind and deaf to all that is going on? It has been the subject of gossip for the past week that Verity and Vivian disappeared on the same day, after spending every waking moment together and flirting madly with each other. The fact that she is having a baby and you apparently knew nothing of it is giving the real scandalmongers food for much imaginative talk. They are saying they met before, in Cambridge."

A muscle twitched in his cheek as his jaw tightened, "Verity has never been in Cambridge. I fear I must take my leave of you, Lady Hartley-Wells."

"Pray do so – but for Heaven's sake, find your wife and my nephew before this goes beyond repair!"

His tone was curiously tight and unemotional as he replied, "I can assure you, my wife is with my mother and certainly *not* with your witless nephew."

"I hope you prove to be correct, sir."

As he reached the door she called to him, "How is the Collinson girl? With all this, I almost forgot to enquire after her."

"Still unconscious – and likely to slip away at any moment."

"I'm sorry for that."

"So am I. She was the only chance I had of saving an innocent man from the gallows."

*

It was with a less than jaunty step that Underwood approached the door of the vicarage, only to be almost bowled off his feet by the sudden advent of his brother, who had jerked open the door and set off down the path at a neck-breaking run. He skidded to a halt when faced with Underwood, "Thank heavens, Chuffy! I was just coming to find you."

"Having found me, might I be allowed to know the reason for this unbecoming haste?"

"I sent an express letter to mother, and she has sent one in reply."

210

Underwood said nothing, but raised an enquiring brow. Gil, for some reason, felt compelled to explain his actions, "I was worried about Verity, so I wrote."

"Presumably mother is on her way here with Verity, thanks to your interference"

Gil's hands dropped helplessly to his sides, the letter drifting from his suddenly nerveless fingers, "I wish to God that were the case, Chuffy. Mother is coming, but she will be alone. Verity is not there."

Underwood had the curious sensation of having been punched directly in the stomach. He had only once before experienced the horrible sickening loss of air which now assailed him, when as a boy he had fallen out of a tree onto his back, and that feeling of fighting for breath was one which he had never forgotten. He stared uncomprehendingly at his sibling, so blank was his expression that Gil felt it necessary to repeat his news, "Chuffy, Verity is not with mother. She has never been there. Mother had no idea she was gone, nor did she know about the baby."

"My God! What have I done?" The anguished whisper went straight to Gil's heart, for in spite of his behaviour over the past few days, he held his brother in the greatest respect and affection.

The sound of footsteps outside the gate and voices floating on the warm afternoon air suddenly reminded him of their situation and he realized this conversation could not be continued on the front path. He took his brother's arm and gently led him indoors, speaking comfortingly as he did so. "Do not blame yourself, Chuffy…"

"Who else should I blame?" was the bitter rejoinder, "Because of my selfishness, my wife is alone in the world! She could be ill, hurt, frightened, dead! And I was so arrogant I thought I knew how her mind worked. I thought I need only wait for her to come crawling back to me."

"Not quite that, old fellow." They had reached the door of Gil's study and the housekeeper's face appeared around the corner of the passageway leading to the kitchen. She opened her mouth to speak, but Gil silenced her with a lifted hand and a shake of his head. She took one look at the ashen-faced Underwood and swiftly retreated. Gil took him into the study and closed the door.

"Oh, yes! Precisely that I was relying on her adoration of me, as I have since the first day I met her."

"I think you are being unnecessarily harsh with yourself. You were in an appalling situation, the like of which you have never dealt with before. Neither of you were thinking clearly."

"Don't make excuses for me, Gil. I have made a rare mess of my marriage from beginning to end! I should have listened to my own fears and objections. I should have known I was too old for her, and too selfish and set in my ways to change."

"Chuffy, Verity loves you, and always has. I'm sure you can be reconciled."

"If I can find her! Gil, you were the last to see her, did she give you no hint of her intentions?"

Gil had the grace to look shame-faced, "I'm sorry, Chuffy, but I suspect she left because I was remiss enough to tell her that you believed she and I were … emotionally involved."

Underwood was incredulous, "You told her that? My God, Gil, what were you thinking of?"

"Well, that was what you said," muttered Gil, in a tone of self-defence which made him sound remarkably like the irritating little brother Underwood had almost forgotten had ever existed.

"You half-wit! No wonder she has left me. Surely your own common sense must have told you those words were spoken in haste and deeply repented."

"I should think they were. Not that Verity or I were ever offered an apology for so gross a slur…"

"I apologise" interrupted Underwood tersely, "Now, can you remember anything she said which might have given some clue to her whereabouts?"

"No, she merely said she was mortified at having come between us and that she knew how to put it right. I never thought for a moment she intended to leave."

"Do you not know of any friend or acquaintance with whom she might stay?"

"I know nothing more than you – she's your wife!"

"Thank you, Gil. Why not just plunge a knife between my ribs and twist it?"

Gil smiled weakly and apologetically, "Sorry," he thought carefully for a moment before adding, "Who was that elderly lady she went to see a few weeks back?"

Underwood pondered the question; "I don't remember the name. Perhaps someone else does. Thank you, Gil."

"Is there anything more I can do?"

Underwood stared at his brother, almost unseeing, before he replied, "Yes, you can stay here and wait for the arrival of mama. I, for once, will turn my much-lauded detective skills towards something vaguely useful. I shall find my wife, if it takes the rest of my worthless life!"

CHAPTER TWENTY-FOUR

'Vulneratus Non Victus' – Bloodied, but unbowed – Literally,
'Wounded but not conquered'

Her face was far more attractive in repose than it had ever
been when animated, probably because only such base interests
as greed and spite had ever caused a flicker of emotion.
Underwood, taking his turn at nursemaid to the still insensible
Collinson, had found ample time to reflect on this fact and
many others besides. He wondered how Gedney could have
brought himself to seduce this unpleasant girl, and having done
so, how he could then coldly dispense with her. What was more
vitally important, he pondered on his own next move. Each day
that passed made her recovery more and more unlikely, and her
death would seal the fate of the unfortunate Dunstable. His new
wife would undoubtedly avoid the hangman's noose by
"pleading her belly" as the parlance went, added to her extreme
youth and naivete, but this did not much comfort the man upon
whom they had both placed their trust and reliance.

Presently he was joined by Toby, who had come to take his
turn at the bedside, "Any change?"

"No, our sleeping beauty still sleeps."

"Well, go and get your own rest, but I may as well warn you,
I'll be gone when you wake."

Underwood looked startled at this sudden announcement,
"I'm sorry to hear that, my friend. Any particular reason?"

The big man shrugged, "I was going to have to go sooner or
later, but frankly it just isn't the same without Mrs Underwood
here."

"True enough. The house is horribly empty without her –
and believe me, no one regrets her absence more than I."

"Do something about it then."

"I'm doing my best, Toby, but she has not left me much to
work upon."

"I'm sure a man of your intelligence can find his wife."

"I've been to every livery stable in town. No one admits to having hired a horse or carriage out to her."

Toby grinned, "And what does that tell you, Mr Underwood?"

"That someone hired it for her – my God! You are not trying to tell me that she really is with that witless Vivian Pepper?"

"For someone so very clever, you can be remarkably obtuse, my dear sir. She left on foot."

Underwood looked relieved for a moment, the his expression clouded again,

"On foot? In her condition? Where the devil is the nearest town where she could catch the Stage?"

"I've no idea. But I'll know tomorrow, because I'll be boarding one myself."

"Would it make any difference if I asked you not to go?"

"No, but thank you for saying it. It means a great deal to have been befriended by you and your family. I heard about your little *contretemps* with Gedney. It was good of you to speak in my defence."

"I just wish he hadn't been drunk, then I could have taken him outside and struck him as he so richly deserved."

Toby laughed, "I'd rather you did not. You have a reputation to uphold."

"My reputation would be well lost for that cause."

"I wasn't talking about your reputation, I meant your brother's."

*

The afternoon sun sent darts and spears of dancing light between the gently stirring leaves of the mossy old apple tree and Underwood felt himself drifting into the first decent sleep he had experienced for weeks. The stone garden bench was not the most comfortable of couches, but his head rested on an

215

ancient velvet cushion which smelled pleasantly musty, rather like the interior of an old country church, reminding him of a time when being in such places had been a pleasure to him and not the trial it had become in later years. After two days of rain the air smelled fragrantly earthy, a slight breeze took the overwhelming heat out of the day and he deliberately cleared his mind and allowed slumber to creep over him, knowing that if he thought about any one of his problems, then all idea of rest would be immediately banished. Callous as it might seem to outside observers, he knew he needed some sleep desperately, or his ever-precarious health would break under the strain.

He heard his name spoken by a woman, but not the feminine tones he longed to hear, so it was languid grace that he opened his heavy-lidded grey eyes and hoisted himself first into a sitting position, then reluctantly to his feet, "Mrs Gedney," he said, with patient resignation, "How may I be of assistance?"

She did not look well, though she had never been a particularly attractive woman, having a bitter set to her thin lips, a long sharp nose and dark rings continually circling her eyes. He observed a tightly controlled panic about her and knew that the moment of truth had arrived. He was immediately alert, though he showed no physical evidence of the sharpening of his every sense.

"I have come to ask a favour of you, sir."

"I'm sure you have, madam, but I fail to see any service which I might render you."

She drew in a deep, exasperated breath, expanding her already ample figure and looking for all the world like a harried hen, "Please stop playing games, Mr Underwood. You know to what I refer!"

"You are mistaken, I have no idea. I was lying here, in my brother's garden, minding my own affairs, taking a well-earned rest. You have trespassed on his property, obtruded into my leisure time, and begun to throw unwarranted accusations about. I cannot charge myself with ever having played games – and certainly not with any member of your family."

She made an obvious effort to not lose her temper and her tone was conciliatory, "Mr Gratten has now arrested Dunstable for my mother's murder. I have come to ask you to allow the matter to follow its logical course."

He gazed at her from beneath a quizzically raised brow, "What makes you think I intend to do anything else?"

"Well, let us not prevaricate! All through this unfortunate affair, you have championed Dunstable, insisting on his innocence, when every shred of evidence pointed to his undoubted guilt. I merely require your word that you will now accept the right man is in gaol."

"Why? I am powerless to change Mr Gratten's mind. What difference does my opinion make?"

She shifted uncomfortably from one foot to the other, then apparently decided she had no choice but to be honest with him, "The Assurance Companies are refusing to pay out, and they have persuaded my mother's solicitor and man of business to hold up the proceedings. We cannot touch any of her money because you have placed a doubt in their minds."

"Ah! I might have known this visit centred upon cold, hard cash. Nothing else could have prompted civility from you."

Her sallow skin took on a hue of dirty red, "Insult me if you must, but spare a thought for my daughter…"

"Pray, do not say another word," he interrupted harshly, holding up his hand as though to ward her off, "Of all the iniquities you could commit, bringing your child into this must be the most base."

"How could I not bring her into it? She is the one who will suffer from your obstinacy. Why will you not accept my husband's innocence?"

"Because, madam, your husband can lie faster than a stray dog trots."

"Mr Underwood," she tried to placate him, realizing that her present line of pleading was leading nowhere, "I understand that you do not like my husband. He is not a conciliating man, but that does not make him a murderer."

"Liking or disliking him has nothing to do with the case. You are either blind or extremely obtuse."

"Say anything you want to about me, or him, for that matter, but take pity on Melissa."

Underwood was suddenly very tired of the conversation, and he desired nothing more than to be rid of the woman. It was with liberation from her in his mind that he replied wearily, "Very well."

She looked startled at gaining so easy a victory, "You mean you are going to do as I ask?"

"I mean you may think whatever you will, with my blessing. If it comforts you to imagine I will ever concede defeat, by all means imagine it."

Her face contorted with fury, "You beast! You are wicked to play such cruel games with me. Do you not think I have trouble enough with my unfortunate daughter, without you mocking me thus?"

It was Underwood's turn to lose his temper, and for once he put no curb upon it, "Wicked? You dare to speak to me of wicked, when you know what your husband had done? I strongly suspect you aided him. You are a pitiful, pathetic woman, Mrs Gedney, but not because of the afflictions of your child. You are prepared to say anything, do anything; sacrifice anybody, for a few grubby gold coins – coins more tainted than Judas' thirty pieces of silver. You are too stupid to understand that the man you seek to protect today, will be the murderer of yourself and your child tomorrow!"

The colour drained from her face, leaving her skin with a yellowish tinge and emphasising the dark staining under her eyes, "You don't know what you are talking about!"

"I know exactly, madam. Gedney is interested only in his own comfort and pleasure. You are only safe whilst he needs you. The moment Dunstable hangs and he feels himself protected from discovery, you and your daughter will merely be awaiting death. It will be slow and subtle. You will gradually weaken and have more and more bouts of illness, each one leaving you frailer than the last. No one will be in the least surprised when you finally succumb to the sicknesses which have dogged you. Count the hours, Mrs Gedney!"

"You are a liar!" she whispered.

"Am I, madam?" he answered coldly, "Well, as I said before, you must believe whatever gives you comfort."

She stared at him for several long seconds before she managed to gasp, "I'll tell you everything. I'll turn King's evidence against him."

"That won't save you, Mrs Gedney. You are of no use to me. A wife cannot testify against her husband. You had better pray Rachael Collinson wakes – and that when she does, she will remember who attacked her."

"Are you not going to help me?" she pleaded, losing all her bravado.

He gave her a glance of withering contempt, "You do not deserve my help madam, but I will do my utmost to save your child." With that he lay back down on the bench, his booted feet crossed at the ankles, his long fingers intertwined on his chest and his eyes determinedly closed. With relief he heard her footsteps die away down the path.

He knew not how much later in the day it was when he was startled awake by an arm flung across his chest and an anguished voice in his ear, "My dear, I'm so sorry!"

He opened weary eyes to find Charlotte Wynter kneeling by his side, her face close to his.

"Good God!" he ejaculated and attempted to extricate himself.

She pressed him back into his prone position, all sweet reasonableness, "Pray do not disturb yourself. I know you must have endured sleepless nights, worrying about the appalling behaviour of that thankless wife of yours. But please believe me when I say I always knew she was not worthy of you. Only I have ever loved you…"

This nonsense prompted him to renew his efforts to escape and eventually he did so by sliding off the far side of the bench, writhing out from under her arm and ending up on the grass, but not much caring how the green stains would ever be removed from his breeches, "Charlotte, you forget yourself!"

She pursued him around the seat, "My darling, my own sweetheart…"

"Charlotte!" he commanded icily, "Stop it at once. I have no desire to hear these endearments from you, and you will regret ever having uttered them."

Since he had evaded her so adroitly, the bench still stood between them. With all the determination of a spoilt child, Charlotte lifted her skirts and climbed up onto the seat, taking him entirely by surprise and leaving him vulnerable to her onslaught. Before he knew what she was about, she was towering over him, her arms around his neck, her lips hovering invitingly above his, "My love," she whispered, "I am yours! I would not leave you to the scorn of others, make a fool of you with another, as Verity has done."

Very uncomfortably, he craned his neck that he might not receive her kisses, "For pity's sake, Charlotte, release me! Anyone might look over the garden wall and witness this folly. And kindly stem your vitriol towards my wife. She has not run off with Vivian Pepper, or anyone else, no matter what the gossips might be intimating."

Firmly he placed his hands on her waist and tried to wrest himself from her grasp, but after years of riding her huge stallion, she had surprisingly strong arms. She began to rain kisses on his face and he despaired of ever managing to regain

220

enough breath to remonstrate with her. Charlotte felt his tacit submission and placed an entirely different explanation on his actions. At last she relented enough to allow him his freedom, thinking she had convinced him he no longer desired it. She discovered how wrong she was with his next words, "Charlotte, if your mother was still alive, she would be mortified to see you behave in such a wanton manner…"

She gasped at his tone, "How dare you call me a wanton! It is not I who has run off with a mere boy."

"Since I seem to be incapable of convincing you that Verity has done no such thing, I will merely state that even if she had done so, she certainly never so far forgot herself and her position as to embrace him in public. Or me, either!"

"That only proves she never loved you – and that I do!"

"Balderdash!" he countered with rising irritation; "You merely show the lack of a mother's discipline. Verity has never misbehaved so grossly, no matter what the provocation."

"I am sick of hearing about Verity's perfection," she sneered, poison dripping from every word.

"Then take yourself off and stop bothering me, you silly girl. To me, Verity is perfection – I had not realized just how perfect until I compared her to you."

Her cheeks flushed at the insult, "*Oh!*" She cried in indignation, "How could you?"

"Quite easily. Go away Charlotte, and please, please *don't come back!*"

With a proud lift to her chin, she flounced away down the garden, and Underwood sank back onto the bench, dragging his handkerchief from his pocket and wiping his heavily perspiring brow, "No wonder Knox called them a 'monstrous regiment'," he muttered weakly, before heading into the vicarage for tea, peace and an aura of sanity.

CHAPTER TWENTY-FIVE

'Non Semper Ea Sunt Quae Videntur' – Things are not always what they appear to be

Major Thornycroft hailed Underwood cheerfully, "Good morning, my friend, no Gil today?"

"No, it is his turn to sit with our invalid."

"Any sign of recovery?"

"No. The doctor is managing to get a little water down her throat, so at least she won't die of thirst just yet. Luckily, despite the damage done to her neck, she still seems able to swallow, but she is unconscious and shows no sign of waking. The bruising is fading now, not so vividly purple, but every other hue you can imagine. God knows how anyone could inflict such injuries on a helpless girl."

"The Law does it every day, and for a host of minor offences."

"Yes," said Underwood thoughtfully, "Would to God they would find some other way of dealing with felons. It is the only thing which gives me pause when I involve myself in such matters as Mrs Dunstable's death."

"But in involving yourself, at least you save the innocent from an undeserved fate."

"One can only hope so. Enough of such dreary thoughts. You must have something to confide that will cheer me."

The Major grinned wickedly, "As a matter of fact, I have."

"Well, don't leave me in suspense. What is it?"

"We have Gedney and his wife frothing at the mouth. I have persuaded Geoffrey and Adeline to contest their mother's Will. In the original their bequest is a small sum of money. Adeline knew that, which is why she insured her adopted mother's life. Poor little soul thought she would never find a husband if she did not have a dowry. Another interesting snippet is that it was

Gedney who suggested the idea of insurance to her, and arranged the meeting with the company."

"You discovered more than I. She would not divulge her reasons for assurance when I asked her."

"You do not have the same charm and easy manner as I."

"Yes, yes! We all know about your innate charm. By Jupiter, Gedney covered himself very well. He lined another up to take his place on the gallows every step of the way, didn't he? If Dunstable had not played into his hands, Adeline would have – and did, until you persuaded her otherwise. But what I want to know is how you thought of contesting the Will? It is a brilliant stroke. I wish I had thought to use the ploy. Gedney is only interested in lining his pockets and is going to be pushed into all manner of folly by his frustration."

"If you are looking for the brilliant author of Gedney's misfortune, look no further than your own wife. It was her idea."

"Verity?" he made no attempt to hide his eagerness, grasping the Major's shoulder in a painfully tight grip and shaking it slightly, "You've heard from her? Where is she?"

Jeremy took his wrist and removed his hand with a theatrical grimace of pain, "Hold hard, old man! These instructions were left with me before she went. Do you really think I would have kept it from you if I had known where she was?"

A deflated Underwood sank onto a nearby bench, "Dammit! Where the devil has she gone, Thornycroft? At every turn I'm reminded how much I miss her, how much I need her. Even at a distance she is helping me find the key to the crime."

"I'm sorry, Underwood. I really have not a notion. But, by God! What a woman she is. Even with all the heartache she has endured, she was level-headed enough to plan ahead, making sure you bring your man to justice, even in her absence."

"I'm sure she would be delighted to know that she possesses so ardent an admirer in you, Jeremy," said Underwood, with unbecoming cynicism.

"Give me half a chance, my friend, and I will take her away from you."

"You'll have to find her first."

*

The two brothers were alone for the first time that evening. Toby had left the previous morning, his meagre belongings wrapped in a warm blanket which Gil had pressed upon him. Both men were unhappy at his obstinate refusal to remain with them until he at least found employment of some kind, knowing that he was condemning himself to a life of vagrancy, but he was adamant he had trespassed on their generosity for long enough. Underwood had pressed a few guineas into his hand and he had reluctantly accepted them, but it was evident he hated doing so. That, more than anything else, made the parting uncomfortable and Underwood almost wished he had not done it, though he knew he could not send the man out onto the road penniless.

Mrs Trent had suddenly announced she was taking a couple of well-earned days off and had gone to see her sister. This was also intensely inconvenient, since neither Gil nor Underwood were particularly talented in the kitchen, and they now expected the arrival of their mother at any moment, but since she had borne the advent of the Herberts, Oliver Dunstable and Toby, and had nursed Rachael Collinson for two days without a word of complaint, they could hardly protest when she declared her utter weariness and left them to their own devices.

They had supped fairly well at the White Boar, accompanied by Major Thornycroft, whilst one of Gil's adoring parishioners had kindly sat with Collinson, and when they returned to the vicarage, she took her leave of them and they retired to the study for an hour or two of relaxation. There was a companionable silence as Underwood read, and Gil wrote notes on his next sermon.

Frenzied hammering on the front door brought them both to their feet and with an exchange of glances which confirmed the panic the sound had instilled in each of them, they set off down the hall of one accord.

Since their arrival home, the light shower they had encountered had been building into a veritable tempest; it was pouring with rain, with buffeting winds lashing the trees. A bedraggled urchin stood on the step as they opened the door, whom neither of them recognised, but even so they urged him to enter out of the rain,

"No, no!" he shouted above the noise of the rain and wind, "I daren't come in. There isn't time, I've to run for the doctor too. You both got to come. I bin sent to fetch you. It's Mrs Underwood, she's ill, real bad. She's bin taken to Lady Hartley-Wells and she begged me bring you both."

"Of course, my boy," exclaimed Gil, genuinely aghast, "We will come right away. Chuffy, get your cloak."

Underwood caught his brother's arm as he turned to the hallstand to grasp his own heavy black cape, "Hold hard, Gil, not so fast! Ask the boy who he is, and who sent him."

Gil looked into Underwood's face, scarcely comprehending the fact that he could hesitate at such a moment, "What difference does that make, for pity's sake? Verity has sent for us…" He broke off, struck by another thought, "My God! He said Mrs Underwood. It may be mother. There must have been an accident with the stage."

He spun round to question the boy further, but was faced with the empty blackness of the rain-soaked night, "Never mind. It does not matter which one of them it is, we are needed now, Chuffy."

Still Underwood did not move, "I don't believe it, Gil. This is a trick. I know in my bones that it is."

Gil wrenched himself furiously from his brother's grasp, "Be damned to your suspicious mind, CH! Have you no heart? How can you even pause for a second at a time like this? Verity has sent for you – or mother. Ill, in pain, perhaps dying and for you to think of logic…"

"You don't understand, Gil. If we both leave here now, Collinson will be alone in the house. What is to stop someone breaking in and smothering her with one of her own pillows? I swear to you that was a false message."

"You don't know that. You can't know it for sure. And even if you are, how can you bear to risk mother or Verity?"

Suddenly all Underwood's resolve crumbled, "Let us go," he said, grabbing his caped great coat, and following his brother out into the wild night, the sound of their feet pounding above the tumult of wind and rain. With every bone-jolting step, Underwood, the man who possessed no religious beliefs, who had not acknowledged the existence of any deity since the love of his youth had died in agony years before, prayed with a fervour of despair, "Please God, let this be the right decision!"

*

Ill-luck dogged them all the way, as Underwood knew it must. There was no sign of life at the White Boar, and their hammering on the door went unheard and unanswered. It became increasingly obvious that they were not going to be able to find a vehicle to carry them to Lady Hartley-Wells, the hour was too late and the weather too wild to hope anyone would still be abroad. They had no choice but to find their way on foot. In daylight the road to her imposing mansion was a pleasant enough walk, now it was a bleak and muddy nightmare of wind and rain, slipping and sliding on greasy soil and grass at the side of the road, or risking a broken ankle in the pot-holed highway, nearly blinded by the driving needles of rain, blown in gusts into their faces.

It took them almost three-quarters of an hour to struggle to the house, and they were faced with the heart-stopping vision of unlit windows and a barred door when they finally reached their destination. No doctor's gig stood outside, with a disgruntled horse turning its haunches to the biting wind and driving rain. No sign of life at all.

Gil skidded to a halt, looked about him in disbelief and turned to his brother, looking absurdly young with his hair plastered to his skull, and a shocked expression on his streaming face, "Chuffy... shouldn't somebody be waiting for us?"

Underwood, feeling sick with dread, but unable to panic the vicar by showing it, answered swiftly, "We have to rouse the house, Gil. We need a carriage to get us back to the parsonage."

"It was a lie then?"

"It was, a cruel and sick hoax, but we must not delay any longer. We have to get back, now!" A sense of urgency at last communicated itself to the staggered Gil and he nobly rose above his own shock and dismay to aid his brother.

Lady Hartley-Wells, being a fairly light sleeper, presently heard their summons and sent Cromer to investigate. Thus, within another half-hour or so, they were ensconced in a chaise and driving fast and wild back to Hanbury. They were rudely rocked and thrown from side to side as Cromer's youngest brother whipped up the horses and took to the road without thought of the pot-holes, stones or other possible road-users. Underwood could only be silently grateful that on such a night they were unlikely to encounter any other vehicles. His initial thought had been to tell the boy not to bother hurrying. He knew now that the plan had been carefully laid, their every movement watched, and the assassination savagely accomplished. The vicarage would, of course, have been entered within minutes of their leaving and the chances were Collinson had been dead for over an hour. Her tenuous hold on life would have been pathetically easy to sever, as he had suggested to Gil, probably by a pillow held over her face. There would not even have been a struggle, no sign that she had been murdered, no proof that would hang the man who had so callously snuffed out the one remaining tiny spark of life.

He grew increasingly depressed as they neared the deserted town, wearily furious with himself for not having resisted Gil's pleas. Why had he not trusted his instincts and sent his brother out alone?

He knew why, of course. That moment of weakness had been prompted by the mention of his wife. Anyone else he could have risked leaving to their fate, even, it had to be admitted, his mother, but not Verity. He had gambled everything in the hope it had really been her who had sent for him. And it had not paid off. Gad, what an idiot he had been – and what was worse, he still did not know where to find her! He realized now that he had never loved anyone as he loved her; not Elinor, nor Charlotte. No one had possessed his soul, matched his mind, gripped his imagination, roused his body as she did – and fool that he was, he had driven her away! With his stupid pride, and pathetic insecurities he had made her feel unwanted and unloved. He did not deserve to have her back, but he would give all he possessed to have her safe by his side once more.

He had lashed himself into a suitably abject state of misery by the time they drew up outside the vicarage, and it was left to Gil to leap from the chaise and head for the front door at a neck-or-nothing run. Underwood stumbled down behind him, his muscles having suddenly decided to stiffen in protest at the unaccustomed action to which he had subjected them. As well as mental anguish, he felt bodily battered and bruised and he hoped he would not have too much to do when he entered the house. He had not mentioned Collinson's peril since those first moments on the doorstep when they had set out on their ill-fated journey, and he hoped Gil had managed to assimilate the knowledge of what they were likely to find. He had no desire to spend the rest of the night treating his brother for the effects of shock.

Gil was still fumbling through his pockets for his key when Underwood joined him and with a tired sigh he reached out, turned the knob and pushed open the door,

"If you recall, Gil, we did not wait to lock the door."

The vicar went deathly white, "Oh, dear Lord! If that girl is dead, the fault will be entirely mine. How could I have been so witless?"

"Don't blame yourself, old fellow. He would have broken in if we had locked and barred every entrance to the house. He was determined to see her dead. He could not risk her coming to and telling all she knew."

"I should have listened to you, Chuffy, the girl is dead because of me." His distress was acute and Underwood knew that nothing he could say would ever ease the anguish felt by the clergyman. He therefore said nothing more, but led his brother into the darkened hall, waving the young whipster away with a lift of his hand, then closing the door behind them, shutting out the easing storm, but unable to shut out the enveloping aura of despair which assailed them both.

He stood for a moment at the bottom of the staircase, unwilling to climb to witness the carnage he feared lay above them.

Gil suddenly stiffened beside him, "I swear I heard a footfall, Chuffy," he hissed, "There is still someone up there!"

In his logical mind, Underwood knew he must be wrong, but still he felt a rush of energy, which was a mixture of fear, excitement and fury, "Damn him to hell! If he is still here, I swear I will despatch him myself. Grab a poker from the parlour fireplace, Gil. I'll have your walking stick from the hall-stand," he whispered fiercely.

He waited until his brother returned, armed, then as quietly as possible they began the long ascent up the, fortunately carpeted, stairs. Those few seconds were the most drawn-out and painful of his life. Every creaking riser sounded like a pistol shot to their ears, and their breathing seemed to rasp like a snoring consumptive.

As they drew level with the landing, they saw that the door leading to Collinson's room was partially closed, letting just one strand of golden light spill across the floor.

"Are you ready?" breathed Underwood. Gil merely nodded, his eyes firmly on the door. They both tightened their grips upon their weapons, then of one accord ran up the last few stairs and burst into the one lighted room in the house.

CHAPTER TWENTY-SIX

'Tarde Venientibus Ossa' – For latecomers, the bones

It would be difficult to say whose expression of surprise was the more ludicrous. Gil and Underwood slithered to a halt just inside the door, faced with the sight of Toby sitting in the light of a single candle, startled out of his wits by their unexpected entrance. They both gaped at him, then cast their eyes about the room.

Collinson lay supine, her breast gently rising and falling, as obviously alive as they were. From this their glance slid to the far side of the room, where an unconscious Gedney lay propped against the wall, bound with ropes and sporting a magnificent black eye and painfully bruised jaw.

"What the devil…" began Underwood, then lapsed into bemused silence.

"Sorry," grinned Toby, swiftly recovering himself, "I didn't hear you arrive or I would have met you downstairs and saved us all a fright."

"What are you doing here, Toby?" asked Gil faintly, feeling that he would never regain possession of his addled wits.

"I never left, sir. Mrs Underwood's instructions. I was to make a great show of going, then let myself back in under cover of darkness and hide in the attic. Mrs Trent has been seeing to my food and drink."

"Mrs Trent knew about this," remarked Underwood grimly, "but we were not made privy to the plot?"

"Mrs Underwood thought you would be more convincing if you knew nothing," explained Toby rather sheepishly.

"Did she indeed? And has she been hiding in the attic too?"

"Unfortunately not."

"And what was her little deception meant to achieve?" Underwood sounded dangerously calm, and Gil looked fearfully at him. Toby seemed unconcerned,

"She knew we needed to force Gedney into an act of rashness, so she decided to give him the opportunity to lure you two from the house, leaving Rachael apparently unguarded. She realized he needed the girl dead, if he was to be safe from betrayal, so taking Mrs Trent and myself away meant he would be left with an irresistible temptation to rid himself of the one person who can – and hopefully will – give evidence against him. His only error throughout the entire episode was to fail to kill Collinson when he first tried. He would have succeeded even in that, had Mr Underwood not been alert to her peril and set me on guard."

"Oh, I am to be given some credit, then?" enquired Underwood, with unbecoming sarcasm.

Toby merely gave his wide, ingenuous grin and continued

"Mrs Underwood was right, of course. Gedney, once he knew the two of you were alone, wasted no time in sending a false message to get you out of the house, then he came straight up here. He did not even bother to risk sending someone to do his dirty work, no doubt having learned the danger of trusting an accomplice. He had the pillow in his hands when I jumped him. Two good punches felled him, and he's been out ever since. I swore I'd never use my fists again, but I admit I felt a rare satisfaction in hitting that little rat!"

"I can imagine," said the peaceable vicar, with unwonted relish.

"Where is Verity, Toby?" Underwood had entirely lost interest in Gedney, Collinson, Dunstable and the rest of the rabble; he just wanted the whole sorry mess finished with and his wife back in his arms.

"I've told you, Mr Underwood, I really don't know. She left these directions with me before she went."

Underwood looked into his eyes, willing him to crack and tell him the truth, but Toby met his stare steadfastly, never flinching or dropping his gaze, "I promise you I don't know.

Would to God, I did. I tell you frankly, I'm worried about her. She should not be alone at a time like this."

Underwood knew it, but he did not want to discuss the situation with a man who so evidently held him responsible for his wife's defection. With a rapid change of subject he said, "We had better fetch Mr Gratten and request him to remove this object from under our roof."

"I'll go for him," offered Toby and promptly suiting words for action, he took up his coat and was gone.

Now the excitement was almost over, Gil felt his knees buckle under him and he sank shakily into a chair, "I can't tell you how relieved I am the girl was unharmed, Chuffy. I really thought to find her here dead."

"She would have been but for Verity."

The vicar looked closely at his brother, noting the weary and depressed air that clung to him, "You know Verity has done all this for you, Chuffy. In spite of her own heartache, she has thought only of you."

"I know it."

"Have you any idea at all how deeply she loves you, and how much hurt you have inflicted upon her?"

"Do you think I am going to find it easy to forgive myself?"

"I hope not."

*

It did not take very much effort to convince Mr Gratten to take Gedney away and place him under lock and key – at the very least he was certainly guilty of entering the vicarage uninvited. Once he was presented with Underwood's findings and Toby's tale of the attempted murder of Collinson, he knew that at last he had the true culprit in his hands. He had brought two henchmen with him and they soon hoisted the now conscious and cursing Gedney to his feet.

233

"I'll kill you, Underwood, if I ever get the chance," he shouted furiously, as he was bodily dragged away, fighting and kicking.

Underwood paled slightly under the onslaught, for he had never been good at handling confrontation, but Gratten merely asserted triumphantly, "You won't be given the chance, my friend." He had quickly overcome his annoyance at being torn from his warm bed in the middle of the night and was positively expansive. He waited until the shouted protests and scuffling footsteps of the still resisting Gedney had died away then he turned to Underwood and continued, "I suggest a meeting in the morning with the magistrate, when you can explain your evidence more fully. Gedney is not going to be able to cover his tracks so easily this time, no matter how glib he is."

"Very well. Shall we say eleven?"

"Certainly; that will give me ample time to send for Sir Alfred Dorrington."

"Whereabouts is this meeting to take place?"

"At my house, for the present. Of course you will be required in Court, but that will not be for some time yet."

When he was gone, the brothers and Toby went to the kitchen for a well-earned cup of tea – made by Gil, naturally.

"Tomorrow is not going to be a pleasant day for you, Chuffy," commented the vicar, as he diligently stirred the pot. Underwood, who had chosen the best seat in the room, a cushioned rocking chair much favoured by Mrs Trent, and was almost on the verge of sleep, unwillingly forced his eyes open, "Not pleasant at all, dear fellow, especially if Gedney is going to be his usual, charming self and disrupt the proceedings with foul invective."

"I've never known him do anything else."

"Nor I. Well, I shall just have to prepared myself to suffer his offensive – in both meanings of the word"

"Will you be all right?" Gil asked the question diffidently, knowing how his brother hated to admit real physical weakness, though he was only too willing to complain of mythical ailments.

"I may not be. I hate to ask it of you, but could you both be there with me? At least that way I can fall back on you to finish my testimony if I feel unwell."

Toby and Gil readily agreed, but unfortunately it meant that they had to spare him another hour or so, thinking longingly of their beds, whilst he explained every nuance of the evidence he and Verity had so painstakingly garnered.

*

Watery sunlight was sparkling on the puddle-strewn, muddy street when the occupants of the parsonage set out for Gratten's house. Catherine had been brought in to mind Rachael, though now there was no longer any need to fear for her life, they had no concerns about leaving her, but they had no wish to find that she had woken alone in a strange place, should that eventuality occur.

Gratten had chosen his dining room for the consultation, it being large enough to seat everyone. He and Sir Alfred sat at the head of the table, Mr and Mrs Gedney and the Dunstables on one side, Adeline Beresford opposite them, and chairs left vacant for Underwood, Gil and Toby.

After formal introductions and greetings were exchanged, Mr Gratten invited Mr Underwood to begin his summing up of the evidence.

"May I begin by saying that without Mrs Gedney's insistence on claiming tansy as the poison which had killed her mother; this crime might very well have gone undetected. Dr Herbert assures me there is, as yet, no way of testing for plant-based poisons. Some, of course, have particular side effects that make their use obvious, but most do not. It was Mr

235

Gedney's greed in trying to have Dunstable hanged for the murder, so that he would forfeit his share of the inheritance, which is the sole reason we are all gathered here today. The sad fact is the Gedneys could have killed a dozen people, and never have been suspected." There was a contemptuous snort from Gedney, but no comment from anyone else, so Underwood smoothly continued, "My first indication that Gedney might be the culprit rather than the suspected Dunstable, was a rather odd circumstance. On visiting Gedney, I noticed that his hands bore a rash, and having just studied various tracts on tansy, I had learned it can cause a violent reaction in the skin of the susceptible. Gedney refused to give an adequate explanation for its presence."

Gedney half rose to his feet, his shackled hands clenched, "I refuse to sit here and listen to this drivel. What the hell right had he to ask me anything? I'm not answerable to him."

"Sit down, Gedney, and be quiet!" roared Gratten, completely losing his temper. He wanted to present Sir Alfred with a measured and intelligent assessment of the situation, and he was not about to allow Gedney and his foul mouth free range. Mr Underwood waited for the furious, but silenced, Gedney, to slump back into his seat before continuing.

"The more I investigated, the more unlikely it seemed to be that Dunstable had killed his wife. Financially, he would have been a far richer man whilst she remained alive, than after her death. He did not know tansy was fatal when taken in overdose, but Mrs Gedney knew all about its properties, even going so far as to claim she recognized the faint aroma of it in the cup on the day of the murder. She had even recommended her own herbalist to Dunstable – a piece of information with which he foolishly failed to provide me, until last week."

He paused for breath and to shuffle through the pile of papers and books he had brought with him – he might also have been accused of building the inevitable tension.

"Unfortunately," he went on presently, "we were never able to fully discover from where Mrs Dunstable had the poison. She had been given bon-bons by various people, and she always drank a full bottle of wine each evening at dinner, either or both of which could have been adulterated at any time, but the bon-bons were all eaten and the wine-bottle rinsed – though that action in itself was suspicious, since I was assured by the staff that the event was unprecedented. Next we come to the drawings my wife makes at every available opportunity. She is an exceptionally talented artist, and not only do her sketches clearly show faces and buildings in fine detail, she is also organized and neat. She always uses these particular notebooks, which as you can see are firmly bound and with the same number of pages, leaving no possibility for pages to be added or removed. She dates each picture and states each location. It was through one of her pictures that she unwittingly provided me with a vital piece of evidence. Mr Gedney lied, on several occasions, about the date he arrived in Hanbury. Without knowing who he was, for this was well before our first formal introduction, Verity captured the likeness of Mr Gedney in the main square of Hanbury three full days before he admitted his presence here."

"That could be anyone," growled Gedney.

Underwood opened the book at the relevant page and passed the book along the table to Mr Gratten and Sir Alfred, who dutifully examined the sketch.

"These are damned good, Underwood," remarked Sir Alfred, obviously much impressed, "And it certainly looks like Mr Gedney to me – with no evidence of erasing or any other form of tampering."

"Quite," said Underwood – he didn't feel the need to say anything more.

"You don't think your wife would be interested in a sitter for a portrait, do you?"

"I'm afraid I have no idea. I shall ask her next time I see her." Sir Alfred, who had been told of the Underwood's marital difficulties by Mr Gratten, had the grace to blush slightly at the gaffe.

A glance revealed that at long last Gedney was beginning to look uncomfortable, though he evidently enjoyed Underwood's irritation at this display of tactlessness. As for Underwood, he continued as though nothing untoward had occurred, determined not to be rattled by anything.

"I realize that anything said to me by Collinson can only be classed as hearsay unless she wakes, but she admitted to sending Gedney messages via the Bluebell Inn, Northcross, telling him when the Dunstable house would be empty, and letting him into the house. The landlord identified a sketch of both Gedney and Collinson, and claimed they not only met at his Inn, but also hired an upstairs room for considerable periods of time."

Mrs Gedney gasped, Gedney cursed, but Underwood ignored them and went on smoothly, "This of course gave Gedney ample opportunity to enter the house at will and lay his traps, like the smearing of the glasses with tansy, as found by Dr Herbert, which would ensure that Dunstable or even Miss Beresford could be accused of handing Mrs Dunstable a poisoned drink. The sketches were also shown to Mr Flynn, the herbalist, and he recognized Mr and Mrs Gedney, Mr Dunstable, and the late Mrs Dunstable. He also asserts that though Gedney did not purchase tansy oil, he did ask how it could be identified in the wild. That led me to conclude that, coupled with his tell-tale rash; Gedney could have picked the plant and placed the dried leaves in the herbal tea brought to Mrs Dunstable by her daughter on the night before her death. The Gedneys kindly provided us with the reasons for using the plant, rather than a faster acting, more predictable poison. It is only fatal in overdose, so no one else in the house could be killed accidentally. I imagine that subtlety was the idea of Mrs

Gedney, concerned for herself and her child. I doubt that Gedney would have cared had the entire household perished, provided his own safety and comfort could be assured."

"Damn you, Underwood," muttered Gedney, apparently stung by this assessment of his character, "You have no proof. This is all conjecture. You have not one shred of evidence to support these wild claims."

Mrs Gedney began to snivel pitifully at this juncture and continued to do so for the remainder of the meeting.

"That is not my concern, Gedney. I will merely present my findings to a jury and let them decide on your innocence or guilt."

He sat down and allowed the debate to begin. There was much discussion. Sir Alfred seemed reluctant to vindicate Dunstable, for he was a firm believer in the age-old theory that in most cases of domestic murder, the spouse is the responsible party. Underwood quickly grew weary of the conflict. He had done his best and could do no more. To either side of him, Gilbert and Toby joined in, growing heated in their frustration at the seemingly deliberate obduracy of the magistrate.

Toby loudly protested that he had seen Collinson and Gedney meet and talk animatedly at an inn, had watched Gedney leave first, then had been called upon to save the unfortunate Collinson from a murderous assailant. Furthermore, he had, only the previous evening, saved her once again from death, this time undoubtedly at the hands of Gedney.

The magistrate's reply was terse. He had no intention of denying Gedney's guilt of the second attack, but there could be many reasons for it – not least the fact that he had apparently been having an illicit relationship with the girl. Perhaps she had threatened to expose his duplicity to his wife. Whatever the explanation, it did not show him to be guilty of the murder of Mrs Dunstable.

Underwood did not particularly like the direction this conversation was taking and so, in an attempt to distract himself from the arguments which raged about him, he took up one of Verity's notebooks and began to flick idly through it. She was damned good; there could be no denying it. Whether landscape, portrait or architecture, she was equally adept. One picture seemed to leap out at him. He stared at it for a moment, then with an exclamation, which brought him silence and the full attention of everyone in the room; he rose to his feet, "By Jupiter! I know where she is."

"Where who is, sir?" asked Sir Alfred, genuinely puzzled.

"Never mind. It has no bearing on the matter in hand. Pray excuse me, Sir Alfred. I fear I must leave. My brother and Mr Hambleton are fully conversant with my notes and can answer any further questions you may have."

"Very well, Mr Underwood, thank you for your time. I trust we can call upon you, should the need arise?"

"Certainly…"

He never finished the sentence for at that moment the door flew open and Mrs Gratten entered, breathless with excitement and pink of cheek, "My dear, forgive the intrusion, but I have just this minute received a message from Mrs Pennington. Miss Collinson regained her senses not a half-hour ago. She seems to be fully cognisant, though suffering a headache."

Underwood glanced towards Gedney and saw the blood drain from his face.

He waited to see no more.

CHAPTER TWENTY-SEVEN

'Dabit Dues His Quoque Finem' – *God will grant an end even to these troubles*

She was sewing by the open window, her head bent industriously over a tiny white garment, her ringlets falling forward and stirring gently in the warm breeze.

He did not think she had heard him enter and so he hesitated for a few moments in the doorway, reluctant not only to startle her, but also to lose the precious seconds of examining her face whilst he was unobserved.

She looked a little pale, perhaps, but otherwise unscathed by the misery Gil had assured him she had suffered. He was astounded to feel that along with the overwhelming relief at seeing her safe and unharmed, fury was also rising rapidly within him. What right had she to look so serene and well when he had been plagued by worry and sleeplessness since she had taken it into her head to run away? Gone now was the memory of the fervent prayers for her safe return.

As if by intuition she gradually became cognisant of another presence and slowly raised her head.

He admired her coolness, for only by the slightest widening of her eyes, and the lightest of in drawn breaths did she betray her surprise, and she very quickly mastered herself, laid aside her occupation and rose to her feet, "Good day, Cadmus. You have found me then?"

If he had expected her to fly, weeping into his embrace, he was sadly disappointed. She merely stood, looking calmly at him, waiting for his response.

"So it would seem," he replied quietly, determined to be as stoic as she, "I trust you are in good health?"

"Fair."

He scarcely heeded her answer for, standing as she was, with the sun behind her, her figure was clearly outlined in the muslin

241

morning dress she wore. The high waist simply served to accentuate the thickening of her body, and he was stunned that the child within her had grown so much in – how long had it been? It seemed months must have passed since he last saw her, but in reality it was less than a fortnight.

She quickly realized he was shocked by her appearance, and immediately placed the wrong explanation entirely upon it. He was disgusted, of course, appalled by her bloated body! She moved away from the unforgiving light of the window and went to the sofa; "Won't you sit down?" She invited him nervously, all her *sang froid* gone now.

"Thank you." He took the proffered seat and waited for her to sit beside him, but she moved away and took one of the chairs across the room from him.

"How did you find me?" It was hardly the most tactful thing she could have said, for it merely reminded him with painful clarity, of just how much anguish she had caused him.

His voice was tightly controlled as he answered; "Your sketchbook showed a drawing of your day out with Mrs Leigh of Draythorp. The rest was easy. It solved the mystery of why no vehicle had been hired by you or Vivian Pepper. You walked here, of course."

"Vivian Pepper? I thought he had gone off to the races, so what has he to do with the matter, pray?"

"Apparently nothing," he retorted, and after a slightly puzzled frown crossed her brow, she decided not to pursue the topic any further and presently changed the subject.

"How are you, Cadmus?" she asked politely, bereft of anything more interesting to say.

"I have been better," he responded, with equal civility, but no emotion, "Worry, of course, tends to have an extremely adverse effect on my nerves, but no doubt I will recover swiftly, now that I know you are safe."

She blushed vividly at the sarcasm, but refused to dignify it with a word of protest, "I'm sorry to hear it, though I must own

I too know something of the effects of insecurity on the system."

He looked into her eyes, no flicker of his fraught feelings showing in his face,

"It was a wretched thing to have done, Verity. I have been half out of my mind, wondering where you were, if you were ill – or worse!"

She gave him stare for stare, "I do not care how you have been feeling," she said, at last, her voice cracking with emotion, "I have worn myself out caring about you and how you are feeling, and never receiving one ounce of regard in return."

He tried not to show it, but his anger was near the surface now, a bubbling brew of pride, passion and resentment, "That is incredibly unjust. I fully admit I have been at fault, but so have you. It was unforgivable to keep the knowledge of your condition from me."

"It was unforgivable of you to spend your days flirting with Charlotte Wynter, then to accuse me of having an affair with your brother." She was no longer calm, nor felt any particular desire to be so.

His face was ashen with suppressed fury, "I? *Flirting?* That is precious, coming from the woman whom half of Hanbury believes to have eloped with Vivian Pepper."

It was her turn to grow pallid, but her emotion was shock and distress, not anger, "*What!*"

"Do not, pray, pretend such surprise, my dear. How could your wanton conduct with the boy prompt any other supposition?"

"*My* conduct? Oh, oh! How I hate being a woman." She jumped to her feet in agitation; "Your behaviour with Charlotte was far more outrageous than mine with Vivian, yet it is I who is vilified. How appallingly unfair it is!"

"Unfair? You use the word very lightly, madam. You do not seem to think your own accusations of wrong-doing on my part to be 'unfair'."

She glared at him, her hands fisted and clamped to her sides, and stamped her foot in utter fury and frustration, "You beast! I don't know why you have come here, except to torment and distress me. What do you want of me?"

"To discuss our divorce, naturally." He didn't even know where the words came from, for they had certainly not been in his mind at the onset of their meeting, but they shot at her like bullets and felled her just as surely.

She stared at him, the cheeks which had reddened with temper only seconds before now grew as white as parchment, she took one tottering step towards him, then dropped like a stone at his feet.

"Oh dear God!" He was on his knees at her side in moments, "Verity, my dear one, my sweet life. What have I done?" He lifted her into his arms and carried her tenderly to the sofa, laying her gently down, then kneeling beside her and patting her hands until she opened her eyes once more.

She looked hazily at him, until the memory of his harsh words came swiftly back with her senses, "You … you said something … about divorcing me?"

He raised her hand to his lips, overcome with remorse, "I deserve to be horsewhipped! I am so very sorry, sweetheart!"

She seemed not to understand what he was saying; "You did not mean it?" she asked pitifully.

"Of course I did not! I was angry – furiously angry. Not an emotion to which I am accustomed. Very few people are capable of making me lose my temper."

She closed her eyes wearily, "Good," she whispered, "then I shall divorce you!"

"I beg your pardon?" he asked incredulously.

"I think you heard me well enough," she said, in a voice growing ever stronger, "Now, please go away. I want Mrs Leigh."

"Do not play silly games, Verity. I have apologised, what more can I do?"

Her eyes opened, the spark of anger hot within them, "You can go to the devil for all I care. You are cruel, completely heartless! You have used me as a convenience since the day we married, never showing one whit of unprompted affection or concern for me, allowing the likes of Charlotte Wynter to look down on me and pity me. If you had, just once, shown me the kind of adoration you profess to feel for me, then she would never have had the impertinence to throw herself at you as she did."

"My dear – be reasonable. I am not a man who easily displays his feelings…"

"Balderdash!" she said rudely, much to his surprise, "I saw you kiss Charlotte in public when you were engaged to her – but have you ever done so to me? No, you have not."

He looked astounded, "Good God! I should have thought you were past the age of wanting idiotic, immature exhibitions of romance."

"*Past the age…*" Her furious tones trailed off into the silence of disbelief and it was a minute or two before she could add coldly, "Just exactly how old do you think I am? One hundred and three? Of course I want you to make an exhibition of yourself for me. You did so for the lovely Miss Wynter."

He stood up and paced about the room, as though trying to escape an awkward situation, "Oh, God preserve me from women. Don't you think I might prefer to forget that I ever made a prize fool of myself over Charlotte?"

To his astonishment she suddenly began to yell, in an extremely unladylike way, for Mrs Leigh, who arrived with an alacrity which suggested she might not have been as far away as Underwood would have desired.

"What is it, my dear?" she asked, her voice gentle with concern.

Verity threw a poisonous glance in her husband's direction and said, with considerable vitriol, "Mr Underwood is distressing me. I should like him to leave."

Underwood, who had already had one battle with the lady of the house, when he demanded to see his wife alone and unannounced, now found himself suffering the ignominy of being ejected from a house. He listened to her stunning pronouncement with a frozen face. Mrs Leigh looked askance at him, so he bowed stiffly, "I shall remain in Hanbury for the present, Verity. Should you wish to contact me, you know where I am – I, at least, accord you that gesture of civility."

Mrs Leigh showed him out.

*

His expression was thunderous when he entered the vicarage, and his mood was not improved by the gathering who were waiting to greet him.

It seemed the stage had arrived in his absence and now, along with Gil and Toby, were his mother and her husband, General Milner.

She immediately rushed towards him as he walked into the parlour, "Chuffy! What have you been doing to upset Verity? Where is she? Why have you not brought her back with you?"

"If you would care to hold your tongue for long enough to allow me to get a word in edgewise…" he began testily, whereupon the General intercepted gruffly.

"Now, now, my boy. No way to address your mother, don't you know?"

Underwood, though seething, recognized the justice of this, however much he might resent the quarter from which the reminder came, and after a deep breath, he forced a smile, and resumed, "I beg your pardon, mama, I'm a little fraught! Verity has taken it into her head to be awkward. No doubt her condition can be blamed, as I understand women can be unpredictable at times like these – but by God! I'd like to throttle her!"

246

"Oh dear," whimpered his mother faintly, "What has she done?"

With great self-control he managed a small, not very convincing, laugh, "She's threatening me with divorce."

Mrs Milner's horrified gaze hurt him more than he cared to admit, "Oh, Chuffy!"

"Be calm, mother, for pity's sake. It is nonsense and she knows it. Quite apart from anything else, the cost would be prohibitive. It takes a debate in both houses of Parliament, and a wife cannot divorce her husband for adultery – even if he had committed it, which I most certainly have not. Her only recourse would be non-consummation – and I doubt very much she would win on that, given her present condition."

"There is no need to be vulgar, Cadmus," said his mother severely, the use of his forename amply demonstrating the depth of her displeasure.

For the first time Underwood began to see a glimmer of humour in the situation. He grinned broadly, "Forgive me, mama. I forget myself."

"You most assuredly do!"

*

Two days later, he was no longer amused. Verity had not contacted him; his mother was frantic, Gil silently condemning. Underwood attempted nonchalance, but was hardly convincing.

He knew his affairs were the staple of Pump-room gossip, along with what was happening to the Gedneys, and though he utterly deplored the situation, there was little he could do to halt the prattle.

Major Thornycroft joined him at the fountain as he collected water for his mother, "How goes it, Underwood?"

"Badly," returned the dutiful son tersely, "What about you?"

"Never been better, my friend. Miss Beresford has done me the honour of accepting my hand."

247

Underwood, relieved at finally having some good news to celebrate, greeted this announcement with delight, "You old rogue! I thought you were too noble to ask her to saddle herself with a gambling, alcoholic, reprobate."

"I was – she asked me – and being a gentleman, I could hardly refuse."

"You, a gentleman? I think not."

"Watch your manners, sir, or I shall ask Toby to stand as my best man in your stead."

It took Underwood a moment to assimilate this invitation, then he smiled with a genuine fondness and shook the Major warmly by the hand, "It would be an honour. When is the wedding to be – and is Gil to officiate?"

"Of course, but it cannot be until the Dunstable and Gedney saga is at an end. Speaking of which, have you heard the latest?"

"I knew, of course, that Miss Collinson and Mrs Gedney have become unlikely allies and have told Gratten everything they know. Gedney is as guilty as sin, his wife an accessory, but likely to be dealt with leniently for turning King's evidence."

"Dunstable has now been released, not a stain on his character."

"I wouldn't say that exactly," murmured Underwood wryly.

"Quite," grinned the Major, "However, he and his new wife have offered to give a home to young Melissa."

"Thank God. I must admit to several sleepless nights on her account. She may have had appalling parents, but at least she had someone. My actions will probably leave her an orphan."

"Well," continued Thornycroft, "Adeline and I were not so sure Dunstable and Frederica were quite capable of raising a child with her problems. Those two can barely control themselves, let alone a difficult child. It also occurred to us that she stands to inherit a fair amount when Josie's will is finally executed. Dunstable may not have murdered Josie for her money, but he did marry her for it."

"Very true, but what alternative is there? We don't want the child ending up in a sanatorium or some such place."

"Adeline and I are going to have her."

"Good Lord!"

Thornycroft laughed, "Thank you so much for that vote of confidence."

"I'm sorry, my friend, but as you so succinctly say, she is a difficult child. Are you sure you will be any more use to her than Dunstable?"

"Not at all, but at least she will have guardians who understand her pain and frustration. When she throws one of her temper tantrums, I shall probably join her on the floor."

This presented a mental image which Underwood found vastly amusing, and it was with his broad, boyish grin on his face that he lifted his head and glanced towards the doors, where newcomers were entering amidst a buzz of excitement.

The smile swiftly slid away as he recognized his wife, and apparently he was not the only person to do so. There fell a profound silence and all eyes were upon them as Verity made her way slowly across the room, a passage forming for her as those in her path fell back.

Gossip had been busy and now almost the entire population of Hanbury knew that Verity had committed the unforgivable act of leaving her husband – very possibly for another man. The whole room was agog to know what Underwood intended to do about this tardy – and judging from the stubborn expression on Verity's face – unrepentant return.

Underwood met her eyes though there was still some distance between them, and she stopped, stock still, no clue in her demeanour to tell him how she wanted him to behave.

He knew their future together depended upon his handling of this moment correctly. Without more ado, he thrust his mother's cup into Thornycroft's hands, not caring that the overfilled vessel spurted water all over the proud red tunic, and he began to walk swiftly towards his wife.

249

He said not a word, but swept her up into his arms and kissed her passionately. There were several shocked gasps from some of the elderly spinsters, but most of their acquaintances were smiling fondly, a blend of relief and amusement adorning their features.

This display was so very unlike Underwood, and so unexpected in the face of tales of desertion and divorce, adultery and elopement, that a loud and spontaneous burst of applause greeted the moment that their lips parted. Verity blushed delicately and hid her pink cheeks against his shoulder. With a triumphant, and wholly ungentlemanly grin, Underwood carried his wife out of the Pump-rooms and bore her away.

Mrs Fancourt rapped her son over the knuckles with her folded fan, "If you had done that to Meg Rowbottham forty years ago, you wouldn't be sitting here with me now!" she exclaimed loudly.

"Oh, hush, mother!" was the vastly irritated reply.

"Eh?"

"HUSH!"

THE END